WHISPERS OF THE STARLIT SEA

WHISPERS OF THE STARLIT SEA

A LITTLE MERMAID RETELLING

ROBYN SARTY

For Katie,

Who always loved Ariel the best,
for the truest songs are those we carry within.

THE CHRONICLES OF
AVALORE
THE KNOWN WORLD

◈ CAPITAL CITY
•• COUNTRY BORDER

BRANAR

HOLGLEN
◈

EADARRIN
◈

CAOLHAIN

DRAKMORE

STONEHOLD
◈

LO
EA

TORAVIK

ISKARRAIG
◈

M A I G H D E A N N   S E A

FENMERE
LOCH SEWEN
BRAEHELM
THORNVAREN
EDELAND
PENHALETH
THALDRAN OCEAN

CHAPTER ONE

THE ARCHITECTS OF OLD had made use of the landscape to build the Iskarraig castle in the most defensible position on the cliffs above the harbor. The harbormasters had protested, pointing out the need for a light in the same spot to warn ships of the deadly rocks and guide them to safety. In the end, a compromise was reached, and the eastern tower was expanded and raised to house the light that now lit up the sky in comforting intervals, a stark contrast to the capricious lightning that cut through the heavy clouds.

The floor below the light was an open terrace with views that stretched from the harbor and the town nestled at the foot of the cliffs to the vast Maighdeann Sea and the steep hills on the far side of the castle.

The rolling thunder made talking almost impossible, but at least Arick knew no one could overhear their conversation. He paced the octagonal floor, careful not to get too close to the open archways. The rain being driven sideways drenched the mosaic tiles, and he wasn't keen on a soaking.

"Are you sure?" he asked his cousin, wishing he were wrong.

The other man nodded. "Yeah. Because I look like this" — he gestured to himself — "they don't think I would make a good king."

The hurt was evident in his voice.

"They're wrong, you know," Arick told him.

Thomas nodded. "I know, but it doesn't feel good to hear it."

A flash of lightning revealed his scrunched-up face as he struggled to hold back tears. Arick moved to him and wrapped him in a hug, a fierce sense of protectiveness filling him. Thomas might have been different, but that didn't mean he didn't know when people were talking about him. And it certainly didn't mean he couldn't fulfill the role he'd been born into.

Lightning rippled across the sky again, casting the two in white light. Arick towered over Thomas, though that wasn't uncommon; he was frequently taller than most. They were both stocky, with ruddy-blond curls. The family resemblance faded there, as Thomas's speckled hazel eyes lifted in the corners while Arick's crinkled. Arick had sharper features than Thomas, whose rounded face often made people think him younger than his true age of twenty.

"I'm glad you're here," Thomas said, his voice thicker than usual.

"Me too." Guilt pricked at Arick. He nearly hadn't come. Thomas's letter couldn't have arrived at a worse time in Arick's training, and the summer storms had made the travel difficult.

But now that he was here... Well, he was here. And he'd support his cousin as best he could, even if he wasn't entirely sure what he could do.

Thomas pulled back from the hug, looking at the ground. "They want you to be king instead."

Arick stared, certain he had heard wrong amid the raging storm. "Me? But I'm not... Why not Princess Ailsa?" Even as he asked the question, another face, another option, crowded in. *Daniel should be here, not me.* He shoved the thought away.

Thomas splashed at the pooling water with his toe. "They figure you could marry her and that would make it right."

Arick shuddered. They weren't direct cousins — their grandfathers had been brothers — but even that was too close a relationship for him to want to marry Thomas's younger sister.

Lightning snapped, blinding them. Before the deafening thunder came a different loud crack.

The two rushed to the railing that overlooked the sea as more lightning lit up the sky.

A ship bucked on the towering waves, struggling to stay upright. Its mast lay broken across the deck.

Ignoring the rain that stung his eyes, Arick scanned the water for lifeboats as tiny figures clung to the ship. A small dot headed for the shore with a directness that surprised him. Waves crashed over it, yet the little boat stayed upright.

"The rocks!" Thomas pointed with a shout.

Arick stared in horror. Surely the sailors in the rowboat could see they were headed for the jagged rocks that lined the coast. Why weren't they turning?

He held his breath as the waves stalled their progress. They had time to turn, to angle away from the waiting jaws of the coastline. Farther into the harbor, they'd have a chance. He glanced at the stairwell, knowing it was impossible for him to reach the shore in time to help them.

The light from the lighthouse washed over them, timed perfectly with a massive wave. The men gave up all semblance of rowing, and instead clung to the sides of the boat.

But it was no use. The wave washed over them, pushing the boat onto the rocks.

Arick pulled Thomas away from the railing. They didn't need to watch the men die.

THE SOUL-PIERCING CRACK OF the ship's mast breaking in two sent splinters into the hearts of the merfolk gathered to wait out the storm. Even at that great distance, the cries of the sailors could be heard over the crash of thunder. Muffled by the water, any sound that reached them carried the promise of devastation.

With every bolt of lightning, the bioluminescent carpeting of the ocean floor flashed in response, turning the sea beyond the cavern into a flickering world of wonder.

Sorcha, the youngest of those gathered, flinched with every flash.

"Please, Mother," her raven-haired eldest sister begged as she swam tight circles around the others. "Let me go help Father."

The largest of the caverns that opened off the grotto belonged to the mermaids. Those who didn't have jobs or family to look after gathered here to wait out the storms. Tonight, there were seven of them, all anxiously looking for the return of those who had gone with the king.

Their mother shook her head, not lifting her hands from her ears. She lounged on a divan draped with seaweed. Even here, it was higher than the others, denoting her status as queen. "It's too dangerous, Ciara. Put your shells back."

Sorcha huddled in the sand with the other mermaids, each of them holding conch shells over their ears. The shells did little more than muffle the sounds, but the echo of the ocean within them disrupted the sonic waves of the human voices. They were uncomfortable, but Sorcha pressed them tightly to her head.

Ciara floated to a stop near her, her expression stubborn. She cast glances at the cave entrance where their father and the others had disappeared when the storm had first started.

"Ciara! Your shells!" Mother snapped.

Reluctantly, Ciara complied, flicking her purple fin.

Sorcha shuddered as her red locks fanned out around her shoulders. She couldn't imagine taking the risks Ciara did. The older girl had finally convinced their father to let her train with the Watchers, but he had refused to let her help this time.

"It's too dangerous. If there's a woman on board, we'll send for you, but for now, you'll stay put," he had told her.

None of the mermaids voiced what they were thinking — that if there was a woman on the ship, by the time one of the Watchers swam back to fetch Ciara and her dolphin, it would be too late.

But going to the surface was far riskier for merfolk. On the surface, there was no ocean to cut through the luring tones of human voices. Nothing to stop a mer from following a man to shore and dying on the beach like a washed-up fish. Or worse.

Father knew the dangers, as did the rest of the Watchers. They wore starfish over their ears and used hand signals to communicate. And they never got too close, using their trained dolphins to nudge bits of the shipwreck to the humans. Occasionally one would drag a human to the shore while the mermen stayed out of sight.

Better for tales of benevolent dolphins to fill their evenings of song than for rumors of merfolk to start up again.

But the storms had arrived early this year, and the humans would insist on sailing anyway. And unless the merfolk wanted their lifeless bodies filling the underwater city, luring sharks to their home, Father and the Watchers would venture out to save the lives of as many as they could.

Another boom echoed through the water. Sorcha couldn't stop the cry bursting from her, her cousins also crying out at the sound. Ciara pulled her close. Rona, the second oldest, began humming a melody. She raised her pointed nose, so like Mother's. And like Mother, she was the only one with her hair pinned up.

"Hush, little mermaid, close your eyes," she sang, motioning for Sorcha to join her.

Mother and some of the others took up the next line, eager for something to do to distract them from the storm. "Let ocean's whispers lull your sighs." The melody flowed around them like the silky water of a sun-kissed day.

"Rest in the embrace of the starlit sea." Ciara's rich soprano carried through the cavern.

Not content, Rona glared at Sorcha. "Sing!" she signed, her hands twisting around each other with her two fingers extended.

With a sigh, Sorcha began to sing on the last line. "Where dreams and peace forever shall be."

As they began the next verse, Sorcha let her voice blend with those around her, the tune familiar and comforting. For a moment, the seven voices rose in perfect harmony. She leaned her head against Ciara's, their air bubbles tumbling together as the song rose and fell. Her eyes drifted shut as she let the song carry away the fear that had gathered around her heart.

A hand grabbed her arm, and she shrieked, a discordant sound that shattered the music.

"You're not singing properly," Rona hissed in her ear.

Sorcha pulled her arm free. "Yes, I am," she insisted. With the spell of the music broken, she could hear the storm again.

"You're not. Look around."

Sorcha looked at the others. Despite the calming music, worry still adorned the faces of the women around her, two of her cousins clinging to each other with white-knuckled hands.

"Sing," Rona told her.

"I can't," Sorcha retorted. She knew what Rona wanted, but stubbornness held her back. Why was it always up to her to solve everything?

"Yes, you can. Use your magic."

"I won't have enough left to heal the men later if I do."

Ciara leaned around Sorcha and pushed Rona away. "Leave her alone."

"She can heal them, but she won't. They're worried and scared."

"And her singing won't fix that."

Around them, the song faltered as the bickering sisters continued. Sorcha shrank away from them as much as she could.

"Are you saying you aren't worried about your fiancé?" Rona demanded.

A stricken look flashed across Ciara's face. "Of course I am. But magic won't take that away, and I wouldn't want it to either."

Rona sat back with a huff. She crossed her arms, her black bracer dull against her sunset scales. "If someone I loved had been taken, I'd at least *care*."

Ciara swirled in the water, looking ready to slap Rona. Sorcha stared at her sister in horror — how could she say such a thing?

With a choking sob, Ciara sped out of the cavern, her tail raising clouds of sand in her wake. Sorcha stared after her, wondering if she should follow.

Mother floated over and put her arms around the two remaining sisters. "Come, girls. Let us sing together and chase away these worries that cling like barnacles."

Sorcha let herself join the circle again. This time, she let a hint of her magic seep into her voice, earning her a smug look from Rona. If it weren't for the approving nod from Mother, she might have stopped.

It felt good to be useful, to do something to assuage the oppressive atmosphere that filled the cavern each time there was a storm. But it didn't stop her from hearing the roaring waves and desperate cries from far above grow worse.

Or maybe she was only imagining them.

CHAPTER TWO

T HE MORNING BROKE BRIGHT and clear, as though the sky were apologizing for the storms of the night. Arick enjoyed his stroll along the cobblestone streets of the waking city as he made his way to the castle. He followed the harbor road, keeping an ear open for any reports of lost ships, but any grieving was being done behind closed doors.

The steward showed him directly to the king's private sitting room, where the barrel-chested king was washing down his breakfast with a massive pot of tea. Thomas grinned up at him from the opposite side of the table, his dog at his feet.

"Arick, lad! Thomas said you'd arrived. Beat the storms. Why aren't you staying at the castle?" He motioned for Arick to sit down and slurped his tea. "Bring another cup for the lad," he shouted at the steward.

Arick smiled at his uncle's exuberance. As a child, he'd loved hearing him recount tales of battles and bravery. "Hullo, Uncle Craig. I wanted the chance to visit with Elsbeth at the inn," he said in response to the king's question.

"Ah, yes, and how is herself?"

"I fear her age is catching up to her, not that she'd let me see." He joined them at the table and accepted a cup of tea with a nod of thanks.

"No, of course not. Let me know if she needs anything."

"I will, thank you," Arick said. Elsbeth was like a grandmother to him, and it saddened him to notice the faint signs of aging on her face and in her mannerisms.

"Now that you're here, I've got a task for you," the king said, around a bite of breakfast, ignoring the crumbs that fell on his doublet.

"Of course, sir," Arick responded, curious. Thomas squirmed.

"We're planning a little something different for Thomas's birthday in two days. Now that you're ready to become a naval officer, I think this is right in your wheelhouse."

Arick nodded, wondering what his uncle meant by that. But more, he was wondering why Thomas wouldn't look at him.

The king outlined more about the party, reassuring Arick that he wasn't in charge of counting spoons or ordering hors d'oeuvres.

"Thomas will take you to the, uh...venue. Are you ready to go, Thomas?"

"I need my coat." Thomas shoved his seat back.

"Well, run and do that."

"Da...you promised." Thomas hopped on one foot.

The king waved his hand at him. "Yes, yes, I won't tell."

Thomas's face stretched in a grin as he ran out of the room. Arick relaxed slightly. Thomas wasn't upset with him. He helped himself to a muffin.

"There's something else I want you to pay attention to while you're here." The king grew serious and leaned forward. "These storms, there's something uncanny about them."

"The one last night was much worse than any I remember as a child," Arick agreed.

"We'd generally get one or two like that, but I worry that they've started so early in the season," the king said.

"Have many been lost?" Arick's stomach turned, thinking of the men he'd seen headed for the rocks below the lighthouse.

The king shook his head. "Two ships have been lost with all their crew. They were outside the harbor, but still — two too many."

Arick pushed his plate away, the muffin half-eaten. "What about last night? Thomas and I saw some in peril."

"Aye, Thomas told me. I had guards check the shore this morning. A lifeboat was on the beach, but no dead."

Arick breathed a prayer of thanks.

The king cleared his throat. "I'd like you to do some investigating and see what you can come up with."

"Sir, don't you have advisers for that?"

"Bah, they're either in denial about the risk of more storms or they blame Cliodna." The chair creaked under his weight as he jerked upright.

"Cliodna? You mean the..."

"Yes, the mythical spirit that supposedly controls the sea." The king shook his head at the thought but sent him on his way without elaborating further.

Arick pondered the idea as he and Thomas made their way to the docks. A mythical being controlling the storms was nonsense. The Creator was the one who controlled all of nature. And yet...

A shadow fell over him, causing him to glance up. All at once, the king's first request made sense.

"Surprise!" Thomas gloated. His small sheltie, Cookie, yipped in agreement, dancing around them.

With a laugh, Arick returned his cousin's hug. "Hardly my surprise though — it's your birthday present."

"Yes, but I've known about it for ages. It's more fun to surprise you."

The ship before them was a sailor's delight — long and sleek, with a foredeck that was designed as a floating ballroom. The yacht could host at least a hundred people yet manage the high seas for a day cruise.

Arick was in love.

The naval vessels he served on were far more utilitarian, and even the cargo ships were designed for one purpose — and it certainly wasn't for comfort.

Councilman MacIsaac joined them, bowing to both of them, though it seemed as though he bowed lower to Arick than to Thomas, his prince. He was a small man, mean of appearance and broad of mustache, and Arick took an instant dislike to him.

"His Majesty informed me that you would be taking point for His Highness's birthday gala." MacIsaac's tone implied he did not think the change of command was necessary.

"The seafaring aspect only. I have no interest in taking over. I'm certain you have put a lot of effort into the celebrations, and there's no need to start changing things now," Arick assured him.

MacIsaac gave him a calculating look, but he let the matter drop.

They climbed the gangway — wider and with sturdier railings than normal — and met Captain Blair, a pleasant, trim fellow who was the kind of man who could be both effusive host and rigid leader as the need arose. MacIsaac immediately bombarded Blair with questions, some quite unnecessary or ridiculous, in Arick's opinion. The captain could no more promise good weather than he could wish for it to rain gold. And there was little reason for MacIsaac to query the number of guests that could fit onboard — surely the councilman already knew that information.

Too excited to wait for the captain to give Arick a proper tour, Thomas led the way, jabbering about the various aspects of the ship. Arick followed him. He'd ask the captain technical things later. For now, he tried to take in all the details, from the hand-carved railings to the elevated platform for the musical ensembles and the polished floor that could be removed and stored safely when a ball wasn't in progress.

"This is my favorite part," Thomas said, guiding him down a level to a large space that had been closed off from the rest of the deck. Cookie ran around the sparsely finished room, sniffing everything. Thomas opened a set of French doors on the side of the ship with a flourish.

Arick stepped out onto the small balcony and looked around. There were no railings, only two guide wires holding the edge of the balcony to the ship.

"It's a swimming platform." Thomas pressed his hands together, as if trying to contain his glee. "See, you can dive from here, and there's the ladder to get back up."

"And these wires?" Arick held onto one to steady himself as he peered over the edge.

Thomas sighed. "Da didn't like the look of it with a full balcony, and the shipwright gave some boring explanation. So the platform has to fold up when we're not using it. See, it tucks into the doorway, here. It blocks the bottom half of the door, and you can still see out the top windows."

Arick studied the neat little system that worked the moving floor. The workmanship was impressive to have made it fit so well and not look out of place when closed. He bounced on the balls of his feet, testing the give of the platform. Despite everything, it had little movement, just enough springiness to be perfect for diving.

From inside the ship, footsteps and murmured conversation drew closer.

"I know what I saw," a gruff voice said from somewhere behind them.

"You're off your head if you think you're seeing mermaids," another retorted.

Arick stilled. He hadn't heard anyone speak of mermaids since Daniel...

E VEN DEEP BENEATH THE waves, the early morning sun brought hope and beauty after the storm. Dappled light filtered through the waves, changing the colors of the underwater flora and turning Sorcha's shelf of bric-a-brac into a glittering collection.

She turned the piece of malachite so it better caught the light, then picked up a jar that held jewelry she'd found on the ocean floor. The gold and silver had tarnished from the saltwater, but the gems still shone. Her favorite, a heart-shaped sapphire set in silver latticework, shimmered a pale blue. She fished it out and slipped it over her head. The faded ribbon was wearing thin, and she freed her hair as gently as she could.

Turning the jar in the light, she pondered what her Aunt Maeve had said about how the humans didn't have their own magic. Instead, she'd told her, they imbued gemstones with it. Were any of her collection magical? Sorcha couldn't help but wonder.

"Morning," Ciara said as she poked her head through the opening to Sorcha's cubbyhole. "A ship sank last night. Want to go take a look?"

Sorcha shivered. "Not until the Watchers have cleared it."

Ciara tugged her hand, pulling her from the tiny cave. All traces of the argument from the night before were hidden behind a teasing smile. "Are you a cuttlefish?"

Sorcha shook her head firmly. "No, but I'd rather not come across a dead human, thank you very much." One already this season was quite enough.

"They can't lure you to shore if they're dead." Ciara rolled her eyes. "Come on. You've been cooped up for weeks. Time to have some fun."

"I promised Aunt Maeve I'd help her in the infirmary today."

"You can help her later."

Sorcha started to protest again, but the pleading look in her sister's eyes stopped her. Ever since Ciara's fiancé, Ewan, had vanished at the end of the last storm season, she'd become increasingly chaotic. At first, she'd spent days scouring the ocean for him, but after weeks of no trace, she'd changed her focus. Their father had given into her pleading and allowed her to join the Watchers. If she hadn't been the oldest, she would have joined when she was eighteen, as her song magic aligned with that of the undersea mammals, like many of the other Watchers. She and her dolphin had been training all winter to be ready to help this season.

No one wanted to give voice to their fears, but only one cause for his disappearance made sense. Humans.

Ewan and Ciara made a good pair, both of them being impulsive and longing for adventure. Mother had only approved the match because she had hoped marriage would encourage them to settle down. Sorcha had her doubts on that.

But would Ewan's impulsivity have caused him to help a human directly? Would he have taken off his starfish ear protection and allowed himself to be lured to his death on dry land?

Sorcha shivered again at the thought. Surely not — he was a trained Watcher after all, and safety was drilled into them. Save the humans, but not at the risk of a mer life.

With a forced smile, Sorcha tapped her sister on the shoulder and swam away as fast as she could. "If you want fun," she called back, "you'll have to catch me first!"

"Tag? Isn't that a little childish?" Ciara retorted, giving chase.

The sisters raced through the grotto, sending fish and merfolk fleeing. The massive underwater grotto was the perfect shelter for the merfolk home, providing the center for their aquatic life. Smaller caverns, tunnels, and caves opened off of it, forming homes for many of the citizens of Muirin. Sorcha's own tiny cave, where she kept her treasures, was too small for anything else, and no one wanted to be tucked up against the cavern ceiling anyway.

"Caught you," Ciara panted, brushing her hand against Sorcha's shimmering blue scales.

Sorcha twisted away, zipping around a group of mermaids discussing hairstyles and the best pronglesnaffers to use for untangling knots. They tsked in annoyance.

"Stop acting like guppies!" one of them shouted.

Too late, Sorcha realized Rona was among them. No chance Mother wouldn't hear about it now. Oh, well.

Ciara grabbed Sorcha's hand. "Come on."

Together, they swam past the palace — a towering structure of rock and coral in the center of the grotto. Along the base of the palace, nestled within small caves and gentle openings, lay the offices of the various guilds and ministers, where the wheels of governance turned with an undercurrent of efficiency and harmony.

Ascending the levels of the palace, Sorcha's eyes were drawn to the regal quarters of the royal family, her own among them. A sense of grace and elegance permeated these private sanctuaries, where the blend of comfort and opulence painted a picture of a cherished retreat. Beyond the royal chambers, the infirmary and apothecary offered healing and solace, attending to the well-being of the merfolk community.

At the pinnacle of the palace, Queen Brigid's throne stood as a testament to the bond between ruler and people. Its intricate patterns and ethereal glow mesmerized Sorcha, drawing her in with their captivating beauty. As a child, she would insist on going up with her mother, then promptly abandon her to play amid the vibrant palette of the coral formations. It was said that with each new reign, the colors and designs would shift, a reflection of the ever-changing tide of leadership. Although Sorcha was too young to recall her grandfather's reign, Ciara said she remembered it being more green than the current yellow tones that matched Mother's tail.

In this wondrous underwater realm, where living organisms melded with the magnificence of nature, Sorcha reveled in the kaleidoscope of colors that embraced her. The grotto's curved ceiling, a tribute to the awe-inspiring craftsmanship of the ocean itself, served as a natural amphitheater, carrying the soothing melodies of Mother's voice to all who gathered. It was a place of unity, where the enchanting beauty of the surroundings mirrored the harmony and solidarity of the merfolk community, bound together by their shared love for this iridescent underwater haven.

No matter how often she saw it, Sorcha never failed to find something new and marvelous in the grotto.

Father waved to them, a smile on his tired face as they swam through the grotto's opening. His own domain lay just outside. There, the Watchers trained and lived in smaller caves or on shelves of coral.

"Any sharks, Father?" Ciara asked.

"Not today, thankfully. You girls are free to explore; just don't stay out too long."

"More storms?" Sorcha frowned.

Father shook his head. "It doesn't look like it, but the weather above has been...unpredictable of late." A Watcher swam to a stop beside them, his fist over his heart in a salute. Father waved the girls off and turned to take the report.

"I still don't want to go to the wreck," Sorcha said. Even without sharks — or the drowned humans who drew them there — the newly sunken ship would be too eerie to explore.

Ciara shook her head, studying her sister's face. "No, not today. Today is for sunshine and gentle breezes."

Sorcha rolled her eyes at her sister again, turning to hide the dark shadows under her eyes. "You know we don't need sunlight the way humans do."

"I disagree. Look at your tail – it's looking so drab lately. The sun will brighten that up."

With a laugh, they shot upward and broke through the surface, where the warmth of the sun beckoned them to play amid the waves. Sorcha had to admit that her scales shimmered a brighter blue in the light, and she enjoyed racing her sister, who swam just below the sea foam that collected on top of the water.

A RICK TURNED TOWARD THE voices and noticed two sailors passing outside the door, carrying something between them.

"Oh, 'scuse us, sirs," the first man said. "We've been told to bring this settee down here to the sitting room."

The men were looking to him for an answer, but Arick deferred to Thomas with a pointed glance.

"Uh, go ahead," Thomas told them. As the men proceeded to find a spot for the settee, he leaned close to Arick. "Do you think mermaids are real?"

Arick laughed. "The stories of merfolk are more than a hundred years old. If they ever did exist, they've died out by now."

"That's just what I said, sir," the gruff one said. "Cliodna don't work with mermaids."

Councilman MacIsaac and the captain chose that moment to join them. MacIsaac glared at the men. "Back to work. And enough of this fanciful talk of mermaids and sea witches. No need to frighten the prince."

Thomas blinked. "I'm not frightened. I'd love to meet a mermaid."

"Be that as it may, there are none to meet," MacIsaac replied dryly.

"I wouldn't go so far as to say that," Blair said, his eyes twinkling.

"You've seen one!" Thomas turned to the captain.

MacIsaac sneered. "Surely you don't believe such tales."

"I'm not saying I do or I don't — but you see some strange things at night when you're out on the water, far from land." He turned to Arick. "But enough of that. We're about to let go the lines, if you'd care to join me on the bridge?" He looked to Thomas as well, making sure to include him in the invitation.

The four of them returned to the top deck and climbed the steps to the bridge. Unlike the near vertical stairs on most ships, these were wide and sweeping, so any ladies who might be onboard would be able to visit the bridge without fear of tripping over their skirts.

The next hour passed pleasantly as the captain put the ship through her paces, calling commands to the sailors who swung from the masts. At last, they slowed as they approached the center of the harbor. No ships were scheduled to be arriving, and any departing would wait for the ebbing tide later to guide them past the rock formations at the entrance, so they could take their time.

MacIsaac's continued displeasure with everything nearly drove Arick mad, and he made every effort to shield Thomas from the man's barbed comments. Guessing MacIsaac would shy away from heavy work, he volunteered to lower the anchor.

Together, he and Thomas worked the windlass and let the anchor go. Even though it would spend a good portion of its life on the ocean floor, the anchor displayed skilled craftsmanship and the ornate emblem of the crown.

With the ship rocking gently in place, there was little else for Arick and Thomas to do. Any time Arick tried to speak to the captain, MacIsaac was there, pestering Blair with questions he had surely asked a hundred times before.

"Let's go swimming!" Thomas suggested. Arick eagerly accepted the distraction. They ran down to the sitting room and changed into bathing costumes. Cookie trotted between their feet and promptly found a patch of sun. He stretched with a yawn, his fluffy tail dusting the floor. Once he had changed, Arick walked out onto the platform, feeling the slight spring beneath his feet. Below him, the water beckoned. The sun glinted off of it.

"Chicken?" Thomas asked.

"No, just waiting for you." Arick grinned. With a shout, he dove off the platform, feeling the sun and air embrace him in a moment of flight.

The ice-cold water wrapped around him as he crashed beneath the waves. The shock drove the air from his lungs, and his eyes popped open. As he sought the surface, he noted how clear the water was, filled with sea life.

As he broke free of the water, he shook his head, sending streams in all directions.

With a shriek of joy, Thomas jumped off the platform and into the waves behind him. "Co-old," he chattered when he reappeared. Above them, Cookie ran in circles, barking at their madness.

"Very," Arick agreed. "Come on, let's swim to warm up."

They raced the length of the ship a few times, staying clear of the bow and stern lest the ship turn unexpectedly. When they grew tired, they floated on their backs and let the sun warm their faces. This was the life. If only being a royal meant he could spend his days on the water, swimming and racing boats. He recalled the letters his brother, Daniel, had sent him, speaking of the endless meetings and countless social obligations he'd been forced to attend. At least, that's how Arick thought of them. Daniel had spoken of them with enthusiasm, proving he had been the better brother to join the Toravik Council. If only —

"They hate me," Thomas said, breaking his reverie.

Arick wasn't surprised Thomas's thoughts were also on the council. "Why do you say that?" The hurt in his cousin's voice made him choose his words carefully.

Thomas slapped the water with his hand. "Look at how MacIsaac treats me! Either he acts like I am a child, or he ignores me!"

Arick rolled over in the water to watch Thomas's reaction. He moved his arms and feet enough to stay afloat. "Do you want to be treated like a child or ignored?"

"No!"

"Then...maybe don't let him?"

Thomas's face creased with concentration. "Why did you say that?" he asked, his voice cracking.

Arick had never seen his cousin as "less than." As children, they had spent much of their time together, and though he knew Thomas was different from other children, he was just Thomas. Even after his father had become the ambassador to Edeland, Arick and his brother, Daniel, had spent their summers visiting the castle. When they turned eighteen, Daniel had moved back to Iskarraig, and Arick had joined the Edelish Navy.

"You're allowed to speak up. You're the prince, and he should be diffident toward you."

"Easy for you to say," Thomas grumbled.

"I know. And I'm sorry they treat you like that." It *was* easy for him. People had been looking up to him physically ever since he'd passed six feet at age sixteen. As part of his training to be captain, he had learned how to be commanding — though being commanding and being listened to were two very different things, he had quickly discovered. "Just remember, you have just as much right to be heard as the next person. If you act like you belong, they'll not be able to ignore you."

"I'll try."

"Good. But for now, I'm freezing. Race you back to the ladder!" He dove under the water, encouraging Thomas to chase after him. He took the outside, planning on letting Thomas win.

When Arick surfaced for air, he saw Thomas several strokes ahead of him. He'd been too slow, and Thomas had been faster than expected. With renewed purpose, Arick struck out again. Even at his fastest speed, however, he only managed to catch up after Thomas had taken hold of the ladder.

Laughing, the two climbed back to the platform, where an ecstatic Cookie danced circles around them as they dried off. Exhausted, they stretched out to let the sun warm them up, letting their feet hang off the edge.

Above them, someone tuned a fiddle and began playing. Thomas hummed along to the traditional song. Arick pushed himself upright, knowing what was coming. He leaned back on his hands, his face tilted toward the sun.

The next tune was one of his favorites, and Thomas could never hear it without begging him to sing. Arick cleared his throat and sang the haunting lyrics of a love lost and a land that separated them. Thomas joined on the chorus, his high tenor voice providing a perfect counterpart.

As he sang, his gaze traveled over the water as though searching for the lost love of the song. Two dots bobbed along with the waves, growing ever closer. They looked like the heads of two women, one with red hair, the other black. But the water out here was far too deep for ladies to risk, and no one would be swimming by the rocks like that.

Mermaids.

He immediately shook the idea free. The music — that must have been the reason behind such fanciful thoughts. They were seals, nothing more.

But why did the thought leave him disappointed?

WHEN THE SISTERS HAD exhausted themselves, they found a rock and leaned against it, letting the sun and wind dry their hair. With only their heads and shoulders out of the water, they could pass for humans, albeit oddly dressed humans, arrayed in garments of scales that covered most of their bodies and faded to skin just below their collar bones. Humans seemed to wrap themselves in layers of fabric, something Sorcha was glad the merfolk didn't need to be concerned about. The scales provided them with what modesty and warmth they needed.

"I wish Father had let me join the Watchers last night," Ciara commented. "I've been training for ages."

"The storms started early, and you've not had your graduation ceremony yet."

"I know, but it's been ages since a mermaid has been a Watcher. With the increase in storms, there's a greater chance for a human female to be on the ship."

Sorcha pushed her red hair out of her face. Out of the water, curls started to form as it dried, tickling her cheeks. "Why do you think the starfish can't block the female's voices?"

Ciara shrugged, watching a small crab dance its way across the rock. "They're higher pitched. But that doesn't explain why mermaids are less susceptible to their voices." She turned to look at the human city in the distance, with its massive gray castle high above them on the cliffs. "I'd love the chance to learn more about them."

Sorcha pushed her off the rocks. "Don't *say* that! You get close, and you know what could happen!"

"I'd cover my ears. Besides, once the human stops talking, the spell releases." Ciara rolled over and leaned back against her perch.

"Not before you are too far up the sand to get back." She'd seen fish die that way — flopping and bouncing as much as they could, until they exhausted themselves and lay twitching on the shore, the vibrant colors of their scales fading.

"Better than being bound to a human," Ciara said, bitterness in her voice.

A seagull floated by, bobbing among the waves.

"What do you think happens to bound ones?" Sorcha asked, following the change in topic.

Ciara shrugged. "They turn into humans and live the rest of their lives on land."

"There has to be more to it than that. Or else merfolk would do it all the time. Aunt Maeve said she once wanted to be human, but it wasn't worth the cost."

"Aunt Maeve wanted to do everything. Maybe I'll rescue a human and we can find out what happens," Ciara mused.

"You wouldn't dare!"

"Wouldn't I?" A teasing gleam appeared in her eye. "Let's go find a human and see!" She sank beneath the waves and zipped away, her purple-blue fins lifting above the water to splash Sorcha.

"Ach!" Sorcha cried in protest. She pushed off from the rocks to swim below the surface. Immediately, her breathing came easier, and the drowsiness she had felt faded. While they were above the surface of the water, merfolk were still able to gain the oxygen they needed, but it was harder. And when they were completely on land, it was almost impossible. "Where are you going?"

Ciara didn't answer as she pulled farther away. Sorcha concentrated on catching her, but Ciara was stronger from her months of training and kept just out of reach. As they swam, they passed the eddy that led back to the grotto, heading for the harbor. For a few minutes, a dolphin joined their race, darting in and out between them. Then, the rock formations that guarded the entrance for ships flashed by. Ciara turned over, swimming backward to taunt Sorcha. "Can't you keep up, then?"

Sorcha looked up, her eyes widening in fear at the sight of the wooden wall that loomed behind her sister. "Ciara!"

Ciara spun around, her shoulder bouncing off the ship. Sorcha grabbed her and pulled her away before she could be caught in the wake.

"Stop, I'm fine." Ciara's voice was shaky, but she hid it behind a toss of her hair.

Sorcha clamped her hands over her ears. If there was a ship, there were humans. "Let's go back."

"No, I want to see what they're doing. No ship passed us outside the harbor, but this one isn't leaving...it's heading back in."

Sorcha let her attention return to the ship, this time noting the shape of the hull. It was wide and long, but not deep like many of the others that passed over the grotto.

"We can watch from the rocks," she offered.

They swam back to the large rocks at the entrance and hid among them. Sorcha kept her hands clamped over her ears, and ducked beneath the water when two men appeared near the back of the boat to release the anchor. She winced at the splash, knowing the fish and sea life would be scattering in fear.

The sailors vanished, then reappeared on a small platform one deck lower. One was several hand-lengths taller than the other, but their blond hair was the same. They stripped off their shirts, then the taller one leapt into the water with a whooping shout. The other followed, shrieking as he fell through the air. On the ship, a fluffy brown and white creature whined and yipped after them.

Mesmerized, Sorcha watched the humans play in the water. She'd never seen humans so close, nor grown ones splash about like that. Occasionally, their voices reached her, but they were having too much fun for conversation. Beside her, Ciara watched with an intense look on her face.

"I wonder what it would be like on land," Ciara mused.

Sorcha shook her head. "Not me. Living on land would be so one dimensional. The water holds freedom."

"Yet water is constrained by land."

Sorcha thought about that. In a way, yes, it was. The land rose from the water, resisting it. But the ocean went on forever.

After some time, the humans climbed up the side of the ship. The small creature spun in excited circles and beat its fluffy tail against the men.

"It's getting late," Sorcha said. They'd been gone most of the morning.

"Not yet," Ciara whispered. "I want to see what they're doing."

But it appeared that they weren't doing much. The pair sat on the small deck, their legs over the edge as they talked. Another sailor appeared above them, holding a flat, oval box with a long handle in one hand and a stick in the other. Sorcha squinted, but she couldn't see what they were for.

"Is that a weapon?"

"Don't be silly. What would they need weapons for?"

"Then what is it?"

Before Ciara could pretend to know its purpose, the man raised the box to his shoulder and put the stick to it. Music filled the air, the notes tripping over each other like a school of clownfish darting through the coral. Sorcha gasped in delight, letting her hands fall from her ears so she could better hear. The vibrant sound pulled her from her hiding spot, and she swam closer, only her head above the water. She could sense Ciara beside her, but she willed her sister to not say anything to interrupt the music.

The song changed to one full of melancholy that made her chest ache. A voice lifted, a rich baritone that blended perfectly with the music. Longing filled her, and with all her heart, she wished to know the meaning of the words sung by the tall blond sailor.

Laughter pulled her back to herself as hands clamped over her ears.

"Look at you, Miss Never-Want-to-Be-near-a-Human." Ciara smirked.

Sorcha gasped to realize how close she'd gotten to the ship. The tall man was staring in their direction, the song fading from his lips.

With a cry of fear, Sorcha dove beneath the waves, losing herself among the rocky formations on the harbor floor.

CHAPTER THREE

T HE SUN WAS SETTING in a glorious banner of purples, pinks, and oranges as the royal yacht cast off from the dock. A cheer went up from those gathered on the deck for the official inaugural voyage.

The plan had been to leave a bit earlier and watch the sun go down as they sailed outside the harbor. But with the unpredictable storms, Arick had advised the king not to take the risk. And so they had pushed back the start time of the party to begin with the floating ball — enough of a novelty in itself to be talked about around every teapot in the city for at least a month.

As the guest of honor, Thomas stood on the bridge, leading the cheer. His parents stood behind him, their expressions more reserved. His sister, the princess, Ailsa, graced the top of the port flight of stairs while Arick positioned himself on the starboard.

He joined in the clapping, again impressed with the gracefulness of the ship. Over the past few days, he'd had the opportunity to speak further with Captain Blair and learn more about the vessel. She would never win any races or haul great cargo long distances. But she was a delight to handle and would be perfect for the royal family to travel to other parts of the kingdom by sea.

The yacht made a sweeping circuit of the harbor, then lowered its anchor in the same spot where they'd gone swimming a few days earlier.

The musicians slid from the jovial tunes that had welcomed everyone on board to the more sedate strains of a dance.

Thomas turned and bowed over the queen's hand. She was a petite lady, but her elegant demeanor made everyone forget her size, and she glided down the stairs on her son's arm with a benevolent smile. Arick crossed the bridge and offered his first dance to Ailsa. She flushed a pretty pink and curtsied in reply. As they descended the staircase to the dance floor, Arick couldn't help noticing the pleased looks they were receiving from several of the councilmen who were gathered along the rail.

Arick guided Ailsa through the dance, concentrating on the steps — and on not stepping on her. At sixteen, Ailsa was full grown, yet her head didn't reach his shoulder.

"They wish for us to marry, you know," she said, proving that she wasn't really a child.

"You noticed them too, then?" he asked wryly.

She nodded. "The topic has been brought up more than once in council meetings of late."

"You attend the council meetings?"

"Why wouldn't I? As princess, it's my duty to know what is happening in my kingdom." She hesitated. "And Thomas appreciates having someone to talk to about the meetings after."

Arick nodded. Even though Thomas was quite smart, there were times when he did struggle to grasp concepts. Although from what Arick had seen, the thing Thomas struggled the most to understand was why the council didn't do more to help the people, a testament to his pure heart.

"You don't seem bothered by the idea of marrying me," Arick said. Etiquette would say he had no right to mention it without being ready to ask for her hand, but she had broached the topic first.

She shrugged a tiny shoulder. "There are worse men they could want to marry me off to for an alliance. At least you're nice and not twice my age."

Arick tamped down his own protests about their close relationship. As a man, and not a royal, he had the choice of whom he would marry. Women had far less freedom, and princesses were expected to wed in a fashion that would be advantageous to the kingdom.

"But our marriage is designed to legitimize my claim to the throne. Would you want to see Thomas stripped of his role?"

She gave him a sharp look. "My brother is perfectly capable of being king, so long as he has advisers he can trust and lean on.

I intend to be one of those advisers. Marrying you won't change that. And I hope it would give Thomas another trusted person on his council."

The music came to an end before Arick needed to reply. He left her with a bow.

Being an unattached man below a certain age, he was expected to dance as much as he could, so he spent the next hour on the dance floor. New partners were introduced to him as soon as he returned one to her chaperones. At this point, he'd forgotten nearly all their names, but Ailsa's keen eyes watched him throughout the evening, and he knew she could recount each of the young ladies he'd been paired with.

Her words continued to nag him. Married to the princess or not, did he owe it to Thomas to set aside his dream of being a captain to serve at his side?

As another song came to an end, he paused his dancing and left the floor in search of a drink. He should have asked the lady he'd been dancing with if she wanted something, but he wasn't in the mood for her constant chatter about sheep.

MacIsaac appeared at his elbow. "You haven't danced with the princess in quite some time," the councilman pointed out.

Arick jerked at his voice.

"If you are to be betrothed, it's good for the people to see you together."

Clenching his fist at his side, Arick kept walking. "'If' is the key word here. And any relationship between the princess and myself shall be kept private."

The corner of MacIsaac's mustache lifted in a shrewd smile. "So you do have a relationship?"

Arick's face flushed. *Confound the man.* "That is not what I said, and you know it."

"Well, hopefully, you'll be able to make your *private* relationship more public before the week is out." He smirked.

For a moment, Arick wondered whether it would be entirely inappropriate to punch the councilman. Fights weren't uncommon in the island courts, the people being much more fiery and passionate than those in the lower countries. But it would ruin Thomas's party, and a fight over her would do nothing for Ailsa's reputation. He clenched his fist and sought a polite way to escape.

Someone jostled him from behind, and he turned to see one of the smartly dressed sailors hurrying to the foremast. His eyes traveled up the mast to the sky. The stars were winking out one by one as clouds swirled overhead.

A storm was coming.

T HE SONG SHE'D HEARD the humans sing continued to play in her ears over the next few days, and Sorcha often found herself humming the melody as she went about her duties. Was it the odd instrument that drew her or the man's voice?

Another storm raged overhead. One ship had already crashed onto the rocks, and several Watchers had been injured trying to free the sailors. Chaos reigned in the infirmary. Sorcha leaned over a merman with a chunk of wood sticking out of his tail. She held him down as her aunt Maeve worked to free it.

Maeve waved a hand in front of her face, drawing Sorcha's attention. Chagrined, Sorcha realized it wasn't the first time Maeve had tried to talk to her. With the seashells tied over her ears, it was hard to hear.

Maeve held her hand near her throat, fingers pinched together, then twisted her wrist back and spread her long, bony fingers at the same time. *Sing*, she mouthed, just in case Sorcha had missed the hand sign.

With a nod, Sorcha cleared her throat and searched for the words of a song. Lyrics from the lullaby came to mind, but as she tried to sing it, her voice kept searching for the tune from the human song. She faltered and tried again, concentrating on the familiarity of the lullaby, letting her magic flow into the music.

The merman writhed as Maeve pulled the wood from him, forcing Sorcha to tighten her hold. She lost her place in the song, and the human melody took over again. As Maeve bandaged the wound, Sorcha focused on her song, and the merman relaxed.

Maeve pulled her aside when they were done. She removed the shells from over her ears and motioned for Sorcha to do the same. "That's a human song. Where did you hear it?" Her fingers were tight around Sorcha's arm, and her unnaturally blue-white hair stood even more on end than usual.

"No...nowhere," Sorcha gulped. Going to the surface wasn't exactly forbidden, but the heat of Maeve's eyes made her feel as though she'd committed the worst offense.

"Humans aren't to be trusted. You forget that song, or before you know it, you'll be flopping on dry land like a dead fish."

Sorcha nodded, her eyes wide. How *dead* fish flopped, she wasn't sure, but it didn't feel like the right time to ask Maeve.

"And you forget the human who sang it, you hear me? You must never go near them again."

Sorcha nodded again.

"Good, now get back to work. Give this to the one by the entrance; he's looking a little green around the gills." She handed Sorcha a vial of turquoise liquid before swimming off to help someone else, her black scales showing purple in the light. Despite her bulk, Maeve floated around the infirmary with grace, bringing an odd sort of comfort to the injured. As long as Maeve was snippy and cantankerous, you knew you'd be okay. She was only kind when there was no hope.

Sorcha settled the shells back over her ears, wishing she could use the starfish the way the Watchers did. But there were only so many that could be convinced to help, and the Watchers needed the extra protection. Picking a different song, she sang as she navigated through the chaos, letting just a bit of her magic seep into the upbeat tune — not enough to drain her, but just enough so that the magic would help ease the pain of any who heard.

She offered a comforting smile to the Watcher reclining on a shelf by the entrance. The merman clung to the coral as he gasped for oxygen.

Studying him, she frowned. There was no mark of injury anywhere on him, yet his eyes were wide, and he shook as he tried to breathe.

His starfish!

One of his starfish was gone, and the other clung to his neck rather than the side of his head. She reached for it, but he let go of his hold on the coral long enough to bat her hand away. He shrank back into the wall. She tapped the side of her own neck, but he just shook his head violently.

Leaning close, she yelled into his ear. "The starfish is on your gill — that's why you can't breathe."

He stared at her, wide-eyed. Taking that as an invitation, she reached for the starfish and gently coaxed it free. He shoved her arm again, but not before she had lifted the starfish partly away from his gills.

As oxygen reached his brain, he understood and ripped the starfish off, flinging it across the room. That was one that wouldn't be interested in helping again.

The merman looked better now that he could breathe, but he still held tightly to the coral wall.

"Don't let them take me," he whimpered as thunder rolled in the distance.

"Who?"

"The humans! I heard their voices!"

She reached to pat his shoulder, then remembered the vial in her hand. Was it capable of canceling the siren spell? Or was it just a tincture to calm him down?

Either would work, if she could convince him to take it. She held it out to him, but he shook his head, refusing to let go.

"This will help?" She swallowed hard. She hadn't meant to make it a question.

He squinted at her doubt. "Will it?"

"Of course." She pulled the stopper out and leaned over to give it to him. If she had to pour it down his throat, she would.

He jerked again, his head knocking into her hand.

The vial flew out of her grasp, the green liquid spilling into the water. It bounced against the coral and smashed.

"That's how you deliver medicine around here?" A sarcastic voice asked.

Sorcha looked up to see Rona in the doorway, her arms folded. Some of the liquid bubbled against the yellow stone in her bracer.

"Sorry," Sorcha muttered, ducking to pick up the glass shards.

"I came to see why you aren't singing. Mother was worried." She moved just out of the way enough so Sorcha wouldn't bump into her, but didn't offer to help.

"Been a little busy here. Ouch!" Sorcha cried as the glass cut her finger.

"Ach, can't you do anything right?" Rona sneered.

Tears filled Sorcha's eyes as she spun away. Why did she think she could help? Everything she did was wrong.

Pushing past Rona, she fled the infirmary. She wanted the solitude of her cavern, but a group of merfolk gathered in that section of the grotto. She turned and headed for the entrance, needing to get away.

Away from her mistakes, away from Rona's judgment, away from the countless expectations.

A sob threatened to choke her as she swam through the opening. Without paying attention to where she was going, she sped away. The knot holding her sea shells on her head came loose, and she let them fall away. Below her, the bioluminescents flashed in response to the lightning above.

"Go TELL HIS MAJESTY there's a storm coming," Arick ordered, his training as an officer taking over any sensibilities of rank on land as the clouds continued to block out the sky.

MacIsaac paled. "Where are you going?"

"To find the captain. Go, but quietly. No sense in causing undue concern."

MacIsaac nodded, then hurried off. Arick headed to the bridge, thankful he didn't have to go far. A familiar head of ruddy curls caught his eye. He leaned over the rail.

"Thomas! What are you doing hiding back there?"

Thomas looked up from his hiding spot behind the sweeping staircase. "I don't want to dance anymore."

"You love dancing."

"Not when everyone keeps asking me about you," he mumbled.

Oh. "That's just because I'm new. Come on, I'm heading to the bridge anyway." If there was a storm coming, he wanted Thomas nearby, his need to protect the prince rooted in the days when young Thomas couldn't speak.

As they started up the stairs again, lightning flickered in the distance.

In the short time it took them to reach the bridge, the ship was already rocking from the increased waves. Cries of alarm came from the main deck, and the music cut off abruptly as the ensemble packed up their instruments. Overhead, thunder rumbled.

"The king and queen are safe in the royal cabin," Captain Blair informed them. "You should join them."

Arick shook his head. "I'd rather stay up here, if that's alright with you, sir."

The captain nodded with a jerk, his focus on the sails as men raced to draw them in. Behind them came a shout.

Two men were winching in the secondary anchor that had been used to keep the ship steady for the party. But the wind had already caused the ship to shift, and the anchor was stuck. Arick raced over to lend his hand to the windlass. Thomas was right beside him. The lantern light glowed orange, but even so, Thomas looked a little green.

"We'll be alright," Arick told him, surprised that he had to shout to be heard. "We're so close to shore."

Thomas nodded.

With the four of them straining, the anchor finally broke free of its hold on the ocean floor. Without it, the ship whipped around in the wind, sending people sprawling. Arick hauled Thomas to his feet, and they returned to stand near Blair.

"The wind is coming from the east. Near impossible to reach the royal docks in this, but we should make it to the far side of the harbor." The captain looked to Thomas for permission.

Thomas swallowed hard, his eyes darting to Arick. He gave him a slight nod. The captain knew what he was doing.

Thomas wet his lips. "Get people back safely," he shouted over the wind.

The skies opened up, drenching them all in seconds. Thomas clung to the railing where he had stood earlier, cheering.

"Take him below," Blair ordered, his voice nearly lost in the storm.

Arick nodded, staggering as he crossed the few feet to reach Thomas. Even with his seasoned sea legs, staying upright was a challenge as the ship bucked beneath them.

Lighting tore across the sky, lasting long seconds. A cry came from the foremast. Fire broke out, and two sailors fled from it, shimmying down the mast as fast as they could.

The wind shifted again. As the ship swung wildly, its masts groaned under the strain. A deafening crack reverberated through the air, sending a chilling shiver down Arick's spine.

Massive waves pummeled the ship. With a scream, one of the sailors lost his grip on the ropes and vanished overboard. Arick kept one arm firmly around Thomas, guiding him to the stairs.

With a blinding crash, lightning struck the mast again. Already cracked, the mast could no longer withstand the ferocity of the storm. It snapped, sending giant splinters and rigging through the air, carried by the gale-force winds. The mast crashed to the deck, splitting open the once pristinely polished dance floor. The ship shuddered under the impact and tilted toward the water. Screams filled the air as the party-goers fell through the broken railing into the seas below.

Arick closed his eyes as nausea swept through him. He searched the horizon for the shore, but darkness met his gaze. The harbor wasn't that large — lights from the city had been visible all around them only moments before.

Waves lashed the ship from all sides. Thomas stumbled beside him, and the two fell. They slid down the stairs, the momentum ripping them apart.

Arick lay on the deck, dazed. Above his head, the crest of a wave threatened to collapse.

Then the ship slammed back down, and the world righted itself.

"*Arick!*" Thomas screamed.

Fighting to sit upright, Arick searched for his cousin. His white shirt stood out against the black a barrel-length away, and Arick leaped for him.

The ship lurched again, sending them sprawling toward the railing.

Something loud and furry tore past Arick. Barking madly, Cookie reached Thomas's side. He bit into Thomas's shirt, tugging.

A wave crashed over them, blinding Arick. He gasped for breath and wiped water from his eyes.

"Thomas!" he yelled. The deck was empty.

Arick shoved himself to his feet and ran across the deck. He clung to the railing as he searched the churning seas for signs of Thomas.

A bark and a flash of white.

He grabbed one of the mooring lines that had been coiled nicely on the deck. Without another thought, Arick flung himself over the rail and into the water below.

"HOLD UP! WHERE ARE you going?" Ciara grabbed her arm, pulling her to a stop.

"Away!" Sorcha sobbed.

Ciara wrapped her in a hug. A rubbery nose bumped against her side as Ciara's dolphin, Cuan, offered her comfort as well. Distant rumblings made her shudder.

"What happened?"

"I just do everything wrong, and Rona…" She rubbed the cut on her finger, the bleeding already stopped. The sting of her sister's words, though, lingered.

"Rona needs to leave things well enough alone." Ciara's voice was hard.

Sorcha glanced around, noticing for the first time how far away from the grotto they were. "What are you doing out here?"

Ciara wouldn't look her in the eye. "Cuan wanted to join his mates, and I couldn't disappoint him."

Sorcha gaped at her sister. "You're going to the surface? In a storm?"

Ciara's jaw tightened. "Yes. I can help. Come with me. There are a lot of humans in trouble up there."

"All the more reason not to go!"

"They're too busy trying not to drown to worry about ensnaring a mer! Come on!" She grabbed Sorcha's hand and took hold of Cuan's fin. He took off, pulling them along as if they weighed nothing, and emitted happy little noises all the way.

They broke the surface just inside the harbor rocks. The waves immediately ripped Sorcha from her sister. She cried out, her voice lost in the thunder that rolled overhead.

Lighting cut across the sky.

The fancy ship she'd seen the other day rocked in the middle of the harbor, its forward mast nothing but splinters. Humans clung to whatever piece of the ship they could, but with each wave, more of them were swept away.

Sorcha covered her ears — not just to protect from the siren call of the human voices but from the deafening roar of the wind and waves. She stared in horror. All around the ship, humans cried out in fear. She could see dolphins darting in and out, nudging people onto pieces of flotsam.

Ciara was in there somewhere, helping, she was sure. As were Father and the Watchers. They would do whatever it took to save the lives of those who belonged on the land.

Everything within her told her to leave, to go back to the safety of the grotto; that she couldn't help here.

That if she were useless doing the one thing she'd been trained to do, she'd be even worse here.

But something held her in place, glued to the surface, even as the waves flung her about. She gave up trying to cover her ears, needing her arms to stay upright. The human siren calls were drowned out by the winds and waves anyway. Surely the Watchers didn't work from the surface. How could they see anything?

She rode a wave to its crest, then plummeted to the trough of the next. A board spun past, scraping her side. In the darkness, she could see nothing, blinded by the wind and rain.

A voice reached her above the tumult of the storm. She cast about, searching for it.

There, floating on a piece of the ship, clung a human and a smaller animal. The waves drove him toward her, but he seemed to be pointing in the direction he had come. She lost sight of him as the waves crashed over them both. When she next saw him, he was much closer, but angling away from her. With a gasp, she recognized him as the shorter of the two men she had watched singing. The small creature barked, a sharp sound that cut through the booming cacophony.

A sleek gray body showed above the water for a second as a dolphin drove him toward the shore. Even knowing he would be okay, the man continued to point back to the center of the harbor.

Sorcha let the next wave pull her high, searching for what the man was so concerned about.

Lightning flashed, blinding her, but not before she spotted a human struggling to hold onto a small board, a piece of white fabric floating near him. She broke free of the hold the storm had on her and dove beneath the waves, deep enough to be able to see again.

None of the Watchers were nearby. She could just make out a cluster of vague shapes in the distance. Too far to be of help.

She swallowed hard, swimming toward the spot she had last seen the human.

But what good would that do? She had no starfish to stop him from entrapping her in his siren voice. No dolphin to send to his aid. No training for how to help a human without cursing herself.

As she drew near, she rose to the surface. He was gone. The board and white fabric were there, but the human was gone.

She dove again, powering through the tempestuous waters to reach the spot. She cast about, searching for any sign of the man until she spotted him below her. He wasn't struggling anymore. He drifted with the water, limp, as the ocean drew him to the floor.

Sorcha hesitated for only a moment. Rescuing a human might mean she would be bound to him for life. But that didn't mean she could let him die.

CHAPTER FOUR

DARKNESS ENCOMPASSED ARICK THE moment his feet left the ship, the rope in his hand his only connection to safety. The wind tugged at him, holding him aloft. Rain whipped from all directions, and he tucked his chin down to get a breath before plunging into the ocean.

The cold enveloped him. The water flung him around. With his lungs screaming for air, he fought for where he believed the surface was.

He broke free of the water as a piercing bark sounded to his left.

"Cookie!" he shouted, his mouth filling with water as a wave sloshed over him. He struck out toward the sound of Cookie's barking. The rope in his hand burned, but he refused to let go and wrapped it around his arm. If there was any chance of getting Thomas back to the ship, he needed to hold fast to the line.

He rode a wave to the top and caught a glimpse of Thomas's white face on the crest of the next. Arick shouted again, then set out with renewed energy to reach his cousin. Cookie had stopped barking, but stayed close to Thomas.

Lightning ripped around him as he angled toward Thomas, the rope tight around his arm. Every wave sought to pull them farther apart. Thomas swam toward Arick, but even with one arm flung over Cookie's back, he faltered.

Arick was only a few strokes away when Thomas sank beneath the waves. For a moment, his white hand clung to Cookie's collar, then that too vanished.

With a sob for breath, Arick dove in search of Thomas. His hand brushed something. The rope jerked him back. His eyes straining, Arick spotted his cousin drifting just out of reach. To reach him, he'd have to let go of the rope. But without the rope, they'd never make it back to the ship. Thomas looked up, his gray-flecked eyes filled with fear — and trust. Arick let go of the rope that was holding him back and kicked with everything he had.

He grasped Thomas's shirt and hauled him up.

Arick's lungs burned. He clamped his lips together to stop the urge to open his mouth and let the water pour in. They broke the surface and gasped.

Arick looked around for any sign of succor. The loss of the rope to guide them back to the ship sat like a weight in his stomach. His sense of direction was gone, but surely safety couldn't be that far away. They were in the harbor, encased by land. If only he could see where it was.

Beside him Thomas floundered, his grip tight on Arick's arm. Still pressed against Thomas's other side, Cookie yelped in pain. The sound barely registered as Arick fought to keep them all above water.

"Arick!" Thomas gasped.

Arick turned to see what Thomas needed.

A piece of the ship about the size of a door floated just out of reach, each second sending it farther away. Arick struck out after it, trusting Thomas to keep hold of him. A wire trailed from the flotsam, and Arick grabbed it. He pulled the door toward him. His hand landed on the ring holding the wire to the wood. It wasn't a door at all...it was the diving platform that had been so cleverly fastened to the side of the ship. The broken mast must have ripped it free.

For a moment, the two rested against the wood, catching their breath. But the storm wasn't so kind, and within a moment, it threatened to tear their salvation from their hands.

His arms trembling, Arick helped Thomas onto the platform, then shoved poor Cookie up after him. The little dog was shivering from cold and fear, his drenched coat making him look half his usual size.

"Come on, Arick!" Thomas shouted. He shifted to one side to make room. The platform rocked. Arick grabbed the side to stop it from flipping over.

His fingers were stiff and cold, and he struggled to hold on and lift himself out of the water.

"Arick!" Thomas screamed, his eyes wide in terror.

Then the world became crushing, whirling water as a massive wave crashed down on them. Arick's head banged against the platform. Pain seared across his vision. The wire ripped from his hand.

Thomas. He had to get back to Thomas.

The water was never-ending — swirling, tearing, crushing, until all thought was gone and only the desperate ache for air remained.

He surfaced, his breaths coming in short gasps. A small board bumped into him, and he clung to it with what little strength he had left. *Was Thomas okay?*

He just had to hold on a little longer. Get back to Thomas. Swim to shore.

Blackness crowded his vision, and he choked as he breathed in water. No, he couldn't give up. He had to...had to...something.

Lightning flashed, and he winced at the glare. With renewed alertness, he tucked the board under his chest and began to swim.

But the ocean was having none of it. The water under him rose and rose until the world turned upside down.

Once again, his lungs burned, and all sense of up or down vanished. He was so tired.

Something brushed against his shoulder, and he reached for it. Forcing his eyes open, he searched the darkness for hope of salvation.

A shape that seemed made of the ocean and yet wholly separate from it loomed before him. The continuous roaring of the storm began to fade as he was wrapped in a lullaby. The ocean sang to him, and he thought he must surely be dying, for before him was an angel, lifting him up.

If this was death, then it was far lovelier than he had thought.

E VEN BELOW THE SURFACE, the water was in turmoil. Sorcha fought her way to the man. Why wasn't he trying to swim?

She grasped his arm, startled at how cold he felt. Turning, she swam upward. He was heavy, pulling her down. She adjusted her grip, holding him under his arms. Thick, dark liquid drifted from his head. Knowing he would die if she didn't do something, she began to sing. The words to the familiar lullaby came easily this time, but she struggled to compel her voice. Dragging the human through the water stole her breath.

The dark spiral from his head slowed, whether from healing, she didn't know. But she kept singing until they broke the surface, her voice changing in the air.

The storm hadn't abated, and they were propelled by the waves. If only she had a dolphin! She held him out of the water as best she could, continuing to sing.

"Rest in the embrace of the starlit sea," she panted, feeling her magic fill the words.

The man coughed once, then sputtered.

A sharp pain filled her chest, and she cried out, losing her grip on him. He gasped for air and flailed about, forcing her farther away.

She swam in a tight circle around him as the pain faded. He gave no further signs of awakening, and now that she could breathe again, she darted in to grab hold of him once more.

Wind pummeled them until she didn't know whether she was above or below the waves. For what seemed like hours, she could do little more than hold him out of the water so he wouldn't drown. Exhaustion clouded her vision, but every time she thought about letting him go, something warned her not to.

At last the crashing thunder faded away, and the lightning no longer blinded her. The waves were still agitated, but she could swim through them.

Ahead was a stretch of sandy shore, just behind the rocks. She flipped the man onto his back and grabbed hold of his collar. It took all her concentration, but she began to make headway against the waves. Rocks lurked along the shore, and despite her best efforts, she was tossed against them repeatedly.

Sand brushed against her fins as she kicked. She pushed the man in front of her and used her arms to propel them both forward onto the beach.

The tide followed them up the sand as though seeking to drag him back into the depths. Sorcha turned so she was sitting in the sand, the water over her waist. Every seventh wave sloshed over her head as she scooted backward. She settled into a rhythm of shuffling back, then hauling the man as far as she could.

Her arms trembled with exhaustion, and the temptation to return to the ocean grew. She panted, unable to catch her breath. The farther she went out of the water, the harder it was to breathe. But the water kept reaching for them, and she couldn't leave the man until he was above the high water line.

His chest rose and fell so slightly she had to put her hand on him to feel it. She should sing for him again, but breathing was too difficult, and she doubted she had the strength to pull her healing magic into it.

Finally he was free, and she collapsed onto the sand beside him. The rain had stopped, and the wind no longer threatened to strangle her with her hair.

A fiery pain rippled through her fin and tail. She cried out. It washed over her like the traitorous tides. Whimpering in agony, she crawled back to the water, seeking its soothing touch.

Swimming back to the grotto was out of the question. She tucked into a corner of the rocks where she couldn't be washed out to sea and laid down in the water. She tried to sing, her voice barely a whisper between the sobs, until at last she passed out.

CHAPTER FIVE

T HE COLD SEEPED THROUGH him, and Arick turned to hide beneath the covers. He rolled over and the mattress beneath him shifted. His pillow scratched his face, and his blanket was gone. Every muscle ached, and his head felt dull and thick. He fought his way from the depths and forced one eye open.

A stretch of sandy beach greeted him, littered by rocks, driftwood, and other debris.

Why was he asleep on a beach?

He'd been at Thomas's birthday party, but surely he hadn't consumed that much wine to end up here. Not even at his graduation at the naval academy had he been so foolish as to drink enough to lose control of his sensibilities.

Memories of the storm came crashing down, and he sat up in a panic.

His stomach and head both protested the movement, and he retched up the saltwater he had swallowed. He flopped back on the sand when he was done.

Where was Thomas? Was everyone okay?

He forced himself upright again. Black spots danced at the edge of his vision. He moved slowly, trying to clear them. He had to get up, had to go find Thomas.

A flicker of light drew his attention to the lighthouse, standing a lonely sentinel on the far clifftop in the gray morning.

The storm had cast him onto the far side of the harbor, and he looked with despair at the city in the distance. Exhaustion settled on him, exacerbating how far he would have to walk.

The sea still showed signs of the turmoil of the night. Pieces of the ship were scattered across the beach and caught on the rocks. He shuddered, not from the cold but from the dread of how anyone could have survived.

No one else was on the beach near him. Only smaller pieces of debris were this far from the water.

How had the storm pushed him so high up on the sand?

It had come up so suddenly — from a near perfect day with a cloudless sky to a storm that had ripped the ship apart.

Only magic could do something like that. He swallowed hard, his throat as rough as the sand.

Magic belonged in old legends, the stories that were told over firelight. No magic users had been heard of in a hundred years.

But how else could he explain the suddenness of the storm? The power and frequency of the tempests that had been plaguing the island of late could only have been caused by magic.

The thought made his head hurt. He let it fall to his hand, wincing as his fingers brushed a sore spot. Dry, crusted blood clung to his hair. Looking down, he could see a streak of it on his shirt. His jacket was gone, as were his boots.

He should care more, but he found he couldn't summon the energy. Thomas needed him. That's what he was supposed to do.

Get up. Walk to the city. Find out where Thomas was. Yes, he would do that. If only his head weren't so fuzzy. He closed his eyes against the pain. What had he been trying to do?

He sank back onto the sand, the memory of the ocean singing to him lulling him back to sleep.

Everything ached.

SORCHA SAT UP, SHIVERING. She was wedged between two rocks, which had kept her from being washed out to sea while she slept. But being in the water had never made her cold before. The rocks had caught seaweed and other debris, but she didn't push it off her, seeking what little warmth it provided.

"Sorcha!" a worried voice called.

"I'm over here!" she cried in relief, blinking at the reflection of the sun on the water.

A moment later, Aunt Maeve appeared around the rock, her face full of worry. When she saw Sorcha, her shoulders dropped, and she let out a deep sigh. "You're alive."

Sorcha nodded, her throat tight.

Aunt Maeve stopped some distance from her, the shallow water preventing her from drawing near. "What happened?" she asked softly.

"Ciara dragged me to the surface." She couldn't stop the hitch in her voice. "It...it was awful. I've never seen a storm that bad. It was unnatural."

Maeve gave her a hard look. "Why do you say that?"

Sorcha flinched. "I don't know. It just felt so wrong. Is that what storms are always like on the surface?"

"That's a topic for another day," Maeve said. She looked away, her face troubled.

"What is it?" Sorcha demanded. She wanted to go to her aunt, but moving brought pain, and she was so cold.

"Ciara was injured."

Horror flooded her. "Is she okay? Did she...?"

"She's fine now." Her aunt looked like she wanted to say something more, but changed her mind. "How did you end up here, so far from the grotto? Everyone's been looking for you."

If everyone was looking for her, how had Maeve been the one to find her? Usually only the Watchers went so far from the grotto. And why wasn't she helping Ciara?

"I got separated from Ciara when she and Cuan went to help the humans." She lowered her eyes, not wanting to admit what she had done. She worked her jaw, trying to clear the odd sensation in her ears.

"And...?" Maeve prompted. Something in her voice told Sorcha she already knew the truth.

"I saved a human," she whispered, wrapping her arms around herself.

"Oh, Sorcha." Her voice was full of pity. "Why?"

The question jolted her. "Why? Because there was no one else!"

"It was the one you heard sing, wasn't it?" Maeve sighed, understanding filling her eyes.

"It's not like that! He would have died!"

"You know what saving him means, don't you?"

Sorcha nodded. At least, she thought she knew. Saving the life of a human bound them together. But none of the stories had explained what that meant.

"You can never return to the ocean, Sorcha. You're bound to him forever."

"Never?" she gasped. But how could she, a mermaid, live on land? She needed the sea to survive.

"Look down, my little guppy," Maeve told her gently.

Sorcha obeyed. The seaweed had slid off her while they talked. Her beautiful sapphire tail and shimmering, iridescent scales were gone.

In their place was a pair of pale human legs and narrow feet.

CHAPTER SIX

"WHAT...WHAT IS HAPPENING TO me?" Sorcha cried out in fear.

"You didn't think you could be bound to a human and remain a mermaid, did you?" Maeve asked.

Sorcha didn't know what she had expected, but not...*this*. Not these pale sticks in place of her powerful sapphire tail. Her new toes were nearly blue from the cold of the water.

"You're going to want to cover up, too," Maeve said. "Humans are rather snooty about clothing."

"What?" She looked down. Of course. Humans had skin everywhere. Her torso, too, was white and smooth, the scales that normally covered her having vanished. Only the blue gem in its lattice cage rested against her chest, the ribbon around her neck somehow having held through the storm. She bit back a sob.

"I don't want to be a human." This couldn't be happening.

"Too late for that," Maeve said dryly.

"What do I do?" she whimpered.

"The only thing you can do is get him to like you."

A strange voice calling out from the other side of the rocks interrupted her next question. With barely a splash, Maeve disappeared.

Sorcha pushed herself free of the rocks and scrambled deeper into the water. "Don't leave me here!"

She flipped over and tried to swim, kicking her new legs together as though they were still joined. She ducked under the water, but she couldn't pull air from the water like she normally did. Why were her gills not working? She opened her mouth to call for her aunt. Water filled her mouth, and she choked.

What was happening to her? The ocean was her world, her whole life. Why was it rejecting her? She flailed, her limbs refusing to work as required.

Arms reached around her, and she was lifted from the water. *No! She had to get home! Ciara needed her!*

She fought against whoever was holding her. The man said something, his voice rough, but she couldn't focus. His voice was so loud! He stumbled as she continued to flail.

"Let me go!" she cried, pushing against his chest.

With a grunt, he released her, and she fell to the sand.

The jolt startled her out of her panic, and she glared up at him. The early morning sun turned his ruddy-blond curls copper, and his hazel eyes were full of concern.

He spoke, words that made no sense. She shook her head and pointed back to the water. Aunt Maeve had vanished, but maybe she was still close enough to help her back to the grotto. If she could just get home, surely Aunt Maeve could help her solve this. How her aunt knew so much about the binding, she didn't know, but she definitely planned on asking.

She pointed more aggressively, her hair shifting with the movement.

He looked away, his cheeks flushing pink. Searching the beach, he muttered to himself. What was he saying? He motioned with his hands for her to stay put, then hurried off. She huddled in the sand, burying her strange toes in it. Her long hair fell in tangled waves, and she let it cover her as she wrapped her arms around her legs.

The man hurried back with a bundle of cloth in his hand. He held it out to her, keeping his head turned away. What did he want her to do with it?

Maeve's words about humans and clothing returned to her. Oh. Right. She didn't have scales to cover her anymore.

With a half-sob for what she had lost, she snatched the cloth from him and wrapped it around herself.

The man crouched down to her level, worry creasing his forehead. He spoke again in a soothing tone. She couldn't understand him. Humans spoke a different language, but whatever magic had transformed her into a human hadn't thought fit to ensure she could speak to any of them. Tears trickled down her sand-dusted cheeks.

"I need to go home," she whispered, knowing he wouldn't understand her.

He reached a hand and patted her shoulder, his hazel eyes full of concern. He stood, looking to the end of the beach. With a sigh, he offered her a hand. Shaking her head, she huddled deeper into her covering. His words came faster, and he motioned to where the sand ended.

He wanted her to go with him. But how could she leave the ocean behind? She dropped her head to her knees, sobs shaking her shoulders.

His hand slapped against his salt-stiff clothing as he sighed. He said something more, his tone full of resignation. When she didn't respond, he turned and walked away, his feet shushing though the sand.

Her chest grew tight, and she raised her head to breathe better. The man continued to walk away from her.

Where was he going? The tightness in her chest grew. Why had he left her there? She knew no one else, and if she was bound to him, shouldn't she go after him? Her breath came in short gasps as she contemplated being abandoned in the human world. Being stuck with him was far preferable to trying to navigate on her own. She rubbed her chest, trying to alleviate the pain. She had to go after him.

But how? She didn't know how to walk. She tied the covering around her so it wouldn't fall. Pushing herself upright, she stood wobbling in the sand, her arms out for balance. She could do this. She could follow him. Swallowing, she lifted one foot...and fell flat on her face.

Spitting the sand out of her mouth, she tried again. Stand. Balance. One foot, just like the humans she'd seen walking.

Sand in her mouth again.

She glared at her traitorous new feet. Experimentally, she told her left foot to move. Both feet flipped in unison like her fin underwater. She leaned forward and grabbed her right foot and moved her left foot again. Her right jerked in her hold.

She wiped away tears from the pain, then pulled her right leg up and sat on her foot. This time her left foot acted on its own. Her cry of triumph was lost in a sob.

Unable to stand it any longer, she folded over in the sand, her hands pressed to her chest, where her heart thudded in a desperate cadence.

The pain grew, as though part of her were being stretched and ripped out.

A RICK GLARED AT THE traitorous blue sky as he hurried across the sand, dodging the plethora of broken pieces of ships. He'd already wasted too much time when he needed to find out what had happened to Thomas and all the others. But he couldn't exactly abandon the poor woman.

Who was she? He didn't recognize her from the party. Perhaps she'd been on one of the smaller vessels that had joined the regatta.

The sand switched from damp to dry beneath his feet, and he struggled to catch his breath. If he was so exhausted he couldn't cross the beach, how was he to make it all the way back to his lodgings? Where was everyone else? Why were they the only two on this beach? The debris proved that the storm had driven whatever had been on the water in all directions.

He stopped on the edge of the bank to rest for a moment, sinking down into the sand. The woman was still huddled under the piece of sail he had found for her. Perhaps her friends would come for her, he reassured himself. Was she from one of the neighboring kingdoms, here for Thomas's birthday celebrations? In that case, he really should try to bring her with him. But she had so adamantly insisted on staying near the water.

The ocean had calmed considerably, but the water was choppy. The rocks that protected the beach blocked the water, sending white spray towering into the air with every wave.

Sitting was doing him no good, so he got to his feet, wavering as the world tilted around him. He was not so out of shape that a short walk like that should wind him. The salt grass cut his feet with each step as he walked and tried not to pant.

Maybe water had gotten into his lungs. He reached the road and paused, his hands on his knees as he breathed against the vice around his chest.

A cry cut across the still beach. He turned in time to see the woman collapse in the sand. As much as he wanted to know whether Thomas was safe, he couldn't leave her there.

He pushed himself upright, the world spinning even more. He took one step, then blackness washed over him.

M INUTES PASSED WHILE ARICK struggled to push aside the blackness. The woman's anguished sobs drew him back to her, and he stumbled forward. No matter how bad of shape he was in, he couldn't leave her.

The sharp salt grass on his legs helped to center him, and as he crossed to the sand, his breathing grew easier until he was able to run the last few steps to her side.

She had ceased crying, though her chest still heaved. For the first time she looked directly at him. And he was lost in the depths of her sapphire-blue eyes.

"Are you alright?" he asked softly, his own pain forgotten.

She offered him a wan smile and sat up. Pushing her hair back, she took a shuddering breath. Her hair had dried and now fell in thick ringlets around her face, the rich red contrasting with her pale skin. She adjusted the sail around her, and he was surprised to see that she'd managed to turn it into a quite modest outfit. She'd tied the top around her neck and wrapped the longer sides around her, knotting them in the front.

"Can you walk?" He doubted that she understood him. He motioned in the direction he'd already traveled, hoping she would understand.

She nodded with a smile and tried to stand. He caught her arm to steady her. She wobbled, her feet close together. Tucking her arm over his, he drew her nearer to offer support. He was surprised to see how tall she was. Most women didn't even reach his shoulder. She lurched forward, crying out in pain as her foot sank into the sand. Her fingers bit into his arm.

"Oh! Is there something there?" He couldn't see anything, but perhaps a piece of shell was buried.

She clung to him, shaking.

"Come on, shall we try again?" Holding her with both hands, he started off again.

She took another awkward, lurching step, with the same result. He glanced down, and those brilliant blue eyes were so full of pain and fear he had to fight the urge to hold her close. Such a move would be wildly inappropriate, and the poor thing was only just beginning to trust him.

"We have to keep going," he said apologetically. "Staying here won't do either of us any good, and I would really like to check on my friends." He kept his voice low and soothing, and the wildness slowly faded from her eyes.

His throat was scratchy, but talking seemed to calm her. "I'm sure your friends are looking for you, but the best place to find them would be back in the city. The harbormaster likely has a list already started to help people find each other."

When she was ready, he took a cautious step forward. She pressed her lips together and slowly lifted one leg without bending her knee, then lowered her foot to the ground a few inches in front of where it had been. Right before it touched the sand, she paused before letting it drop. She whimpered and clung to him.

"Shh, it's okay," he reassured her. "You're hurt. Let me see."

He helped her sit down again, and with gentle hands, he lifted her foot. Her feet were long and slender. He'd never before touched a woman's foot, but he told himself this was for medical purposes. His fingers hesitated, and he swallowed hard before starting his examination. He could see no sign of injury — certainly nothing that would cause her to cry out like that. As he ran his thumbs lightly over the sole, he watched her for any indications he was hurting her. She stared back at him with those blue eyes he could get lost in.

"Does that hurt?" he asked to distract himself from the sapphire pools. "Let me know if you feel anything."

Her skin was smooth, soft, without the usual calluses people gained from years of being on their feet. He frowned. Maybe she had a disability that prevented her from walking. That would explain why the movement seemed so unnatural to her and caused her so much pain.

At last he sat back, gently placing her foot on the ground. He'd taken the liberty of checking her ankle for swelling as well, but it was cool to the touch. Unless it was her knee or something else bothering her, he had no idea why she was so in pain when she walked. But he was not bold enough to look further without her express approval.

She looked at him curiously, with no trace of the pain that seemed to affect her so acutely at times. He let his breath out in a huff.

"Well, this isn't getting us anywhere, is it? I hope you don't think this is too forward, but I do believe the only solution is for me to carry you."

He helped her stand once more, chatting as he did so. "Up like this. There you go."

Hoping she would forgive him for acting without being able to explain his intentions, he scooped her into his arms.

"Oh!" she said, clutching him around the neck.

Her wide eyes were so close to his, and he found he couldn't think of a single thing to say. She offered him a shy smile, then cocked her head, as if asking what he was doing now.

"Right. I do hope I'm not hurting you, but I dare say it's best if we get a move on." His stomach rumbled loudly, and she giggled. "It appears that I've missed breakfast."

This time as he crossed the sand, he moved with ease and none of the shortness of breath from earlier. He found a path that avoided most of the salt grass, and they soon reached the road.

He took a moment to get his bearings. The city lay to the left, but a small town might be closer in the opposite direction. Only moors and hills dotted with distant white sheep called to him, so he turned to the city.

CHAPTER SEVEN

A FEW MINUTES AFTER they started walking, a cart rattled up behind them. Arick's shoulders dropped in
relief. The woman wasn't heavy, but he was fatigued from his
night in the ocean, and he wasn't looking forward to carrying
her all the way to the city, especially with no boots. He stepped
to the side of the road and waited for the cart to slow.

The pretty little highland pony leading the cart immediately began scrounging for pockets of grass. The driver studied
them, a pipe hanging from a corner of his mouth.

"Is it a ride you're after, then?" he asked around the pipe.

Arick nodded in relief. "Please. We were caught in the
storm last night, and Iskarraig is a far way to walk."

"Aye, it is," the man agreed, then turned back to face the
road.

Arick took that as all the invitation he needed and hurried to the back of the cart. It was half full of bundles, with just enough space for them to sit with their feet dangling off the edge. He set the woman down and helped her swing her legs around. Sitting didn't seem to bother her, so he hoped the bumpy ride wouldn't cause her undue pain.

He hoisted himself up beside her. Once he was settled, the driver muttered, "G'wan witcha," and the little pony trotted off, seemingly unaffected by the additional burden. Arick thought about striking up a conversation with the driver, but the man was content with his pipe, and the rocking of the cart lulled him into a stupor. The rich, earthy scent of the tobacco blended with the wild perfume of heather on the nearby hills.

Beside him, the woman held onto the cart rail and stared at the world around them. She gasped at the first real bump, then giggled at the vibrations caused by the wooden bridge that spanned the little creek.

She pointed at the carpet of purple heather as they passed and exclaimed something. Arick wished he could understand her.

"She does speak, then, does she?" the driver commented with no expectation of a response.

A shaggy cow, with long white horns, lowed at them, and the woman watched it until it disappeared from view. After some time, she sank back against the bundles and appeared to doze. Arick contemplated doing the same, but his thoughts wouldn't rest.

"Were there any reports of castaways out your way?" he asked.

The driver was silent so long he doubted his intention to answer at all. "On the hills, no. I dinnae think there'd be much chance of the storm blowing them that far."

Arick laughed, but stayed quiet after that.

"Were you heading for the city, then?" The driver asked after some time.

Arick turned around to see the first structures coming into town.

The driver waved with his pipe. "It's to the right I'm heading, at the wee crossroads."

"That's fine, thank you," Arick replied. "The inn isn't far."

"Ach, if it's to the Coorie Inn you're going, then I can take you that far."

"That would be immeasurably kind. Thank you, sir."

A few minutes later, the cart slowed in front of the inn. Even at midday, the windows glowed bright with flickering lanterns, exuding a sense of warmth and hospitality. The building's timeworn walls seemed to hold countless stories within their embrace.

Arick jumped down and lifted the woman in his arms. He set her on a bench near the oak door and returned to the cart.

"I'm sorry that I have no coin with me today, but if you find yourself at the castle, tell them Arick sent you, and they'll see you're adequately compensated."

The driver gave him a hard look. "You're the young laird, then."

Arick squirmed. His brother was to have been the one to inherit their father's title, and Arick was still adjusting to the fact that one day it would be his. "You've done me a great service, so I see no need for formality between us. You have my gratitude."

The driver nodded, then removed the pipe from his mouth to point at the woman. "She's an odd one, isn't she?"

Arick shrugged, for he couldn't deny it. He thanked the man again and walked back over to the woman. She looked small, sitting under the second story overhang, though there was a wild elegance to her. Her pale skin and red curls stood out against the dark wooden shingles of the building. Another cart trundled by, followed by a pair of riders on tall horses. From the nearby dock came shouts as sailors and stevedores worked on a ship.

He pulled his gaze away. He could ask there later whether anyone had been pulled from the water, but he needed to take care of the woman first.

"Shall we go in?"

The tension in her shoulders fell away as she spotted him, and a slight smile played on her lips. He wondered why everything seemed so new and overwhelming to her, and he made a note to check with the harbormaster about whether any foreign ships had been due to arrive last night.

He lifted her and walked around the side of the inn. Although it wouldn't be busy this time of day, it wasn't appropriate for him to haul her through the public room, clad as she was in nothing but a piece of sail.

"Elsbeth!" He called at the back door. "Give a lad a hand, would you?"

"Enough of your hollerin', I'm coming," a harried voice snipped in reply.

The door pushed open to reveal an apron-ensconced woman. A tartan scarf covered most of her silver-streaked hair, but flour dusted scarf and braids alike. Her rich brown eyes opened wide when she spotted him.

"Arick, lad, what happened to you?" She bustled him and his burden into the kitchen and motioned to a bench where he could set the woman down. "Is she alright?"

"I think so. She's not been able to tell me what's wrong, but her feet hurt when she tries to walk."

"What do you mean, she can't tell you?"

He helped the woman settle on the bench and gave her a reassuring smile. "I think she speaks a different language."

Elsbeth frowned. "How did you find her?"

"On the beach. We were shipwrecked in the storm last night." He pressed his lips together, still angry that the storm had ruined what should have been a beautiful night. "Have you heard anything?"

Elsbeth stoked the fire and moved the teakettle closer. "Just that seven ships were lost, and who knows how many smaller boats."

"Was anyone...?"

"Not that I've heard, but there were stories all morning of close escapes, and the usual tall tales of dolphins." She pulled two teacups from the cupboard and set a strainer over one.

"Thomas?"

She gave him a soft look. "If your cousin were missing, you know there'd be an outcry up and down the island, and there's been nothing. I'm sure he's fine."

His shoulders dropped in relief. He lifted the cloth covering the plate of cookies she always kept on the corner of the counter and took two. He handed one to the young woman — he really needed to figure out her name — and took a bite out of the other.

Elsbeth's cookies were what he considered to be the best baked good in the seven kingdoms. The woman stared at it a minute, then looked at him. After he took his bite, she nibbled at hers. A look of concentration pulled her brows down as she tasted it. Her eyes widened in delight, and she bit into the cookie with greater urgency.

Elsbeth poured the tea, adding honey and a generous helping of milk to each, an indulgence he was sure she only offered due to their disheveled appearances. She handed him one cup, then brought the other to the young woman.

"Arick!" she cried out. "What is she wearing?"

His ears burned, and he hid behind his teacup. "A sail."

"A sail? You're telling me you brought this poor creature into my kitchen and you didn't even think to tell me she needed a dress?"

He mumbled his excuse into his cup. It was snatched from his hand before he could sip the soothing liquid.

"You bring her back to my rooms right this second."

Knowing he wouldn't get his tea back until he did, he obeyed. His punishment was being relegated to the kitchen bench as Elsbeth bustled back and forth to her private rooms at the rear of the inn, first with pitchers of hot water, then a tray laden with food.

He sipped his tea, wondering if it was safe to help himself to another cookie. As he lifted the cloth, he spotted a plate on the kitchen table with a thick slice of brown bread dripping with honey. Bless the woman. He stuffed a cookie into his mouth, and with a fresh cup of tea and his plate of bread, he returned to his bench. When he was done, he set the plate and cup on the table and headed upstairs to his own room, where he'd been staying since his arrival in Toravik.

WHATEVER THIS ROUND HUMAN food was, Sorcha wanted more. With each nibble, the buttery richness danced upon her tongue, complemented by a subtle sweetness. The texture, delicate yet satisfying, melted away in her mouth. The crumbs were the color of sand, but never had sand tasted so good.

Before she could ask for another, the woman started scolding the man, and then she was whisked away to another room.

It took a minute for her to figure out what the woman expected her to do with the hot water and the soft square of cloth, but she found it was soothing to wash away the salt and sand.

The clothing was a bigger concern, as she had no idea how to put all the various pieces on. In the end, the woman helped her, under the impression that Sorcha was too frail to do it herself.

The dress was too big and too short, but the woman tucked and pinned, chatting away as she worked. Sorcha tried to stand a couple of times to make whatever the woman was trying to do easier, but she kept pushing her back down to sit on the bed. The only time the woman paused was when she caught sight of the ribbon and pendant around her neck. She stared at it, then shook her head, continuing on with her administrations.

At last she left her alone with a tray of strange-looking food.

The small round cup held a fragrant brown liquid, and she found herself drawn to it. She sipped it carefully as she studied the rest of what was laid out before her. With not a small amount of trepidation and a growing sense of curiosity, she sampled each of the foods.

A bowl of stew made her stomach growl, but she could find no oyster shells to scoop it with. A metal tool on the tray seemed designed for the same purpose, so she picked it up, pondering the need of the long bit attached. She held it at the base of the stick portion, and scooped up a small amount of the stew. The stick quickly grew to be a frustration, so she tried a few different ways of holding it.

Although the stew was warm and thick with different colored lumps, she found it bland. When she'd eaten all she could, she set the tray aside and curled up by the foot of the bed. The woman hadn't come back for a while, and she didn't know if she was allowed to leave the room. Could she even walk by herself?

She sat upright and lowered her feet to the floor again. She was not going to spend her entire life on land being carried about by the man. He'd been kind, but to be so constrained went against her very nature as a mer.

The floor felt smooth and hard beneath her stockinged feet. She wiggled her toes, still fascinated by the stubby little fingers that were attached to her new appendages. Holding onto the corner post of the bed, she stood.

No little daggers stabbed her soles. With a deep breath, she concentrated on lifting one foot. Both of them slid on the floor, and she clutched the post for balance.

Why did her feet insist on working at the same time? Humans operated them separately. She had to figure this out. She sat down on the bed and glared at her new legs. Holding on to one, she commanded her legs, her feet, her toes to move.

She laughed when she finally managed to wiggle the toes of one foot without the other joining in. For the next while, she worked on making each of her feet and legs do something independently of the other. When she could close her eyes and lift each leg and wiggle the foot without the other moving, she decided it was time to try walking again.

Holding the post tightly once more, she stood. To her delight, one foot lifted, and the other didn't follow. Slowly, she lowered it back to the floor.

Tiny prickles of pain ran along the bottom of her foot. She snatched it up again. Why did everything about being a human hurt?

She couldn't keep standing there on one foot. With renewed focus, she put her foot down, bracing against the sharp pain. Once her foot was solidly on the ground again, the pain faded.

Relieved, she tried with the other foot. Lifting it was easy, and she laughed at the way her foot vanished under her skirts. Setting it down again brought the same prickles of pain, but she pushed through it, and when she was standing on two feet again, the pain was gone.

After several rounds of walking back and forth along the end of the bed, she faced the far wall. A square in the middle of the wall let in light, and she wanted to see what lay beyond it. Perhaps it was an exit to the outside world.

A deep breath and a step forward. She held her arms out for balance, wobbling. Another step. If only each step didn't offer the sensation of brushing against hard coral, she might enjoy walking. A third step brought her close to her destination. Something filmy hung in front of the square, but she could see movement beyond it.

The strange pain in her chest returned, and she stumbled against the desk that was under the opening.

Outside, the man was walking away.

No, no, no. He can't leave me here!

"Wait!" she cried, shoving the filmy material aside so she could follow him.

Her hand banged on something hard. He turned, a frown on his face only growing when he spotted her in the window. She smacked the opening again. What magic was this that refused to let her out? He rubbed his chest, undecided.

The square didn't move.

Pushing herself upright, she looked to the part of the wall that the woman had opened when she'd come in and out of the room. It was farther than she'd walked so far, but she couldn't let the man leave. The pain that had threatened to rip her apart the last time he'd walked away drove her to brave the distance.

She staggered to the spot in the wall, leaning against it as she gasped for breath. How did it open? Had she been trapped in here? What had the humans done?

As the pain and panic grew, she banged her hand on the wall.

"Let me out!" she cried.

Soft thuds hurried toward her, then the wall was being pushed open. The woman with the kind face stood there, her forehead creased. She saw Sorcha's tears and immediately enveloped her in a hug. Despite being taller, Sorcha melted into the comforting embrace.

Her panic subsided, but her breaths still came in choked sobs. She motioned to the window. "Where is he going? I need to go with him."

The woman shook her head and said something that ended with "Arick."

It was a word she'd used before when the man was around. She latched onto it as a connection to the man.

"Yes, yes, Arick. Please."

The woman released Sorcha and hurried away, leaving the opening ajar. Not wanting to be left behind, she followed. Her feet hurt, and she lurched as she walked, trying to find a way to put them down that didn't cause pain. As she neared the large room that was full of smells that made her mouth water, her breathing came more easily.

The man was standing by the opening to the outside, looking paler than he had earlier. The woman was scolding him.

Deciding to test a theory, Sorcha pulled herself upright and said, "Arick."

The man looked at her, his hazel eyes wide. He said something in reply, words too fast for her to understand. He walked over to her and tapped his chest.

"Arick." A small smile danced over his lips.

She took a deep breath and tried again. "Arick."

His smile grew, and he gave a small cheer. He said more words, a question.

"Sorcha," she replied, guessing what he wanted.

"Sershe?" He frowned, his tongue stumbling on the strange word.

She giggled, shaking her head. "Sorcha."

He tried again, getting closer this time. When she nodded her approval, he laughed. He said more words, then turned to include the woman. "Elsbeth," he said, placing his hand on the woman's shoulder. The woman pointed at herself and repeated the word.

"El-bet." The unfamiliar sounds were hard to make. She touched her hand to her chin and brought it forward in a gesture often used under the sea. Even knowing Elsbeth wouldn't understand her, she wanted to express her gratitude. "Thank you for your kindness."

Elsbeth's brows raised, then she smiled, and replied in a gentle tone.

Arick shifted, then said something. Elsbeth shook her head. The two argued for a minute, their words flying too fast for her to understand anything. In the end, Arick raised his hands in defeat. He laughed at Elsbeth's smug look, then bowed to Sorcha. He straightened and offered her his elbow.

She looked at it a moment, wondering whether this was some strange human tradition. He seemed to be waiting for something, so she turned her own elbow out and bumped it against his.

Elsbeth let out a peal of laughter. Arick's ears turned pink. At prompting from Elsbeth, he reached for Sorcha's hand, so she let him take it. He stepped closer and tucked her hand under his elbow.

Ah, so that's what he wanted. She made a note to avoid elbow-bumping in the future — though perhaps it was a custom humans could take up. It seemed preferable to being this close to someone.

He tugged her forward, and she clutched his arm as the daggers shot up through her foot.

Elsbeth frowned, then gave Arick an order. He bent and swooped her into his arms with ease and carried her outside to the bench she'd sat on before. She'd been too distraught earlier to notice how strong he was.

"'tay," he told her, holding his palms out flat. He hurried around the corner of the building, and she braced herself for the sharp pain that wrapped around her lungs every time he walked away. Her chest grew tight, and she focused on keeping her breathing steady. As the minutes dragged on, the pain grew no worse, and she found she could bear it.

Outside of the building, the noises grew louder. She'd always missed the way the ocean muffled sounds when she surfaced, but here, there were just so many things to make noise. She pressed her hands over her ears, wishing she had shells to tie over her head.

While she waited, Elsbeth approached with two odd-looking items in her hands. She showed Sorcha how to put them on her feet and lace them up. At least she seemed to accept that Sorcha had no concept of human things, but she wondered how much the older woman knew. Elsbeth went back inside, and Sorcha stared at the strange leather wraps around her feet, wondering if they'd help with the pain.

The tightness released.

Arick appeared around the corner, leading another of the funny animals with long legs and shaggy fur, a cart attached behind it. She stood and took a tentative step forward. To her surprise, the pain dulled slightly. She shuffled closer. Arick hurried over to support her, but she pulled against his guidance.

"I want to touch it," she told him, pointing at the round shaggy beast.

He laughed and brought her closer. He showed her where to pet it, with firm strokes along its muscular neck. The hair was rougher than she'd expected, a gold that reflected the light like sunbeams on the waves. The creature nuzzled her with its velvet-soft nose.

"Oh!" she couldn't help exclaim. "What do you call it?" She gave Arick a questioning look.

"Pony." He rubbed the little creature's back and repeated the word a few times.

"Pony." She liked it.

This time when he tugged her hand, she let him. He had an urgency to leave here, so she didn't want to hold him up any longer. He lifted her into the front of the cart this time. She stood in the narrow space until he climbed up and sat on the bench.

Right. Like the other man had done. She pressed her lips together, determined to pay better attention. She didn't know how Arick would react when he found out she was a mermaid. He had been kind, but the cautionary tales of how humans treated merfolk existed for a reason.

THE LITTLE PONY TROTTED along the street, its head held high as if it knew how pretty it was. Sorcha took in everything around her. Arick talked, pointing every so often, repeating important words so she could learn the names of things.

She tried telling him the merfolk equivalent, but he tripped over many of them until she struggled to hold back her laughter.

"Street," he said, pointing at the cobblestone road in front of them. "Street."

"Sraid," she tried. He nodded in approval. She pondered what she would have called it at home. There were no cleared spaces on the ocean floor, but they did have familiar paths. That was it. "Slighe," she said.

"Slee-ee," he tried.

She giggled. "Slighe."

"Slee-ai." Little lines formed between his eyes as he tried again. "Slee-ay."

The ride passed with them sharing words back and forth until she grew tired. Arick took over the conversation, telling her stories she couldn't understand. The cart rumbled over the cobblestone street, passing the little structures that seemed to house the humans. Ahead, the street climbed toward the castle that loomed over them. She observed everything — the way the structures grew larger the closer they were to the castle, the little creatures that roamed around free, the humans as they went about their day, the pockets of flowers growing on and around the buildings, casting bright spots of pink, purple, blue, and white.

Shortly before they reached the castle gates, Arick guided Pony down another street. This one wound around the hill, and soon the buildings on the right stopped, leaving only the steep hillside below the castle. The road curved, and the town fell away behind them.

Sorcha stared. The land rolled before them, broken by sharp crags and columns of stone. The greens and browns were contrasted by pockets of color that had a wildness to them. It reminded her of the sea, yet it was so much more. The ocean was predictable, never-ending. This was beauty, untamed and wild. And terrifying.

Arick drew the cart into a field and climbed down. He lifted her down and helped her to sit beside a patch of the purple-pink flowers. She brushed her hands over them in wonder.

"Heather," he said, his hazel eyes tinted green from the surrounding flora.

She repeated the word, wondering how such a word could so perfectly encapsulate the heady perfume, the sturdy stalks, and the dainty flowers.

Despite his earlier haste, Arick relaxed beside her, showing her things and teaching her more words. Her favorite was "moors," for he described it with a sweeping gesture at all that lay before them. She loved that he had a word that tried to pocket the wildness.

A shaggy animal with long curved horns trotted over to greet them. It moved with a boisterous grace for one so large, its long tail swinging from the movement. Sorcha scurried behind Arick, but he laughed and scratched the creature's head. He guided her hand to its side, and her fingers disappeared within the coarse hair that was nearly the same shade as her own.

"Heilan' coo," he told her as she stroked the animal in delight.

A shout echoed over the hills, followed by a series of yips, causing the coo to run off.

"Arick!"

He stood with a laugh. A figure ran toward them, shouting. At his side was a small furry animal, the source of the yipping. Arick waved his arms over his head. Sorcha took a steadying breath, prepared for him to leave her, but he stayed until the other was close. They embraced, laughing, both talking over the other.

They broke apart, and Arick stepped back so she could see the other man. With a start, she recognized him as the other man in the water — the one who had pointed her to rescue Arick.

"Sor-she," Arick said, motioning to her. He then placed a hand on the other man's shoulder. "Thomas."

She gave a shy smile. "Sorcha," she corrected. "Tah-mas?"

A wet nose shoved into her face, and she fell back with a squeal. The small furry creature placed its paws on her chest and licked her face. The wet tongue tickled, and she couldn't stop her giggles.

"Cookie!" The two men rushed to save her, pulling it off her.

Thomas sat down, holding onto the animal. "Sor-ry," he said, rubbing his fist over his chest in a circle. That was a sign she recognized. More words followed that she didn't understand.

Arick helped her sit up. She pointed to the animal, and Arick nodded. Thomas shifted so she could pet it. This one was soft, much softer than the pony. She buried her fingers in the long white hair of the animal's chest.

Thomas spoke, then repeated the word from earlier. "Cook-ie."

"Coo-ky," she tried. She filed away the information. Pony for the taller ones, cooky for the smaller ones.

The cooky settled on the heather beside her, stretching out his paws until he was nearly twice as long as before. His fluffy tail curled up over his back, and his ears disappeared as he yawned. She ran her fingers through his soft fur as the two men talked.

Their words flew too fast for her to understand, but every once in a while Thomas made a motion with his hands. It reminded her of the signs the merfolk often used. Water distorted sound, so unless someone was close by, it was easier to use their hands to talk.

Whatever they were discussing had them both upset. The more agitated Thomas got, the more he used the signs. More than once, he waved his hands back and forth, his fingers separated. He followed this up with sharp zigzags with his index finger.

She leaned over and touched his arm, then repeated the movement. Looking up, she wiped her hand across the sky, then did the waves and zigzags again. *Storm?*

Thomas grinned and copied the motion, nodding. He repeated the one for storm, followed by moving his fists in a circle, then bursting them open. *Magic? He thought the storms were magic?*

They tried a few more movements, and she was startled to learn how many of them were similar. Tears prickled her eyes. Arick was patient with her, but being able to communicate with someone lifted a weight. She could be part of the human world after all.

CHAPTER EIGHT

T HE REST OF THE day passed in a flurry of activity. Sorcha followed along as Arick drove the little cart around the city. Thomas and the cooky went back to the castle, but after their meeting, Arick relaxed a lot more.

They went back to the harbor, where Arick spoke to several people. Most of the time, she stayed in the cart or got out to pet the pony. The port was bustling, with people hurrying around and shouting. Two groups of men wielded long poles to pull debris from the water, stacking it in large carts pulled by taller ponies with long ears.

As long as Arick stayed in sight, her chest didn't hurt. She wondered whether he ever had that tightness. Probably not. The curse was hers.

But Aunt Maeve had said she had to get him to like her. Why? Life would be much more pleasant if he didn't hate her, true; but Aunt Maeve's words seemed to have held a meaning she didn't understand. She scratched the pony's neck and wondered what humans did to garner friendships.

Wait — Aunt Maeve hadn't meant *that*, had she? Sorcha shuddered. Being stuck near a human was bad enough; no way did she want to wed one. She'd never be able to return to the ocean if that were the case.

Arick reappeared and handed her a small pocket of food. She cupped it in her hands, absorbing the warmth. She followed his example and bit into the edge. The pastry flaked to the ground. The inside was filled with rich sauce and bites of food that melted in her mouth.

"Pie," he told her, after swallowing his own first bite.

She nodded her understanding, too busy enjoying it to try the new word.

After they finished, he offered his handkerchief for her to wipe her hands, then tucked her arm under his elbow. With an apologetic tone, he spoke as he pointed to a far building. She grasped his arm tighter and readied herself for the long walk.

It was her longest distance since gaining her human legs, and she was quite proud of herself, even though her legs were shaking from exhaustion by the time they arrived. If she stepped firmly, the stabbing pain came and went faster, so she focused on not being afraid to walk. They passed through a door, and Arick guided her to a bench and pointed to a nearby cave that opened off the larger one they were currently in. He stepped inside and greeted an older man. A boy brought her a cup of the hot fragrant beverage Elsbeth had given her. This one smelled different, and wasn't quite as enjoyable, but the warmth was soothing.

Sorcha sipped the drink and watched the people around her. A line of people waited near a long shelf. The officials on the other side looked harried. Most were men, but a few women mingled in the busy space as well. The noise rose and fell, and she wondered if it would be rude to cover her ears. She turned her attention back to Arick.

The older man held an air of importance, his voice authoritative. As with his other conversations, Arick often turned to face the ocean and gestured to the sky as he spoke. The older man looked grave, shaking his head. A few times she heard the word Thomas had taught her — *storm*.

Were the humans as bothered by them as the merfolk? Of course they would be. They were the ones who lost ships in the storms. And if it weren't for the Watchers, they'd also lose their lives. She listened for the other word "magic," but she was too far away to distinguish much of what they said, most of which she didn't understand.

Arick's shoulders drooped as they left. They were silent on the walk back to the cart. He joined her on the bench and covered his face with his hands.

After a few minutes, he looked up and spoke in a quiet tone. The pain in his eyes made her want to sing to take it away, but she could find no song that fit.

He pointed to the ships tied to the piers, repeating the word "ship" each time. He then put his fists together and turned them away in a quick motion. "Broken," he said.

These words were important to him, so she concentrated on his face and what he was trying to tell her, repeating each word as he said it.

"Water." This time he pointed at the harbor, then moved his hands side to side as he wiggled his fingers. She frowned, not sure what he was indicating. "Water," he said a few more times, repeating the movement.

"Wah-der," she tried cautiously. The word was easy, but what part of the harbor did he mean?

He moved on to one last sign, holding one hand flat and moving the other under it. "Under."

"Un-der."

He gave her a slight smile, and she found she missed it when it faded. A light breeze teased his curls. He held up one hand, fingers splayed. With his other hand, he tapped each finger, counting up to seven. She filed away some of the words, but this didn't feel like a language lesson.

Next he pointed at the ships. "Seven ships."

The fists together, then snapping apart. "Broken."

One hand tucking under the other. "Under."

Fingers wiggling back and forth. "Water."

Tears pricked her eyes as she put the words and their meaning together. Never before had she heard of so many ships being sunk in one night.

Memories of the chaos of the storm threatened to choke her. She pointed at him, her hand shaking, then repeated his movement for "under."

He shook his head, not understanding.

What was the human word for "human"?

Or "death"?

"Arick — Ta-mas — El-bet." She strung the words together in quick succession. "Under?" She followed the hand movement for the word by holding her hand out as he had for counting the number of ships.

Understanding filled his eyes, and he caught her hands in his, stilling their agitated motions. "None." He shook his head and smiled softly. Shifting to hold her hands in one of his, he pointed at himself, then her, then the men walking by. "People." He shook his head again. "No people under."

She sank back in relief. Father and the Watchers worked so hard to rescue the humans. She hoped none of them had been hurt saving their lives last night.

But Ciara had been. Had Ciara gone searching for her? Had she been caught up in a sinking ship? Why hadn't Sorcha asked Aunt Maeve for more information about her?

A sob escaped, and she buried her face in her hands.

Strong arms wrapped around her, and she cried as Arick held her.

T HE KING'S EARLIER REQUEST to look into the cause of the storms suddenly made sense. The more he spoke to people around the harbor, the more Arick understood why King Craig wanted someone outside his usual circle to investigate.

Now that he had reassured himself that Thomas was okay, with only a minor earache after his ordeal, Arick wanted to speak to everyone who had been on the water during any of the storms.

He'd taken a risk, going to the moors instead of straight to the castle in search of Thomas. But explaining Sorcha's presence to the guards, not to mention the crowds of nobles who often hung around, would take time he was loath to waste. Thankfully Thomas had remembered their old meeting place — a hillside that could be seen from the prince's window and easily accessed by one of the back stairs.

Thomas's signs had come in handy too, as he was able to communicate with the woman far more than Arick had managed so far. Thomas had been born differently, and as he'd grown, some of those differences had become more evident. When he didn't speak as early as other children, the queen had sought a way to communicate with her bright, happy baby. Arick and Daniel had learned the hand signs as well, incorporating them easily into their play with their cousins. In the years since he'd moved away, however, he'd had little use for them and had forgotten much.

He tried not to mind that her first true smile had been aimed at Thomas and not him.

Thomas had offered to take her back to the castle with him so Arick wouldn't have to worry about her while he investigated, but a fierce protectiveness had taken over him. He had found her on the beach, and until he knew where she had come from, he would look after her. Something deep inside him compelled him to stay near her.

As he made his way along the docks, talking to all the captains and sailors who would give him the time, he watched her. More often than not, she was watching him in return. Whenever he got too far away, she would fidget and show signs of wanting to go after him.

He stopped at the far end to catch his breath. He must still be tired from the night in the water. A heavenly scent drifted past, and he followed his nose to an old woman with a basket of meat pies.

"How much for two, Mother?" he asked.

The old woman grinned up at him from under her shawl, taking in his well-cut clothing, and held up three fingers. He laughed and handed her four coins. He wrapped the hot pies in his handkerchief and hurried back to Sorcha, delighting in her enjoyment of his favorite snack.

The meeting with the harbormaster was the last on his list for the day. The man confirmed what he'd learned talking to the sailors, but with less fanciful theories than placing the blame on a mythical being.

Even having spent most of his adult life among sailors, he was still amazed at how many believed in the supernatural. As he guided the little pony back up the hill to the castle, he wondered what Sorcha believed. He wished he could communicate better with her.

Her tears, which he could only assume were of relief, had torn at his heart. Had she been on one of the ships that had gone down? Was her family washed up on another beach somewhere, equally lost and afraid?

He'd asked around about whether any foreign ships had been spotted in the harbor, but no one had heard of any, and the harbormaster had none on record.

The castle guards gave him odd looks as he handed off the reins and helped Sorcha down.

Even though she couldn't understand him, he chatted away as they made their way across the courtyard and through the castle. He was pleased that walking didn't pain her as much as before, but he still kept his arm firmly around her.

A short man who looked as though something had died in his shoe cut off their progress through the great hall. Arick kicked himself. Councilman Murray was known for being close with MacIsaac, and even more unpleasant.

"Who's this?" he snapped.

"Murray, this is Lady Sorcha." He bowed, just enough to be polite. The councilman had forgone the preliminaries of polite society, so he could too.

Murray sniffed. "Never heard of her. Who's her father?"

Oh, right. He should have remembered that giving her a title would mean she'd be tied to one of the landed families. But she carried herself with such grace he could only assume she was part of the nobility. "She's from Edeland," he replied, pulling himself to his full height.

"Hmm," Murray sneered. "Does Princess Aisla know about your *lady*?"

Arick bit his tongue. Responding to the man's insinuations as to who Sorcha was would only confirm the man's beliefs, and he was all too aware of the guards, servants, and other nobles who wandered the hall. "We were just on our way to meet her. Do you know whether she's with the king?"

There. Any within hearing would know that Sorcha was someone worthy of meeting the king.

"You dare to introduce her to your betrothed?"

Arick had a sudden desire to not have to support Sorcha. If his hands had been free, then he could have demonstrated just what he thought of this man. As it was, he bit back his anger and focused on getting out of the situation without causing further damage.

"The princess is my cousin, and a child. I would thank you to remember that, Councilman Murray."

It was a low blow, but reminding the man that he held no title beyond that which the king allowed him to use was necessary to put him in his place. Not wanting to give the man a chance to respond, he led Sorcha away, hoping Ailsa would forgive him for calling her a child.

Beside him, Sorcha shuddered. He glanced at her, and she gave him a look with her nose scrunched up. He couldn't help the laugh that spilled forth. She had perfectly captured how it felt to be stuck talking to Murray.

THE CASTLE WAS FAR grander than the grotto, but oh, so harsh. The ubiquitous gray of the stone walls was impressive in its uniformity, yet the sameness reminded her of the moody ocean on a cloudy day. Where was the color? The delightful outcropping of coral that revealed a new nook full of surprises or the kelp that waved to her each morning?

Even the humans that stood outside were dressed the same, albeit in greens and blues woven together.

Inside there were even more people. She was grateful for Arick. He was so tall that if she hadn't needed his help walking, she could have hidden behind him. Most of the people nodded politely, but that one man was odious. The sneer on his face made her glad she couldn't understand what he was saying. Arick led her away, his arm tight and rigid under her hand.

"He looks like a blobfish," she told him. She made sure her voice held laughter so he knew she was teasing. Maybe she could draw him a picture later, if they went back to the sandy beach.

Arick guided her down a long hallway, then through a heavy wooden door to where the floor rose in increments, merging with the wall. Arick walked straight to it and put his foot on the first step. She followed suit, but her foot banged into the riser. He bent to pick her up, but she pushed him away. Although it was nice that he was willing to do so, she wanted to learn how to do human things.

And this odd floor wasn't about to defeat her.

She ignored Arick's confused looks as she struggled to lift her foot up to place it on the next step. Pushing him, she motioned upward. He caught on, walking up a few steps before pausing.

She concentrated on how he did it.

Lift one foot, then slide it forward onto the higher part of the floor.

She tried it, and nearly fell over backward. Arick caught her hands and tugged her forward. After a couple of steps, he resumed his position beside her, and they went up in unison. He talked as they went, naming the various things around them, but she was so busy not wanting to fall back down that she didn't pay much attention.

At the top, he grinned at her, and she couldn't resist a little hop of joy for her achievement.

Pain shot through her feet, and she collapsed against him.

He steadied her with the most adorable look of concern mingled with confusion. Her cheeks warmed, and she pulled away, shuffling her feet to avoid the daggers again.

She could see he wanted to question her, but what could she say that he would understand? Even if they spoke the same language, she wasn't sure she could explain this to him. She could barely understand it herself.

After a moment, he gently took her arm again and opened another heavy wooden door. The hallway here was devoid of people, and the quiet was welcoming. They hurried to another door. Arick placed his finger over his mouth and made a shushing sound.

She repeated it, wondering what it was for. He made a face, shrugged, and opened the door.

The sound of voices greeted them, but she could only see Thomas and the cooky sitting on the floor beside a low wall. Arick ducked, and tugged her down with him. With great care, he pulled the door shut quietly. He shuffled over to Thomas.

Sorcha followed and sat next to the cooky. Its mouth opened in what she took to be a friendly expression, the long tail thumping on the floor.

Arick and Thomas leaned against the low wall. The voices continued, rising and falling over one another. Some spoke with urgency while others held a mocking tone. One droned on as if talking in his sleep. She sat up on her knees to peer over the wall.

A large man was sitting in a raised seat, looking out over the room. A guard stood on either side of him, and two people sat quietly at little desks below him. A man in a gray coat focused fully on making little scribbles on a white block while the woman watched the speakers.

The voices were coming from the rows of people. Two were facing her, and more voices were coming from below her.

Arick grabbed her arm and pulled her down, placing his finger over his mouth again.

Oh. They were hiding.

She grinned at the thought of these two men hiding from whoever was in the room below. She wondered what the room was for. It was large, and fashioned with greater care than the other human places she'd seen so far.

The voices pinged back and forth, rising and falling. She couldn't make out any of the words, but at times, anger bounced around the room. A higher-pitched voice, a woman's, spoke passionately for an extended time, but she was soon cut off by the divisive tones from several men.

Sorcha grew bored of trying to understand the conversations, and settled more comfortably near the cooky. She tapped his feet, and he'd shift them away. Any time she tapped his nose, he'd lick her chin.

Below, the voices grew more heated, and Arick and Thomas listened with great interest, their faces creased in concern.

A booming voice broke across the cacophony. "Thomas…!"

She couldn't understand the rest, but Thomas had turned pink. Arick set a hand on his shoulder.

The cooky padded over to Thomas and pawed at him. When Thomas didn't pet him, he let out a short bark.

The voices below stilled. Arick and Thomas exchanged a look.

The booming voice called out again. "Arick! Thomas!" followed by what sounded like a command.

Thomas hopped up and peered over the edge. With a forced smile, he waved at those below and greeted them.

Arick motioned for her to stay there. The two men walked to a door at the end of the balcony and disappeared down a spiral version of the uneven floor. The cooky went with them, hopping down.

Sorcha huddled down in the corner, and waited for the pain to come.

T HE KING'S FAVORITE SITTING room opened off the council chambers. He led Arick and Thomas through without even looking at them. The massive fireplace held a crackling fire, despite the summer sun outside the slit windows.

King Craig took off his cape and tossed it over a hook. His favorite chair groaned under his weight as he settled in and picked up his pipe.

"Eavesdropping, boys? You're both welcome to attend council meetings any time you like." He leveled a stern look at Arick and Thomas as they stood before him.

Arick held himself rigidly at attention. Being caught eavesdropping filled him with shame. As children, he, Daniel, and Thomas had often hidden up there to hear what the adults had refused to tell them.

But they were no longer children, and sneaking around was inexcusable.

"They wouldn't have said all that stuff if they'd known we were listening," Thomas mumbled.

"The council has a right to express concerns about the future of the kingdom. That's their role." The king focused on filling his pipe from a leather pouch of fragrant tobacco.

Thomas muttered something, not wanting to outrightly refute his father's claims.

"Arick? What are your thoughts?" The king pointed with his unlit pipe.

His thoughts? He wasn't sure his uncle was ready to hear them. "Sir?"

"You can speak freely here. I won't throw you in the prisons for being honest, lad."

"Yes, sir." He took a steadying breath. "The things they were saying about Thomas were...unkind."

"And?"

"And you didn't defend him, sir! He's your son, the prince. You could have told them to stop."

"Being king is not always about hearing only what you want to hear. Sometimes you have to listen to what others say."

"But what they said was untrue, sir."

The king sighed, pushing himself to his feet. "Thomas, do you want to rule?"

Thomas pulled himself upright. "I can be a good king, Da. I've learned from you since I was little. I want to help the people and do what's right."

"I know you do, my boy. But that tender heart of yours may just get you into trouble. Being king means making difficult decisions sometimes, and I fear that would cause you undue stress in trying to determine what was right for your people."

"But isn't that why you have the council? To help you make the decisions?"

"Yes, it is. But did we not just discuss listening to them even when we don't agree?"

Thomas nodded, his head down. "Yes, sir."

The king clasped his shoulder a minute before turning to Arick. "You spoke to the harbormaster and the captains who were on the water last evening?"

Arick nodded, pretending not to notice as Thomas turned away with his handkerchief to his face. "They all said the same thing — the storm came out of nowhere. A few injuries, but no one was lost."

"I'm incredibly relieved to hear that, but doesn't it seem a bit odd to you?" The king strode closer to the fire, his unlit pipe clamped in his teeth.

"It does, sir." He paused, wondering whether the king was aware of the rumors that swirled among the townsfolk. "Do you know the last time someone was lost in the Iskarraig Harbor prior to these storms?"

"I do." The king gave him a hard look.

"Ten years. Except for..." His throat closed, and he couldn't say it.

The king took the pipe from his mouth to speak, his voice quiet. "Except for the ship your brother was on."

"Yes sir."

"Why do you think that is? We've had storms, the passage is treacherous, yet all are saved from the depths." He made large circles in the air with his pipe as he talked.

"The sailors have theories." Theories that some part of him believed to be true — the part that vaguely remembered the figure that had appeared in the water as the sea had threatened to swallow him.

"What are they?"

He opted for the more believable answer. "Dolphins, sir."

"Dolphins?" The king let out a bark of laughter. "Have you spoken with anyone who claims to have been rescued by one?"

"There's one woman I want to visit. She was injured, and something pulled her from the water, but..."

"But what? Spit it out, lad."

Arick plunged ahead. The king had the right to know what the people believed. "The scuttlebutt says that it wasn't a dolphin that saved her."

"Well, is it dolphins, or isn't it?"

"I don't know, sir." The voice he had heard belonged to no sea creature he had ever seen.

The king stopped his pacing and studied Arick's face. "There's something you need to see." He raised his voice. "Hughan!"

The door opened to admit the captain of the king's guard. His face was passive, yet his eyes darted around the room and his hand hovered near the hilt of his sword until he ascertained that no danger threatened his king. He gave a slight bow. "Sire."

"Hughan, I want you to take Sir Arick" — the king glanced at his son — "and Thomas to see our...guests."

Something flickered over the man's face, but he made no sign of protest. "Yes, sir."

"Go along with the captain, lads. I'd best return to the council."

With that, he left, leaving Arick even more unsure of what was expected of him.

WHEN THE PAIN DID come, it was so subtle at first she didn't notice it. She'd been dozing to the sound of the voices below as the exhaustion of the day caught up with her. The drowsiness shifted as she found herself needing deeper breaths. Then the invisible bands tightened around her chest, and breathing took great concentration.

Sorcha pulled herself to her feet, grasping the edge of the balcony that overlooked the room below. Arick had told her to stay out of sight from the group of arguing people, but the panic that came with the pain drove all thought from her. She had to find him, that was all that mattered.

The room below was empty. No, no, no. How did she miss them leaving?

She stumbled to the door and tripped into the hallway. Daggers bit at her feet with every step, but she had to find Arick. The pull in her chest guided her along the deserted hall. She hesitated at the door to the uneven floor. Without Arick's help to climb down the steps, she'd surely fall to her death.

No one was around to watch her limping progress, but with each agonizing step, she grew to wish someone would appear to help her. Someone who could find Arick for her.

Did Arick not know that being apart from him was slowly killing her?

The hall ended ahead, and she bit back a sob. The thread kept tugging her forward, and she couldn't bear the thought of turning back. She staggered against the end of the wall, grasping a knobby bit for support.

The knob turned under her hand, and the wall opened, depositing her on the floor.

Cool, salty breeze caressed her teary cheeks.

A long open-air walkway stretched out before her. Columns rose on either side, holding the roof aloft. A carved railing connected each column. She pulled herself over to the railing, her feet grateful for the respite.

But the pain in her chest only grew. Why did it feel as though Arick was getting farther and farther away?

Did he not feel the agony that ripped at her very soul? Was this curse designed only to torment her?

Far below lay her home. The ocean swirled among the rocks. Each wave crashed high on the cliffs as though trying to reach her.

She shuffled along the low railing, trying to save her feet. The columns were too wide to reach around, so she hugged them for support.

Beside her, a soft voice asked a question.

Sorcha turned to see a girl with large eyes and hair like Thomas's.

"I..." Talking was a wasted effort when the girl wouldn't be able to understand her. Sorcha pointed toward the end of the walkway.

The girl slipped her arm around Sorcha's waist and pulled Sorcha's over her shoulders. Despite being shorter than Sorcha, she took her weight without faltering. She spoke gently, slow words that Sorcha didn't recognize until the end. "...Arick?"

"Arick. Yes, Arick!" She lifted her hand and made a knocking motion with it.

Ahead, the walkway opened up into a large circle. To distract herself from the pain, she counted the columns.

Ten.

Nine.

Eight more to go.

The floor of the circle shone different colors, a design she couldn't make out.

Almost there; only three left.

The girl kept up a soothing monologue, her voice rising and falling with the sea.

Sorcha could bear it no longer and collapsed onto the mosaic floor, the tiles cool against her flushed skin. Her necklace tinked as it struck the floor, a sharp sound amid the hum that filled her ears. She lay in a stupor, needing to move but unable to get up.

The girl kneeled beside her, a warm hand on her arm. Sorcha knew she should say something, thank her, but she couldn't. She just knew, whoever this girl was, that she had saved Sorcha.

Sunlight glinted off the center of the floor. Sorcha watched it, mesmerized.

She pulled herself across the mosaic.

The call of the light warred with the pull to find Arick.

Her fingers brushed the piece of glass. Fire ripped up her hand and her arm.

Sorcha screamed.

"W HERE ARE WE HEADED, Captain?" Arick asked as he followed the soldier through the castle. The guest chambers filled the east wing of the castle, and even though they were following a circuitous route, Arick did not believe that was where their destination lay.

"The dungeons, sir." The captain offered no other explanation. He was twice Arick's age, with a lean, muscular build.

"But the dungeons are back that way." Thomas pointed to the hall they had just passed.

"Yes, sir."

"Then why aren't we going that way?"

"We're going to the other section."

Thomas stopped. "There's only one dungeon in this castle. And it's empty. There's no 'guests.'"

"Your Highness is correct," the guard said, his expression blank, yet he made no move to return to the hall Thomas had mentioned.

Arick tossed his hands in the air with a sigh. "Captain, I appreciate the king did not expressly order you to tell us everything, but you might as well explain some of it and stop being so cryptic."

The soldier blinked, his gaze flicking from Arick to Thomas.

Thomas crossed his arms, his chin raised. "I'm not going anywhere until you tell us."

"If my prince so commands."

"I do."

Captain Hughan relented, his shoulders softening ever so slightly. "The lower level of the castle was damaged in the storms at the end of last summer, splitting off access to the dungeons. Thankfully, we have little need for using them. With the cold of winter and constant storms, the flooded portion has yet to be repaired." He paused.

"Which section are we going to?" Arick asked.

"The flooded section, sir."

"But if it's flooded, why would we have prisoners there? That's horrible!" Thomas protested.

"I think it best if I just show you," Hughan said.

They continued on their way, Hughan politely refusing to answer any more of their questions, insisting they would understand when they arrived. They stopped in the soldiers' wing as Hughan fetched torches for each of them. Beyond the barracks, they entered a passageway that had been hewn from the cliffs. Arick and Thomas had explored it as children, often using it to escape to the lighthouse, where their tutors wouldn't follow.

This time, when they reached the curving stone stairs, they went down rather than up. Several years had passed since Arick had last been here, but he couldn't remember whether the stairs had gone down before. Surely they would have explored it if that had been the case.

The further they descended, the mustier the air smelled, and the steps grew damp under their feet. Arick was soon panting.

Hughan stopped before a heavy oak door. "When you enter, you have to stay quiet. No talking at all, unless you are in danger. Is that clear?"

Arick nodded, as did Thomas, but he couldn't help wondering what lay beyond the barred door that demanded such a warning.

The captain pounded thrice on the door. It was opened from the inside, and they were immediately buffeted by warm, salty air. Continual thunder sounded in the distance. Arick followed a ledge around to the left, taking in the large cavern. Two guards stood just inside the door, their eyes locked on a large pool of water before them. Captain Hughan motioned for them to step into the stairwell. As they turned, Arick noticed they wore scarves over their mouths. Before he could ask Hughan about it, a giggle from farther along caught his attention.

He turned to see a short, chubby man who bore an uncanny resemblance to a mouse. He giggled again, clapping his tiny hands together. He beckoned them to follow him as he hurried along the ledge. Every few steps, he'd pause to put his finger over his lips, a giggle escaping each time.

Torches were mounted on the walls, their orange glow reflecting off the water so Arick couldn't tell how deep it was. They rounded a corner, and the floor leveled out as a large cavern opened up. All around were drawings and sketches tacked to the walls. He was too far to discern their subject matter with any accuracy, but he wondered at them. The far end of the cavern narrowed to a tunnel that led to the sea, and now he knew the thunder he'd been hearing was caused by the waves beating against the cliffs. The glow of the late afternoon sun illuminated the columns of stone, casting them in shades of purples and pinks.

"Wha—" Thomas breathed, before Hughan clamped a hand over his mouth.

"Ah, ah," whispered the mouse-like man, wagging his finger in the air. "They mustn't hear you!"

Wide-eyed, Thomas nodded, and Hughan released him.

"They?" Arick mouthed, confused.

The man nodded. He grabbed Arick's arm with a surprisingly strong grip and pulled him to the other side of the level floor. Giggling, he pointed out over the pool of water. Arick leaned forward, wincing at a pain in his chest.

Beneath the water, long pale shapes floated past. Arick stared at one, the features slowly becoming clearer. All at once, the merman broke the surface, his teeth bared as he hissed at Arick.

He stumbled back, his hand going to his aching chest.

Hughan was at his shoulder. "Are you well, my lord?" He spoke directly into Arick's ear.

"I...yes." He nodded, but he was far from well. He took a shuddering breath, winching as his lungs protested.

Thomas grabbed his arm, pointing. The younger man's lips were pressed together to keep words from escaping, but his meaning was clear.

Another mer was shackled to the wall, half out of the water. His pale face held a sheen, and Arick recognized the shallow breaths. He walked closer to the water's edge. Agony and defiance warred for dominance in the merman's expression.

"Release him," Arick hissed. The king must have had his reasons for holding the merfolk prisoner, but torture wasn't necessary. He bent over, bracing his hands on his knees.

"My lord, he tried to escape." The captain broke his own rule of speaking aloud. The other merfolk that had been watching them dove beneath the water.

"Can he get out?" Arick waved at the cave opening. The shackled merman writhed against his bonds, his fin splashing feebly.

"No, my lord, but..."

"Release him," Arick panted, dizziness washing over him. His lungs were being ripped from his body, and he felt as though he would be sick.

Beside him, Thomas's voice cracked as he repeated the order. "Release the merman. He doesn't need to be in chains!"

Thrashing in the water and strange shouts from the merfolk blocked out all other sound. Arick stumbled toward the door, clutching his side. Guards rushed past as the chaos and cries from the merfolk continued. He fell through the opening and collided with the stone wall. A groan escaped him.

Thomas appeared, his face lined with worry. "A-Arick...can...w-what?" He stumbled over the question.

Arick tossed his arm over Thomas's shoulder before he fell face-first onto the stairs. "Sorcha," he managed to say.

He didn't know why, but everything in him said to return to her.

Each step was agony. His muscles screamed for the oxygen his lungs couldn't provide. Thomas was a rock, supporting him. Slowly, slowly, the waves of nausea subsided. By the time they reached the passage to the barracks, the pain had dissipated enough for him to start thinking clearly. But the pull in his chest said to keep going up.

Arick glared at the steep stairs, wondering if his legs would even carry him further. Thomas turned to the door.

"No. Up," Arick told him. Speaking still required more breath than he had to spare.

"But that's the lighthouse." Thomas said in confusion.

"Yes."

Thankfully, Thomas didn't argue, and they continued their climb. Soon, the ache in his legs exceeded the tightness at his chest.

Light from the tower windows fell across their path, and he breathed in the ocean air, hope filling him. Soon he would see Sorcha, and all would be okay.

Thomas groaned. "Too many stairs."

With an apology, Arick removed his arm from Thomas's shoulders, finding he could walk on his own. The curving stairs were easier to traverse single file, and the dizziness faded completely when he moved to the outer wall.

Finally, Arick stepped out of the darkness and onto the edge of the mosaic. His sigh of relief froze in his throat.

"Sorcha!" he cried, stumbling to where she lay prone on the tile floor.

She stirred as he gathered her in his arms.

"Please be okay," he murmured, brushing her hair away from her damp face. Her startling blue eyes blinked up at him.

"Arick," she whispered.

CHAPTER NINE

"**H**AD A BIT OF a hurkle-durkle this morning, did you?"

Arick blinked the lingering sleep from his eyes as he emerged from the stairs into the mostly deserted dining room. Elsbeth shook her head at him from a table by the fireplace. Across from her sat Sorcha, who hid a laugh behind her hands. His worry for her, which had plagued him half the night, drifted away at the sight.

He waved off Elsbeth's teasing, his response lost in a yawn. "Have you got anything for a starving sailor to eat, Mother?" he asked, joining them at the table.

"I'm not your mother, and lie-a-beds don't deserve breakfast." She didn't look up from her knitting. "But there might be a spot of porridge left in the crock."

He got up and fetched the iron pot she'd indicated from where it was tucked into the coals. The remains of the morning's fire were dying down, and he basked in the warmth for a moment. He set the pot on the scarred wooden table and helped himself to a spoon from the jar of clean ones on the mantel.

"Ack, you're not eating out of my pot, are you?" Elsbeth scolded, even as she poured him a cup of tea.

"I was trying to save you an extra dish to wash."

"I've already finished the washing up. Anything you dirty is yours to clean."

"Then I think I'll eat from the pot, if it's all the same to you."

She clicked her tongue. "Good thing I know your mother; otherwise I'd believe you were raised in a barn."

Arick ignored her, his growling stomach demanding to be fed. While he ate, his mind drifted to what he had learned the day before. Merfolk were real. Not only real, but living in the very waters he sailed through — swam in. He'd always assumed they had vanished with the magic all those years ago. Where had they been hiding? And why? Did they know what had happened to the magic?

To avoid the plethora of unanswered questions, he changed his focus to Sorcha. The young woman had been watching their exchange with curious eyes, but now she returned to the lines of wool she had laid out on the table before her. He was relieved to see the shadows that had haunted her yesterday were gone. Although he couldn't say she seemed happy, at least she appeared rested and pain-free.

Her fingers plucked at the wool, weaving two colors together. Although not as fast as Elsbeth's clicking needles, Sorcha's piece grew steadily.

He rubbed his chest absently, the memory of the pain still lingering. What could have caused such a feeling, like his heart was being ripped out of him?

And why had returning to Sorcha made it stop?

A worrying thought stirred in his mind. He knew so little about her. Had she...done something to him?

He shook his head. No. Magic, if it was real, hadn't been heard of in one hundred years. Besides, he'd seen her suffer as much as him, if not more, when they'd been drawn apart. Why would she cast a spell that caused her such pain? He sipped his tea, not noticing it had gone cold.

"Head lost in the clouds?"

Elsbeth's words jolted him from his reverie, and he dropped the teacup. The thin china cup bounced off the edge of the table and smashed to the floor, tea spilling everywhere.

Sorcha jumped with a small shriek.

"Apologies, Elsbeth," Arick said, getting up to pick up the pieces.

"No mind. I'll fetch a rag." She hurried to the kitchen.

Sorcha crouched on the floor and reached for the shattered cup.

"Careful," Arick warned, joining her. He lifted the largest piece, shaking off the tea.

"Ow!" Sorcha jerked her hand back and sucked on her finger. She glared at the broken pieces, then an odd look crossed her face. She reached for the china again, her palm flat.

Arick moved to stop her, but she shook him off. Gently, she touched the sharp edges with her hand, then again, harder. When she pulled her hand back, it was covered in tiny flecks of blood.

She bit her lip and looked at him, her brows drawn together. Twisting around, she sat on the floor and pulled one foot into her lap. She pointed to the bottom of her foot, then to her hand, then to the broken teacup, talking the whole time.

He gave an exaggerated shrug. "I'm sorry. I hate that I don't understand you, but I don't know what you mean."

Elsbeth set a bowl beside him and began sopping up the tea. Sorcha repeated her pointing, her speech slower.

Arick dropped the pieces of china into the bowl. "I wish I could understand what she's saying. I feel so bad that I can't talk to her."

Elsbeth gave him an odd look, then watched Sorcha for a minute. "She's saying the bottom of her feet feel like she's walking on shards."

"Oh." Now that she explained, he could see it. "Has she let you examine her feet to see why?"

"Other than a few bumps and scrapes, there's not a mark on her."

Arick pondered the question as he finished picking up the broken china and cleaning up breakfast. Often his hand drifted to his chest, leaving a damp spot from the dishwater. Once he was done, he returned to the dining room.

"I need to head out. Do you mind if I take the cart again?" Speaking to as many people as he could about the storms was not going to be a quick task, so he wanted to get started on it. It wouldn't be easy, either, so he was mentally preparing himself for the anger and frustration he'd have to face.

Elsbeth cast a shrewd look between him and Sorcha, then nodded. "I won't need it today. You two have fun."

Arick couldn't stop the heat rising to his cheeks. "It's not like that."

She waved a knitting needle at him. "I never said it was, my dear boy."

Protesting would only make her more convinced, so he turned to Sorcha. "Do you want to come with me, or stay with Elsbeth?" He used his hands to mime it out as he spoke.

"Arick," she replied promptly, then ducked her head.

He wondered if the lightness that filled him at her choice was joy that she'd chosen him or relief that he wouldn't be risking the agony of the day before if he was separated from her.

OVER THE NEXT FEW days, Sorcha and Arick visited many homes around the town. Everyone was kind, but most ignored her once they discovered she couldn't speak their language. After the first house, she asked Arick what they'd said. The man had been so angry, and she couldn't see why.

"Storm," Arick told her, using the hand signs Thomas had used to indicate lightning. He pointed to the sun and motioned backward twice.

Of course. The storm that had changed everything.

She frowned and pointed back to the house. "Why that man?"

Arick ran a hand over his mouth, his eyes sad. "Broken ship," he said simply, putting his two fists together and breaking them apart.

Oh.

No wonder the poor man was so upset. Arick was asking him to relive a harrowing experience.

They continued on to visit others. Sorcha paid more attention, gleaning as much as she could from the few words she knew and piecing things together from expressions and hand movements. She was quiet as Arick helped her into the cart after the fourth house. She should have understood sooner.

"What is "dol-fem'?" she asked, fearing the answer. All the people they'd spoken to had used the word.

"Dolphin," he corrected her. "Big fish…" He pointed to the water, then put his palms together and wove his hands back and forth. Next, he held his arms out wide to show size.

She swallowed as he confirmed her fears. He was trying to figure out how all the people had been rescued.

Father and the Watchers were always so careful. But never had there been that many people in the water, so many lives that had needed saving at once.

What if someone had seen one of the merfolk?

What if Arick remembered seeing her?

A lifelong habit of hiding her existence from the humans fueled her hope that he would never learn the truth. The tiny part of her that longed to be truly seen by someone wished he could.

On this morning, Arick kept up his usual chatter as they drove. At first, she thought he was doing it only for her benefit as he pointed out the landmarks and taught her his language. But today there was a heaviness to his words. He wasn't talking aimlessly; he was thinking aloud, inviting her into his thoughts. She listened quietly, able to make out only a few words yet sensing his meaning from his tone. Was this what her life would be like from now on? Only a partial participant to what was going on around her? In time, she would learn more of the language, she was sure. But that would only resolve one of her troubles.

Her fingers brushed the hollow below her throat, seeking the caged heart necklace. It had gone missing after her fall, but she couldn't break the habit of worrying it when something was bothering her.

The cart stopped outside a little thatched house. A low stone fence enclosed the tiny garden. Sorcha looked at the stone path and sighed. Even that short distance would be painful. But waiting in the cart would be worse. Arick offered his arm as always and led the way to the door.

A small girl answered his knock. Only after a voice from inside called out did she allow them entry.

Arick ducked his head as he entered, his hair grazing the doorframe. Heavy beams across the ceiling weren't much higher, and he stood with his head tilted. Sorcha blinked at the gloom after the gray brightness of the sky outside.

The house was tiny, with only one room. The hearth took up most of one wall, with a table and low counter at one end and a bed at the other.

With a start, Sorcha noticed the small woman lying in the bed.

He introduced himself, then her. "— friend, Sorcha. — storms —."

The woman gave a wan smile and dabbed her forehead with a handkerchief. She motioned for them to sit as the girl clattered dishes in the other corner. Sorcha took the low chair beside the woman while Arick perched on a narrow settee.

The woman shifted positions, hissing softly.

Arick made an apology, half-standing to help her. The woman shook her head and asked him a question.

He nodded. "— storms — bad — many people. — you —?"

Sorcha struggled to follow along with his questions. At first the woman did not want to answer, and she watched her as the conversation continued. Despite being confined to her bed, the woman wore a pretty gown of faded flowers, with her hair in a neat bun. Sorcha tugged at her own tangled curls. The humid day had undone whatever order she had managed to tame it into that morning.

"— dolphin?" Arick asked.

Sorcha watched the woman for signs that she was hiding anything.

The woman pursed her mouth. "No, — dolphin... Something —"

Arick glanced at Sorcha before he continued, this time speaking so quickly, Sorcha couldn't make out any words.

"— people — water —"

Sorcha swallowed. People as in humans? Or merfolk?

Had this woman been saved directly by one of the Watchers? Was there another merfolk experiencing the torturous life on land that she was?

Nothing more was said that Sorcha understood, and after a few minutes of talking, the woman struggled to sit up and pulled the blanket from her legs. She tugged her skirt up to show the start of a bandage wrapped around her calf. Arick sucked in his breath and stood for a closer look. He reached out a hand, stilling when the woman murmured a protest. Her face turned red.

Arick let his hand drop, his face full of indecision.

Sorcha stood, pushing Arick away. He wasn't a healer, and the woman wasn't comfortable with him looking at her leg. She hurried him to the door. Once he was outside, she turned back to the woman, a question in her eyes. The woman nodded.

With gentle hands, Sorcha lifted the woman's skirt, revealing the blood-soaked bandages.

Was that how humans treated their wounds? She shuddered and peeled the layers off. Once the bandage was free, she could see that the wound wasn't bleeding as badly as she'd expected, but the edges were red, angry. The bandage, too, was stained and fraying. She tossed it into the fire.

The woman and the girl both gasped at her.

"None of that — that was horrid! You need clean ones!" she retorted, hands on her hips. They stared back. Maybe they had no others. She limped to the door to find Arick. He was moving bits of broken tree around and lining them up neatly against the house.

"Arick!" she called, pleased when he responded right away. "I need seaweed." She bent down and picked a few blades of grass, then pointed at the water.

He fumbled over it for a minute, before understanding lit his eyes. She tapped his coat and shook her head, then pointed back at the grass. To make sure he understood, she found a few more brown items and shook her head no, and then pointed at green ones and nodded yes. He hurried off, and she hoped he would find what she needed.

When she re-entered the house, the girl had a blue cloth in her hand and was about to lay it over the open cut. "No!" she cried, pushing the girl away.

How did humans ever heal if they constantly put dirty things on top? She took the cloth and used it to wipe away the crusted blood from the edges. With trembling hands, the girl offered her a bowl of steaming water, setting it on the chair. She mimed dipping the cloth in the water.

To her surprise, it worked. The blood and dirt came off more easily, but the water was soon filthy. She handed the bowl back to the girl and sank into the chair, wondering what was taking Arick so long.

The woman reached for her hand, squeezing it. Sorcha nodded, frustrated that she could do so little for this woman. If she were home, she'd have no issue healing her. Aunt Maeve would have a tonic, and she would sing.

Sing. She could sing.

She hadn't tried since becoming a human. Everything had been so overwhelming that she hadn't wanted to. Closing her eyes, she sought a melody.

"Hush, little mermaid, close your eyes." Her voice faltered. The song didn't feel right. Although her mouth was able to form the words, the sound was off. She kept going, searching for her magic.

There. A tiny spark. She pulled on it, feeding the thread of light into her song. The music was all wrong, though, and the magic didn't grow like it should have. She pitched her voice differently but couldn't find the note. She broke off with a gasp. How did humans ever sing? How did they pull air in yet breathe out the notes at the same time? She opened her eyes as she caught her breath. The woman was looking at her oddly. Her cheeks burned. Had she sounded that bad?

The wound hadn't healed at all. All that effort for nothing.

A knock sounded at the door, and the girl jumped up. Arick handed her a bundle of seaweed — the green kind — and backed away. Sorcha pushed aside her despondent thoughts. At least she could do this for the woman. The healing properties of the seaweed would keep infection out of the wound while it healed.

As she wrapped the seaweed in strips around the woman's leg, she caught herself humming. The familiar movements of helping someone were soothing, and she hoped her voice wasn't displeasing to the woman.

When she was done, she put the rest of the seaweed in a bowl of water to keep it fresh, and signaled to the girl that she should change them once a day. The woman had fallen asleep, her breaths coming soft and even. Perhaps the magic had worked a little bit after all.

Exhaustion settled on her like a cloak as she limped out the door. As soon as he saw her, Arick rushed over to offer his arm. She took it gratefully, the daggers in her feet easing as she leaned her weight into him.

He pointed at the sky. "Storm —"

She looked up. The haziness from earlier was gone, replaced by heavy clouds that gathered even as they watched. White caps formed on the waves, and tiny sailors ran back and forth on the pier far below them.

Sorcha swallowed against the dread of another night of terror and devastation.

Yet she couldn't deny the hope that filled her. Maybe in the storm she could return home. To her family. To where she belonged.

CHAPTER TEN

BY THE TIME SORCHA and Arick had returned to the
inn, the skies had opened. She climbed out of the cart
and raced to the shelter of the building as he guided the pony
back to the stables. She couldn't bring herself to go inside,
instead pressing against the rough walls.

Lightning flashed, and she gaped at the brightness, the
vibrant white overpowering what little light was able to
penetrate the clouds from the sun.

Arick ran through the rain, joining her in the narrow
space under the eaves. "— help. — here, safe," he said, his
hands moving as he spoke. His signs were jerky, but the more
he used them, the more amazed she was at how similar they
were to the ones the merfolk used.

She shook her head, and started signing. "No, I'm coming with you." Anything to avoid the pain of separation.

And she couldn't deny the hope of seeing her family.

Seeing her resolution, Arick nodded. "Wait —" He hurried inside, and returned a few minutes later wearing a heavy coat with a hood drawn low over his head. He handed her a similar one and helped her into it. Thunder rumbled overhead, and she shivered. Everything was so much louder on land, the sounds sharper without the muffling effect of the water.

Thunder was not just louder; it was oppressive.

His hands settled on her shoulders, and he leaned down. Worry lines drew his hazel eyes together as he studied her face. Even through the heavy cloak, she could feel the warmth of his hands.

"— close. — water —"

She gave him a reassuring smile. He didn't need to be worried about her. He couldn't know, but she could swim far better than she could walk.

Except —

She couldn't. Heat flooded her face as she remembered him pulling her from the water right after she'd gotten her legs.

She couldn't swim as a human. Couldn't breathe underwater as a human.

She was useless as a human.

Not that she'd been much more useful as a mermaid.

Swallowing back the lump in her throat, she tossed her head and forced a smile. "I'll be careful."

He grabbed her hand and hurried toward the harbor front. The rain grew heavier, and she gratefully tugged her hood lower. She bit her lip against the pain that came with each step. It was easier to run, springing away from the daggers, than to step carefully, and she kept pace with Arick.

Along the fingerlike piers, ships were tossing in the choppy water. Only a few smaller vessels had been out that day, and all around, sailors lent their hands to help secure them as they raced for safety.

Arick guided her to stand under the eaves of the building they'd visited a few days before. He leaned close to shout over the rain.

"Stay — help."

She nodded her understanding and watched as he dashed through the rain to give what aid he could. The all-too-familiar feeling of waiting by the sidelines settled on her as she stood there. She couldn't help here any more than she could underwater.

Waiting. Always waiting.

A sound broke through her thoughts, one that was both above the storm and part of it. All around was chaos. The men shouted as they worked to tie off a ship that threatened to buck the crew off her deck. The sound came again, from the opposite direction, wrapping around her.

Tears pricked her eyes as she recognized it.

Another glance at Arick. He had a rope wound around his arms, and he braced himself as another man attempted to tie off the line. He wouldn't miss her if she left for just a minute.

The sound continued as the song grew stronger. Sorcha ran to the far pier, past the abandoned ships that groaned against their restraints.

She dropped to her knees at the end of the dock. "Ciara!" she called out, a smile splitting her face.

Her sister rose with the waves, a matching smile forming. "You're okay." She reached a hand up to clasp Sorcha's. "Auntie said you were, but I had to see for myself. I thought... I turned around and you were gone." She looked at Sorcha's dress, the boots that replaced her once-shimmering fin. "I'm sorry. I'm so sorry."

Sorcha shook her head, her own tears mingling with the rain. "Not your fault. The storm was awful, and I couldn't just let him drown."

Ciara's face turned dark. "You should have."

Sorcha pulled back. "What? Just because I'm not a Watcher doesn't mean I can't help."

"No, you don't get it. Another Watcher went missing after the storm. The humans lured him away."

Bands tightened around her chest, but this time it wasn't due to Arick's absence. Why would the humans want a merman?

"They don't even think we're real," she whispered.

"Some of them do," a third voice interrupted.

"Aunt Maeve!" Sorcha couldn't help the surge of joy that filled her despite everything. "What are you doing on the surface?"

"I had to check on this one," her aunt replied, nodding her head at Ciara.

Ciara rolled her eyes in the gray light. "I'm a Watcher. I'm supposed to be up here."

Something felt off, but she couldn't place it. Maybe it was her... She had changed.

"But I'm glad you're here," Maeve continued as though Ciara hadn't spoken. "I found some old texts. There might be a way to break your curse."

Sorcha startled, nearly falling in the water in her eagerness. "There is? How?"

"You took the curse of being human by rescuing one. Magic has a give and take. In order to undo the curse, an opposite action must be performed."

Thunder clapped, covering her gasp. "I have to *kill* a human?"

"No, my little guppy. A human must do something of equal sacrifice to you. Specifically, your man must perform an act of selfless love. Only then will you return to your true form."

Sorcha stared at her, a million questions swirling through her head. She opened her mouth to ask, then closed it again, unsure of where to start. Arick was kind, but he wouldn't risk his life for her. He barely knew her.

"We have to go — humans are coming," Ciara cut her off. "Take care, cuttlefish. I'll try to come back in the next storm."

Maeve and Ciara vanished beneath the waves.

"No!" she cried. "Come back!"

She had more questions. More things she wanted to say to them. But the waves hid all trace of the mermaids as it had for centuries, keeping their secrets.

Alone, she shivered in the cold rain. Wind buffeted her, threatening to hand her over to the reaching waves.

"Sorcha!" Arick's voice pulled her back from the temptation to follow her family into the depths.

With a last look at the tossing waves, she hurried to join him. Lightning flashed, showing him in stark relief against the dark town beyond. He stood with his head tossed back, one hand reaching for her.

But his eyes were watching the water, not her.

No. He wouldn't sacrifice himself for her. She was nothing, and he would protect his own.

T HE SHOCK OF PAIN that ripped through him when Arick realized Sorcha wasn't at the harbormaster's wasn't caused by their separation.

It was fear.

The storm was getting worse, and she still couldn't walk that well. What if she were injured somewhere? He raced along the harbor front, searching for her.

A shout in an unfamiliar tongue drew him to the far pier. A forlorn figure huddled at the very end. Visions of her falling in tore her name from him.

"Sorcha!"

He froze as she stood lest he startle her more.

Her gaze lingered on the water. What was she looking for?

Lightning blinded him, and then she was there, a welcome shape among the spots that danced in his vision.

"We need to go," he said, taking her hand. "The storm's getting worse."

She nodded and followed him away from the water's edge. He drew her arm through his, telling himself it was to help her walk.

Definitely not his own need to know she was safe.

He led her back to the inn. The harbormaster had assured him all the ships were secured and the crews safely ashore. If any inbound ships were outside the harbor, then there was little they could do to help. Extra lookouts had been sent to the lighthouse, but no rescues would be mounted until the storm faded in the morning.

They ducked their heads and ran through the pouring rain. The short reprieve seemed only designed to allow the storm to gather strength. Arick held tight to Sorcha lest she be blown away by the gusts of wind. Their boots slid on the slick boards, sending them sprawling into the muck at the edge of the pier. He pulled them up, ignoring the mud splattered over them.

At least the wind was behind them, and they didn't have to fight it. They tumbled through the kitchen door in a whirl of wind and rain. Arick hauled the door shut and leaned against it, panting. Sorcha looked up at him from where she'd collapsed on the floor. Mud smeared across her cheek, and she looked like a half-drowned waif. She blinked at him, her lips trembling.

"Please don't cr—" His blurted words were cut off by a giggle.

Clamping a hand over her mouth, Sorcha stared at him, her eyes round. A glob of mud slid from his hair and plopped onto the floor. He stared back before his own laughter broke out. She giggled again, letting it ring forth.

She leaned against the bench, holding her sides. Her laugh was like dolphins dancing through the surf, and he found himself unable to resist laughing in response. He sank onto the bench beside her, his legs weak.

Tears were streaming down both their cheeks by the time they caught their breath.

"Don't you be bringing mud into my kitchen now," Elsbeth, unfazed, scolded from where she was standing by the hearth. She pointed at the boot rack, and Arick dutifully hauled Sorcha up to sit on the bench to remove her footwear. A puddle on the floor marked where she'd been sitting. He hung up their drenched coats. The heavy fabric would need to hang by the fire to properly dry out, but best to let as much water as possible drip out of them in the entry and not in Elsbeth's spotless kitchen.

She'd been busy while they took off their wet things, and when he helped Sorcha limp over to the fire, Elsbeth handed them both a steaming cup of fragrant tea.

"*Tapadh leat*," Sorcha said.

"You're very welcome, my dear," Elsbeth told her as she settled into the second rocking chair.

"Wait, you can understand her?" His heart leapt at the thought that maybe they could finally learn more about where Sorcha was from.

Elsbeth snorted, her eyes on her knitting. "Context helps a lot, lad."

Of course. He tapped down his disappointment, wondering at it. When had understanding Sorcha gone from being helpful to something he desperately wanted?

The image of her reaching toward the waves was seared into his mind. For a moment, he had thought she was about to jump into the raging sea.

He shook off the thought and pulled a chair out from the table. Elsbeth gave him a knowing look, but he pretended not to see it. Sorcha was there, safe, and it was only his foolish brain thinking such outrageous thoughts. He sneaked a glance at her. Her hands were wrapped around the teacup, but the laughter that had lit up her face moments ago was gone. Now she looked sad, alone. He flexed his hand, restraining himself from reaching out to her.

He stood abruptly.

"Alright there, lad?" Elsbeth asked, the creaking of her rocking chair keeping time with her clacking needles.

"Aye. But these storms... I don't know what I'm going to do about them." He set his tea down, then picked it up again.

"Are you the Creator, then?"

"No, of course not."

"Then there's not much you can do, is there?"

He blinked at her. She was right, of course, but...

"The king has asked me to find out what's causing them." He lowered his voice, even though Sorcha couldn't understand them.

"Ah, so he's finally realized there's something unnatural about the storms."

Arick took a slow drink as he tried to decipher the contradiction in Elsbeth's words.

"The Creator might be allowing the anomaly, but that still doesn't make it your fault, lad," she explained. "Unless you're the one causing the storms?"

He let the smile she was angling for quirk the side of his mouth. "I am thankful no more have been lost recently."

"Do you think that will last?"

"No. It's a blessing, but the storms are getting worse."

Elsbeth nodded. "Then I suggest you go get some rest and figure out what you need to do tomorrow."

"I'm not sure what else I can do," he admitted.

"Maybe you need to start at the beginning and look harder."

They lapsed into a shared silence for a time as the fire crackled in determined defiance of the storm raging outside.

Sorcha was asleep, her cheek propped up on her hand. After a whispered word from Elsbeth, he gathered her in his arms, careful not to wake her. He carried her to her room behind the kitchen, amazed at how holding her had become so natural over the past short days. Glancing down, he could see her damp lashes resting on her pale cheeks. Had she been crying? He was a cad for not noticing.

He set her down gently on the bed and tucked a blanket over her.

"Good night, Sorcha," he whispered, her name a caress on his lips. Climbing the stairs to his own room, he couldn't shake the cold that replaced her warmth.

CHAPTER ELEVEN

A RICK AWOKE WITH THE dawn, the soft gray light creeping around his curtains. Worry about what might have happened overnight drove him as he hurried into his breeches and laced up his shirt before slipping down the back stairs. Outside, fog drifted over the water, curling around him. The water was still. Waves lapped against the pier as if apologizing for making a disturbance. He sighed, letting his concerns slip from his shoulders.

He didn't go far; the pain that came when he was too far from Sorcha would surely wake her up. Small bits of debris littered the docks, but he could see no sign of damage to any of the ships.

The world around him was coming to life with the sounds of fishermen readying their ships for the day. Someone whistled a jaunty tune, and a dog barked in the distance.

A normal day.

He heaved a sigh and turned back to the inn. Elsbeth's words from the night before clung to him like the mist beading on his jacket. He needed to go back to the beginning and find out when the unnatural storms had started.

The inn came into view as he rounded the corner, and he couldn't stop the smile that tugged at his lips. Peering around the corner as though waiting for him was Sorcha. No pain drew shadows over her blue eyes, and he didn't think it was wishful thinking on his part that she looked pleased to see him.

"Good morning," he said, offering his arm.

"Guh mooring," she replied.

"If you're up for it, I'd like to head to the castle and..." The blank expression on her face made him stop. Elsbeth was right; if he wanted to communicate with Sorcha, he would need to provide her context to be able to respond to him. He switched tactics and added in more hand motions.

"We go to the castle. Visit Thomas and Ailsa?"

Her face lit up as she recognized the names. "The cooky?"

He laughed. "Yes, Cookie too."

She beamed at him.

Immediately after a breakfast of bannock cakes and bacon, they set out for the castle. They took the cart, but he noticed that Sorcha was able to walk with greater ease than before. He waited while she detoured to pet the little pony, something she made a point to do after every journey. He wished he could understand what she whispered into the little velvet ears.

They slipped in a side door to avoid the central hall — and hopefully all the council members who frequented that space. A servant let him know that Thomas was in the family's sitting room, so they made their way there.

Cookie greeted them with happy barks, his paws dancing on the stone floor as his tail fanned back and forth. Arick guided Sorcha to the settee by Ailsa, who greeted her with a hug. Immediately the two women began conversing, using both their voices and hands to convey their meaning. Arick watched a moment, regretting he had let his knowledge of signs dissipate over the years. Once Thomas had learned to speak, there had seemed little use for it. But now...

He looked up to see his cousin watching him with a huge grin on his face. He puckered his lips and brought his two hands together, making the fingertips twist against each other. Warmth flooded Arick's cheeks as he glared at Thomas, grateful Sorcha couldn't see the prince.

"A letter came for you," Thomas said, moving to the narrow table along the wall. "From a girrrrrl." He gave a pointed look at Sorcha.

Arick cuffed him lightly as he reached for the letter. "Can't be her. We're both staying with Elsbeth. Plus, she can't speak our language. Stands to reason she also can't write it."

"Then who..." His eyes grew wide. "Are you stepping out on her?"

"What? No! Besides, we're not... She's..." he stammered an objection, then redirected his attention to the envelope in his hand at the sight of Thomas's broad grin.

"Then who's it from?" Thomas tilted his head and scrubbed at his ear.

Arick studied the handwriting. He didn't recognize it. A thin string was knotted around it. "No idea. Do you have a knife?"

Thomas pulled open the drawer hidden in the table and rifled through the contents. Arick turned and leaned against the wall, tapping the letter on his hand.

"Thom, do you remember when the storms first started? The bad ones, I mean?"

Thomas paused his search, his face scrunched up in thought. "They've been getting worse the past couple of months. But..."

"But what?"

Thomas chewed on his thumb, avoiding eye contact.

"Thomas?"

"The first bad one...the first that felt...wrong..."

"Yes?" Why wouldn't he just spit it out?

"Six months ago."

Cold swept over Arick as the truth sank in. Daniel's ship had vanished in an unseasonal storm. Was his brother's demise caused by the same mess that threatened them now?

"Here." Thomas held out a thin knife. Arick stared at it a moment before remembering the letter in his hand. He cut the knot and unfolded the page. The page was covered in a tight hand, as though the author was unsure about writing at all.

Arick frowned at the message as he read, then read it again.

Sir Arick,

I should have told you this when you stopped by, but I could hardly believe it myself. However, I wish to repay the kindness that you and your nurse friend showed me. Thanks to her administrations, my leg has already begun to heal, allowing me to return to my duties as a governess in a few days.

You were asking how I came to survive the storm despite being tossed from my ship into the raging sea. You were right to question my story; I was hardly forthright with my tale. But allow me to correct that now.

When the storm blew in and the waves washed over my ship, I believed my life to be forfeit. But I was rescued. There was something — someone — under the water with me. Not a dolphin as you believed; a man. Or something like a man. He appeared afraid to come too near to me, yet he ensured I had something to cling to and guided me to safety.

Please, sir. I know how this sounds. I read the fairy tales to my charges. But I know what I saw. Not once did he need to break the surface for air. And he had no legs but rather a tail like a fish. He sang as we moved through the water, a beautiful melody I couldn't understand. His hair was of copper, his alabaster skin faded to scales of the same color on his torso. I include these details only so you know I am being truthful.

I know I have no position to ask of you anything, yet I find myself unable to conclude this letter without one humble plea: If you find that such beings do exist within our waters, I beg you not to harm them. He had no reason to save my life, yet he was resolute in doing so. Such altruism deserves to be repaid in kind.

Your humble servant,

Miss Nicol Greene

SORCHA SLID OFF THE settee to sit on the floor. The cooky danced around her, sniffing and nudging her face until he was satisfied with her greeting. He lay down beside her, his head and one paw on her leg.

Ailsa laughed and switched seats so she was facing Sorcha. She asked something, her hands moving in unison to make the signs "dancing" and "enjoy."

Sorcha nodded eagerly. Dancing was a release, a way to express music through movement.

Ailsa clapped her hands in delight, then signed her response. Sorcha listened and watched, piecing together the words. "I'm glad. Ball for Thomas soon. Celebrate being crowned."

"He'll be king?" Sorcha asked.

"Well, no. Officially the next king."

The cooky pawed for more pets, and Sorcha obliged as she pondered the human government. She supposed it mattered little to her as she'd be returning to the ocean as soon as she could figure out how. But a dance might be nice. Moving through the water, weightless... No. Humans didn't dance under water, and air didn't have the same properties. Her shoulders slumped.

"I can't dance," she signed.

"I'll teach you," Ailsa reassured her.

"No...my feet hurt." Tears prickled at the backs of her eyes. Not from the pain. She was surprised to find it was the thought of not feeling the escape dancing always brought that had her growing misty-eyed.

A look of mischief crossed Ailsa's face. "We could find you help." She glanced pointedly over her shoulder.

Sorcha followed her gaze. Arick.

Oh.

Her ears burned, and she ducked her head, certain that the cooky needed lots of attention immediately. What would dancing with Arick be like? Would he hold her in his arms like she'd seen humans do?

Ailsa's giggles made her look up again in time to see Arick and Thomas leave the room. She waited for the tightness to form in her chest, but it didn't come.

Still. It was unlikely to lay dormant the entire time he was gone.

"Where?" she signed, needing to know where the men were going.

Ailsa shrugged and stood. "Follow."

Sorcha scrambled up, to the delight of the cooky, who scampered to the door and down the hall. She limped after him. Ailsa intertwined their arms, and they stepped out of the room. The two men disappeared into a door at the far end of the hall.

Despite their efforts to keep up, the girls fell behind, but Ailsa knew the castle well enough to not lose them entirely. It reminded Sorcha of the first time she'd met the princess, and she sought for a way to ask Ailsa about her missing necklace. They wound through long halls and twisting stairs, until they reached a flight of stairs that trailed down below the castle.

"Dungeons." Ailsa signed, but her voice was uncertain. "Damaged, in a storm last year. Flooded. Not used." After a moment's hesitation, she led the way down into the darkness.

Sorcha nodded, her lips pressed together to hold back the whimpers of pain each step caused.

She wasn't sure what "dungeons" meant, but Ailsa clearly wasn't fond of them. They passed a man holding a spear similar to those used by the mer hunters. He said nothing, merely nodded at the princess. At last they reached the bottom, and Ailsa pushed open the door to reveal a large cavern of rough, gray stone. Voices immediately greeted them.

Arick was speaking, his voice louder than she'd ever heard it. Commanding, even as he asked a question.

A chorus of voices cut across his, some crying in fear, some demanding he stop.

Stop.

That wasn't a word she knew in their tongue. It wasn't spoken in the human language.

It was said in hers.

She untangled herself from Ailsa and ran, limping, to where Arick stood at the end of a dark body of water. "Who's there?" she called, eagerly searching the water.

Chains rattled.

"Here."

"How do you speak our language?"

"Stop."

The voices drowned out her words.

She spotted one of the speakers at last. A merman lay half immersed in the underground lake, his arms chained above his head. He glared at her, his chest rising and falling as he fought for breath. His pale skin was beaded with sweat, and the flickering candlelight cast deep shadows under his eyes. The face was familiar, though ghastly altered.

She fell to her knees, her heart thumping against her ribs. "Why are you here?"

"The humans blame us for the storms," another voice answered as a younger merman drew closer. He still wore the armband of the Watchers, but she didn't recognize him.

"Merfolk can't..."

He nodded. "But they don't believe us. They..." He swallowed, unable to speak further. He motioned to the one chained up, unable to reach the water he so desperately needed to breathe properly.

"Can you not free yourselves?"

Damp pale heads shook all around her. "Many of us are chained," the Watcher explained.

"And there's no path to the sea," another added. "Only stones. We're trapped."

She turned to Arick, her eyes wide. She fought to find the words, her mouth moving but no sound coming. "What did you *do?*" She managed at last, forgetting to try his language.

Arick stared back. He reached for her. "I..."

She spun out of his reach and ran. Tears blinded her, and she stumbled toward the first escape she could see. Pain wound its way around her chest, but she ignored it. She wanted nothing to do with Arick ever again.

Even if it killed her.

Sharp rocks jabbed through the soles of her boots, combining with the never-ending stabbing at every step. Her shoulder bounced off the uneven wall of the tunnel. Ahead, the glare of daylight beckoned her forward. She stumbled through the tunnel, her entire body aching. Gasping for air in between her sobs, she staggered out of the darkness onto a rocky shore.

She fell to her knees, clutching her chest. Was this pain because she was too far from Arick? Or a deeper hurt?

The image of him standing in front of the imprisoned merfolk cut across her memory, and she let out a cry of rage.

How could he? She had trusted him.

A soothing voice filled the air, a melody that offered comfort she couldn't reach. The singer drew closer, and Sorcha battled her sobs to see who it was.

"Oh, my dear little guppy." Her aunt's voice carried healing magic, but this was no physical ailment that could be mended with a song.

Sorcha threw herself into the water, desperate for comfort. "Oh, Aunt Maeve! They have merfolk in chains!"

Maeve patted her shoulder. "I know, I know."

Her words sank in, as cold as the water soaking her dress. She drew back. "You *knew*?"

"I suspected."

"And you said nothing. How could you?"

"Now, now. I needed to find out for sure, to find a way to free them."

Sorcha turned to stand, her feet sliding on the wet rocks. "Free them. I...why didn't I try to free them?"

Her aunt caught her arm. "You can't. They have guards."

She fell back, staring at her aunt in horror. "How many...? How long?" She couldn't even ask what she so desperately needed to know.

"All of them. Ciara's fiancé, Ewan, was the first."

Sorcha clamped a hand over her mouth as another cry threatened to escape. "That was *months* ago. You let Ciara believe he was dead!"

"I thought so, at the time." She hesitated, as though unsure whether she should share more. "You have to understand —"

"No, I don't!" She wrapped her arms around herself, sobs choking her.

"Sorcha —"

"I want to go home," she signed, unable to speak against the tears. To be home. Safe. Surrounded by her sisters, her parents.

"You can't. Not until the bond is broken."

"I don't want to be bound to him. He lied." Her fingers formed the words.

"Well, you are bound to him." Maeve was now signing as she spoke, as if to emphasize her words. "Only he can break it. And it must be soon."

Sorcha didn't want to hear it. She scrambled back up the rocks, out of her aunt's reach. A vice wrapped around her chest, far worse than when Arick left her behind.

"Leave me be!"

"Listen, child," Maeve shouted. "You only have until the next full moon to break the binding. Or else you'll turn to sea-foam."

"Go!" she screamed, not listening to her aunt's words. Nothing the older mermaid said was worth listening to. "Go!"

Magic filled her voice, but not the warm embrace of healing. A jagged edge cut her throat. Waves twisted and crashed, and rocks tumbled from the cliffs above.

Her aunt looked ready to argue, then an odd look crossed her face, and she dove beneath the waves.

Sorcha collapsed on the rocks.

Arick had betrayed her.

Her aunt had lied to her.

She had nowhere to go.

A RICK HURRIED ALONG THE rocky tunnel after Sorcha. What had made her so upset? Why had she looked at him like that? As he stepped out of the darkness of the tunnel, Arick froze in place, certain his eyes were deceiving him. Sorcha huddled on the hard ground, speaking to a woman in the water.

No, not a woman. A mermaid.

And they understood each other. Sorcha's hands formed a series of signs, her shoulders shaking with sobs. The mermaid replied, repeating one of the signs. Arick copied the motion, committing it to memory.

Whatever the older mermaid said only angered Sorcha more. She screamed, her voice harsh and desolate. Full of agony. Arick flinched, knowing he was partly to blame. The mermaid looked up and spotted him as loose dirt from the cliff showered around him. She vanished in the tumultuous waves as he ran forward.

Even if she hated him, he wasn't leaving Sorcha unprotected with stones falling down on her head. He spared a glance at the sky, wondering whether this was a precursor to another storm, but the overcast day grew no darker.

He pulled her to her feet and tugged her along the shore. She resisted, shoving him away. He pointed ahead. "Let's go inside. We'll find Ailsa and Thomas and talk."

She shouted at him, but there was only one word he was able to understand: "No."

His mind reeled as he watched her.

She had spoken to the merfolk in the dungeons. They had understood each other.

And the woman in the water, with the shimmering black scales.

He'd been trying for over a week to understand Sorcha. The scholars had been trying to communicate with the captives for far longer.

They'd first met on the shore after the storm. She'd been completely devoid of clothing. Unsure how to walk. He glanced back at her, and a memory flashed across his vision. A face in the water. Hands reaching for him. A voice so beautiful it had made him desire nothing more than to hear it again.

Her.

Sorcha had saved him.

Had only been able to save him because she was a mermaid.

He stumbled away from her.

Why hadn't she told him?

She stood swaying in the light wind like a sapling alone in a field. Her head hung down, her hair loose and covering her face.

A shout heralded the arrival of several guards, pulling his attention from her. They gathered around, asking if he was alright. Arick nodded, still dazed by his revelation.

"You're needed inside, sir," a guard told him.

He hesitated, not wanting to leave her alone.

"Keep an eye on her. Take her to the infirmary, if she'll go," he ordered one of the guards. He didn't know whether she was a prisoner. Surely she wasn't their enemy. But...she had lied, hadn't told him who she was. So it was safer to have them take her somewhere she could be watched.

He trailed behind the other guards as they entered the castle's shore entrance. He would go find the king and tell him what he knew. As he climbed the stairs to the main level, he thought of how to approach the topic.

"Yes, Your Majesty," he muttered under his breath. "I did bring an enemy into the castle and introduce them to your children."

But how was he to know? Mermaids were a thing of the past — creatures of stories and lore. They weren't *real*.

Yet they were. The dungeon was full of proof of that.

He clenched his fist. That was another thing he needed to speak to the king about. That creature studying the mermaids hadn't loosed the one in chains as he'd been ordered. Arick should have stayed and ensured it was done this time, but he'd been too distracted by Sorcha.

His mind was so busy he didn't pay attention to who else was near until a dour figure stepped in front of him.

"Ah, Sir Arick. Just who I was hoping to speak to." MacIsaac smoothed his lapel. "Do be so kind as to join us for a moment, won't you?"

Arick kicked himself for not noticing in time to escape. "I'm sorry, Councilman. I'm on my way to a hearing with the king, so if you —"

"The king has just left for a ride with his queen, so you'll have plenty of time to hear us out."

He was cornered with no way out, so he followed MacIsaac to a large room near the council chambers. A quick glance around the room proved that most of the council was present. Remnants of tea and sandwiches testified they'd been there for quite some time. The chatter stopped as he entered, and all turned to face him.

The door clicked shut behind him, and MacIsaac strode to the center of the room. "I'll cut to the chase, my lord. It's time for you to stop running about town with that bungaid of a woman and step up to your responsibilities."

"I beg your pardon?" Arick demanded. He wasn't sure whether he was more offended at the insult to Sorcha or the implication he was neglecting his duties. "I am doing exactly what the king has requested of me."

"Making a weather report can happen any time. We have less than a week until the prince's coronation, and we all know what needs to be done before that date."

Murmurs of agreement rippled around the room.

"Well, I don't, so why don't you make it plain to me?"

MacIsaac looked around the room, as if someone else would step up, but the others avoided eye contact. "Very well. I'll be frank. Thomas is not fit to rule the kingdom."

"*Prince* Thomas," Arick bit out, "is as capable as any other to rule."

"I know how you feel. It pains me to say it, but it is true. Thom— the prince is...simple-minded. He doesn't understand enough to make the difficult decisions required of a monarch." MacIsaac looked anything but pained as he spread his hands as if to say, *What else could we do?*

A barrel-shaped man leveraged himself out of a chair and approached. Lord Beattie smirked. "There's also the fact that the crown will inevitably fall to you anyway. We're just skipping a step."

Arick looked back and forth between them, baffled by what he was hearing. "Why is that?"

"Well, it's unlikely he will find someone to marry him, and even if he could, do we think him capable of siring children?"

The fire that had been smoldering in his belly since he'd discovered the truth about Sorcha spilled forth.

"How dare you?" Arick's hands tightened into fists that he barely kept by his sides. "How dare you speak of your prince like that? And to be such cowards? To wait until your king was out of the castle to hold this in *his* house?"

"Now, lad, calm down," Lord Beattie said. "Your brother —"

"My brother would never have participated in this...this *treason.*" Arick spun on his heel, no longer trusting himself to stay in the room with them.

"If you won't, we'll find someone else," MacIsaac called after him.

The slam of the door was Arick's only reply.

CHAPTER TWELVE

T HE CRYING OF GULLS pulled Sorcha from sleep. Shivering, she sat up, her entire body aching. Smooth pebbles shifted beneath her. Her eyes itched, and she rubbed her face, trying to remember why she was on the shore alone.

Her aunt. Arick. The merfolk.

She twisted around in search of the tunnel. The tide had come in while she slept, hiding the treacherous pathway she'd used. She rubbed her chest, the familiar ache telling her Arick wasn't close by. She had a vague memory that he'd been there. Had he seen Maeve?

At any rate, he hadn't pieced together yet that she was a mermaid, or else she'd be in the dungeons with the others.

She pulled her knees up and wrapped her arms around them as she stared out to sea. The gray ocean showed no sign of the intricate life that swirled beneath the waves. A steady breeze carried the spray over her, mingling with the tears that fell anew.

Her thoughts churned as she watched the uneasy ocean. Why were the humans taking merfolk prisoner? They could have easily used their siren voices to lure them onto land, but they'd had the decency not to do that. But what was the point?

Arick was convinced the storms were magical. Did he think the merfolk were behind them? She could almost understand that then.

She shifted, the hard rocks beneath her digging into her legs, but she wasn't ready to move yet.

If someone from Muirin was causing the storms, who was it? Aunt Maeve came to mind. No, that was all wrong. Maeve only ever used her magic to heal people. She wouldn't cause harm — would she even know how?

A cold shudder rippled through her, and she reluctantly got to her feet. As much as she didn't want to, she needed to find Arick. Despite what she'd learned about him, he was still the only one who could break her curse and save her from inevitable death.

The uneven shore made walking difficult, and she stumbled with each step. The ever-persistent daggers added to her struggles.

"Sorcha!"

She looked up to see Thomas waving at her, his round, youthful face pinched in worry. The cooky trotted over the rocks to greet her, his tail wagging in delight. Thomas offered his arm as he joined her.

"Cold?" he asked, using a sign she was familiar with.

She hesitated before replying "yes."

He rubbed her arm and guided her to a door in the side of the cliff. She hadn't noticed before, but the castle wall extended down to the shore. They slipped inside, and Sorcha blinked against the sudden gloom. Thomas whispered something to the guard, then led her to a small comfortable room. A fire danced cheerily, filling the air with the rich scent of burning heath.

Thomas directed her to a chair and pushed a footstool over for her. He scampered around the room, moving tables and tugging another chair closer. The cooky leaned against her legs, lifting one paw to beg for pets. She obliged while waiting for Thomas to finish whatever it was he was doing.

He dropped a blanket in her lap. "Sorry," he signed. "I should have brought that first."

The door opened, and a young woman in a gray dress backed in, pushing the door open to not spill the tray of tea she carried. When she turned and saw Thomas, she blushed pink and gave a little bob. Thomas's ears flushed red, and he stood awkwardly in the middle of the room until she'd set the tray down and left.

With deliberate movements, Thomas poured two cups of tea and added generous amounts of milk and sugar to both. He carried over one cup in both hands, mincing his steps to avoid spills. His hand jarred it as he set the cup down, sloshing tea into the saucer. He let out a deep sigh.

"Sorry. Too clumsy."

Sorcha helped him mop it up and took the second cup from him so he didn't have to lower it to the small table. She took a sip, expecting the same earthy flavors as the tea Elsbeth served. To her surprise, this one tasted of fruit and was much sweeter.

The ache in her limbs faded as the warmth from the tea and the fire soothed her, but the burning one in her chest lingered. She didn't know whether it was caused by her separation from Arick or the deeper rift he'd torn between them.

After some time, she gave in and asked where he was, using slow hand motions to ensure Thomas understood her meaning.

He fidgeted, then shuffled his seat over so they could see each other's hands easily. "He's with the councilmen. They wanted to talk to him...about me."

"You? Why?"

Thomas squirmed again, looking down at his hands. "They don't think I'm a fit prince. They want Arick to have the crown."

Sorcha frowned as she followed his hands. So many of their signs were the same, but some were different, so she wasn't sure whether she understood correctly. "But you're the king's son."

He nodded, rubbing a hand across his face. "I am. But I'm...different. I know I'm not as smart as Arick. He'd make a good king."

"What do you want?"

Thomas looked surprised at the question, then nodded. "I want my people to be happy. To be protected." He paused, his hands starting to form words, then stopping. "I believe I could be a good king. But if Arick would do a better job, then maybe I should step down."

The dejection on his face made her heart ache. She leaned forward to touch his hand. When he finally met her gaze, she gave him an encouraging smile. "I think...if you're willing to do that for your people — to step aside to let someone else rule for the good of your country — then you're just the sort of king they need."

He dashed a hand across his eyes and smiled at her in return. "Thanks, Sorcha. You're pretty smart yourself."

They sat quietly until a servant summoned him away, leaving Sorcha alone. The warmth made her drowsy, but she couldn't help thinking of what she and Thomas had talked of. As much as she wanted nothing more to do with Arick, maybe she needed to put her feelings aside and do what was right for everyone — merfolk and humans alike.

A RICK STORMED THROUGH THE castle, seeking an escape, but no matter which way he turned, there was always someone lingering. He didn't want even a servant to see how angry he was.

How dare those fools use his brother's death to manipulate him?

And how dare Sorcha not tell him she was a mermaid?

"Maybe because she knew you wouldn't have been able to understand her?"

He jumped. His wanderings had taken him into the long gallery that he hadn't realized was occupied. Or that he'd spoken aloud.

Aisla set her book aside and stood to join him.

"Still," he grumbled, "she could have found a way to tell me."

"Oh, sure, that would have gone well," his cousin replied. "'Hi there, human man who has never seen a mermaid. I am one, and I'd greatly appreciate it if you'd help me get back home.'" She crossed her arms. "And you'd have believed her, then?"

"I...yes."

Ailsa quirked an eyebrow at him. "Right. Because when you did learn about mermaids being real, the first thing you did was...?"

"Blame them for the storms." His shoulders drooped.

"Right."

He dropped into a chair beside the one she'd abandoned and held his head. "What am I going to do, Ailsa? Everyone has all these expectations of me."

"Who?" She didn't seem surprised at his abrupt change of topic.

"The council just cornered me," he admitted. "They want me to become the heir instead of Thomas. What's worse, they said Daniel would have done it."

Ailsa snorted. "Daniel was ambitious, but he was never *that* ambitious."

He ignored the twinge of guilt that she had known his brother better than he did. "If I don't agree, they'll just find someone else."

"Not if you and I stand up for Thomas. He deserves the chance to rule. If he steps down, it should be his own decision, not one that was forced on him." The heat in her words reminded him of the tiny fireball who had defended her big brother even when they were all small children.

"Even so — Daniel was the one who liked all this political stuff. And I can't help feeling that I owe it to him to continue." He stood and moved to study a painting on the wall, that of their shared great-grandfather.

"What do you mean?"

"What if the mermaids *are* causing the storms? What if they're the reason Daniel died?" he whispered.

After a minute of following his convoluted logic, understanding dawned on her face. "And by being friends with a mermaid, you feel you're betraying Daniel?"

He could only nod.

"You love her, don't you?"

Arick tried to deny it, but the ache in his heart refused to let him. "What does this mean?" He showed her the sign that he'd seen the other mermaid use when she was talking to Sorcha.

Ailsa copied his movements, her brows furrowed. "Oh! Was it more like this?" She changed her hand placement and made the motion more crisp.

"Yes, that's it."

"It means...bound, or to bind. Why?"

The frown returned to his face. "The other mermaid said Sorcha and I were bound together. I don't understand what she meant though."

Ailsa shook her head at him. "You're going to have to talk to Sorcha about that."

Right. The exact thing he did *not* want to do.

Chapter Thirteen

T HE GENTLE FLICKERING OF the fire mesmerized Sorcha. Despite seeing flames almost daily since becoming human, they never ceased to amaze her, this wavering source of light and heat that ate whatever was fed to it.

She'd tried touching it once, her finger bearing a red mark for a few days after. The sting was similar to that of a jellyfish, and she'd quickly learned not to put her hand too close. The humans seemed to have many uses for the fire, warmth being a common one. Elsbeth used it to change the consistency of foods, which was a whole source of fascination on its own.

Humans also carried it around in little boxes or on short sticks to bring light with them. Apparently no bioluminescent plants lived above the surface to chase away the darkness.

The thought of home curled around her heart and squeezed. Oh, how she missed her family — even Rona with her constant pushing for Sorcha to do more, be more. Aunt Maeve said that in order to return home, Arick must perform an equally selfless task. But she hadn't explained what would happen to him when he did so. Would he become a merman?

If he did, she could show him her undersea world — the grotto, the coral throne, her cave of treasures. Her hand drifted to her neck, where the necklace should have been. Maybe he wouldn't be impressed with her discoveries; he'd probably seen far better on land. But they could swim with the dolphins and explore the shipwrecks together. She imagined his smile, his hazel eyes filled with wonder...

The door opened, and a blush spread across her face as the object of her musings stepped into the room. The frown on his face reminded her of what he had done. How he had allowed her people to be imprisoned and chained up below the castle. A shudder ran through her.

No, Arick would have no interest in exploring Muirin. If he knew about the grotto, he would want to destroy it.

He held out his hand to help her up. "— home?" he asked.

Yes, she was ready to go home, just not the one he meant. But the inn was better than this tucked-away corner of the castle. She ignored his help and stood on her own, determined not to show him any further weakness.

He hovered by her side as they walked through the castle. She stepped deliberately, clenching her jaw to hide the pain. The little cart was drawn up to the door, and as much as she wanted to pet the pony as usual, she couldn't bear the thought of the extra steps.

Arick drew closer as she reached the side of the cart, but she refused to glance his way as she pulled herself up, keeping her face turned to hide her sigh of relief as she sat on the bench.

"Sorcha?" he asked, and she shoved aside the thrill that ran through her at the way he said her name. He stepped to the corner of the cart, where she could see him. He said something else, then lifted his fist to his chest and rubbed it in a circle. "I'm sorry."

Fire rippled through her. How dare he be sorry yet continue to keep the merfolk imprisoned? She lifted her chin and stared straight ahead.

After a moment, he walked around the cart and climbed up beside her. As they drove through the cobblestone streets in silence, he tried to speak to her more than once, but each time, she turned away, refusing to look at him.

As soon as he pulled up by the inn's door, she stood to get down on her own, but she couldn't figure out how to do it. It was too far to step, and when she tried to lower herself, her foot tangled in her skirt.

Then Arick was there, his warm hands wrapping around her waist as always. From her first morning on land, he had been there to help her, to show her kindness, to guide her. An ache filled her. Would he be the same if he knew what she was? She turned away as tears filled her eyes.

His hands on her shoulders stopped her. "Sorcha, please."

She waited, not daring to meet his eyes. He held out his hands, wrists pressed together. Then he crossed his forearms, pulling them apart as he firmly said, "No." More words followed that she didn't understand, but the earnest look on his face gave her hope, until she heard the word "storms."

She turned away from him and limped into the inn. Ignoring Elsbeth, she made her way to the little room and curled up on the bed. Guilt flooded her as she thought about the merfolk held captive, some unable to breathe as the chains kept them out of the water.

How could the humans be so cruel?

What had Arick been trying to say? What did the merfolk have to do with the storms? She sat up abruptly. Surely they didn't think the merfolk were the cause of the storms, did they? She had seen no evidence of magic among the humans. Did they believe merfolk were powerful enough to control the weather?

She snorted. Her mother was the most powerful of the merfolk, and even she couldn't do something like that.

Her hand brushed her throat again, searching for her necklace. Despite it being a human trinket, it reminded her of home. Of showing her discoveries to her aunt, something she'd done since she was a child.

A frown crossed her face. What had Aunt Maeve told her? That humans long ago had hidden magic in the precious stones because they couldn't contain it themselves?

Had Aunt Maeve found such an object? What would human magic combined with a merfolk's power be like? Would it be enough to control a storm?

Sorcha tried to push the thought aside, but more crowded in. Her aunt being on the surface during the most recent storm. Maeve being late to the infirmary. Not joining the others in the cavern while waiting for the Watchers.

No. Her aunt wouldn't do such a thing, she was sure of it. No mer would.

But that didn't change the fact that humans held merfolk captive, and that they would die if not able to breathe underwater.

And as the only merfolk on land, it was her responsibility to save them. Which meant facing Arick once more.

"ELSBETH, WHAT DO YOU know of magic?" Arick asked as he plunged his hands into the dishwater.

"Magic?" She gave him an odd look as she set a stack of dirty plates on the cupboard beside him. "Magic hasn't been around for a hundred years, lad."

"I know, and I've only heard the legends. I was just wondering if you remembered something more."

"I'm not as old as all that, young man."

"You're not a day over thirty, and you look even younger," he declared gallantly. "And I've no doubt you'll live long past the time I've taken my final voyage. But..."

"But you still want to know about magic," she finished for him, a fond smile on her face. "Very well; your flattery has won you points with this old lady." She dug a clean cloth out of a drawer and began to dry the dishes he'd already washed.

"These days, magic is spoken of with wonder, like it's beautiful and good. But when I was a child, there were many who refused to hear even the word itself. The stories were told in fear. Those who controlled the magic in the end used it for evil and not good."

"Do you think all magic is bad, then?"

She nodded at the knife in his hand. "Does the knife control whether you use it to chop a carrot or to harm someone?"

"No?"

"Exactly. And magic is the same. It's a tool."

"You speak of it as if it's real — as if it's still here."

"You wouldn't be asking me about magic if you didn't think you had seen it."

He hesitated, risking a glance toward Sorcha's room. But he wasn't ready for that conversation. Not yet.

"The storms. They're not natural. I think something is causing them, but I don't know where to look.

"Hmm...I might have something that could help." Elsbeth set aside her drying cloth and disappeared down the hall.

He couldn't stop his thoughts from drifting to Sorcha once more. Knowing she was a mermaid answered so many questions he'd had: where she had come from, how she had ended up on the beach — without any clothing no less, why she didn't understand his language.

Her confused face at their meeting flooded his mind. The way she had struggled to walk.

"I found it," Elsbeth said, returning with a heavy book in her hands. She set it on the table and opened the stained leather cover.

He dried his hands and joined her, peering over her thin shoulder at the yellowing pages. The first page she opened to had a charcoal drawing of a great winged creature, which resembled a horned lizard. Opposite, another serpent-like creature was labeled "beithir."

"I thought this was a book of magic, not mythical beings?" he asked, flipping forward a few pages before stopping at a sketch of a horse leaping from a pond. An anchor, fashioned from a piece of copper wire, hammered and twisted with care, marked the page.

"And you think these beings couldn't exist without magic?"

"Fair," he said, shuddering at the kelpie. Like most children, he'd been warned to return home before dusk lest the horse-like wraith emerge from the swamps and devour him. He wasn't sure how he felt about the possibility of such creatures being real.

The bell from the front room rang, signaling the arrival of a guest. Elsbeth left him with the book as she hurried through the swinging door to greet the newcomer.

Arick flipped a few more pages, skimming the information jotted down beside the sketches. The artist had a hauntingly surreal style, exaggerating the features of many of his subjects. The rendering of the caoineag, a banshee who reportedly lived in the high country, was particularly grotesque with an elongated nose and dark shadows curling from her cape.

The next spread of pages had two vastly different images with the same label: Bean Nighe. The first was an old hag, with scraggly long hair and webbed feet, her hand raised as a wave crashed behind her. The second depicted a beautiful young woman with the ocean lapping at her ankles. An unsettled feeling came over him as he read that "the sea hag may signal death by singing a lament." Echoes of a half-remembered lullaby swirled through his head.

He turned the page again, and sucked in air as his eyes fell on the new sets of sketches. Human shapes, yet their lower halves were fused together in a long tail resembling a mackerel. Tiny notes in a fluid hand surrounded the merfolk. He skimmed them.

Human voices are as the call of the siren to the mer. Upon hearing a human speak, a mer would be compelled to follow until that human did cease to speak or the mer was stranded on land, where they would perish as like any fish.

A shudder ran through him. No wonder the imprisoned merfolk shouted any time a human spoke near them.

How had all this information been lost in only a hundred years? Surely the castle library had similar notes that the man in charge of the merfolk would have had access to?

His eyes drifted farther down the page, past another line of spidery scrawl.

Curse of the Bond.

What was that? He leaned down to decipher the text.

A slender hand appeared, and a rose-tipped finger tapped the scaled beings.

He looked up to see Sorcha. She gave him a trepidatious smile, her eyes wide. She tapped her finger against her sternum, then pointed to the drawing again.

"Sorcha...under water...people." She moved her hands as she spoke the unfamiliar words.

He'd been right. She was a mermaid. He smiled at her, reaching across the table to take her hand in his. She hesitated, searching his face before accepting.

"I want to know everything about you," he told her, hoping she could hear the sincerity in his voice. With her hand still in his, he looked down at the page again, reading the few lines under the header he'd seen before Sorcha arrived.

The last line had him squeezing her hand tighter as he forgot how to breathe.

If the curse be not broke by the rising of the next moon at her height, then the mer shall return to the sea as foam.

CHAPTER FOURTEEN

S ORCHA SAT ON THE edge of the pier, her feet skimming the top of the frigid water. She'd discarded the boots, hoping the ocean would offer a soothing touch to her poor, aching feet, but the sun hadn't yet had a chance to warm it.

Another storm had raged overnight. She'd lain awake as the wind ripped past her window, threatening to tear the thatch from the roof and the ships from their moorings. She'd slipped out before dawn as the rain stilled. Without Arick, she couldn't go far, but she found she didn't want to.

When she'd first thought of telling him, she was sure he would run away, maybe even throw her into the dungeon with the others. If he'd even understood what she was telling him.

In the end, the telling had been easier than she'd assumed. She'd pointed to the image of the mer in the book he'd been reading, and he'd quickly understood. But his reaction wasn't quite what she had expected. At first, he'd been almost...excited? But then he had looked at the squiggles on the paper, and that excitement had drained away; he'd become worried, sad.

She pulled her shawl closer around herself to ward off a shiver. Even now, she could feel the way his hand had tightened on hers, how reluctant he'd been to let go. The waves sloshed lazily against the pillars below her, as if apologizing for the tantrum of the night.

A whistling tune carried up from the wharf as sailors appeared to check on their ships, but it was the lilting tones coming to her across the waves that drew her attention.

Two heads bobbed in time with the sea, flashes of light blinding her as the early morning sun reflected off their iridescent scales. Even from that distance, Sorcha could tell that Maeve and Rona were arguing. But why — and why were either of them above the surface in the daylight, so close to shore?

"Sorcha!" Arick's deep voice broke her bubble of isolation, but she found herself turning to him with a smile.

She shouldn't be so happy to see him. He was the reason she was trapped on land, away from her family. Yet when he smiled at her like that, with his hazel eyes crinkling at the edges, she let him take her hand and pull her to her feet. She picked up her boots.

"— shoes?" he asked with a frown. "— feet hurt?"

She gave a shrug with a half smile. Although the human's language was becoming easier to understand, her tongue had yet to master the sounds.

He gave her a fond smile and scooped her up. "Too cold..." he said and turned back to the inn.

She couldn't deny that he was much warmer than her previous perch, and she snuggled against him. Glancing over his shoulder, she saw her sister and aunt staring in her direction, though she couldn't make out their expressions. She gave a small wave. They didn't return the gesture, and after a moment, they sank beneath the surf.

She sighed, nestling deeper into Arick's embrace. Would her family even miss her if she were forced to remain on land forever? She would miss them — *did* miss them. She missed her parents, her sisters, Aunt Maeve. She was adrift without the sense of purpose the infirmary gave her, lost in a world with a strange language, different customs, where pain dogged her every step.

Yet there was also a sense of belonging that settled over her when Arick was near. Or maybe it was nothing more than relief that the pain was gone.

She contemplated this as they prepared breakfast together. Elsbeth was already awake, cooking for her guests. Sorcha sat in a chair near the hearth, turning the toast to keep it from blackening — a fascinating result, albeit one that earned her many frowns from the humans — and spreading the golden brown slices with a sticky substance Arick called "jam."

He took over manning the frypan, the contents snapping and cracking as they cooked. He sang as he worked, his lilting baritone filling the kitchen.

Sorcha's breath caught as she recognized the song. He'd been singing it the first day she saw him, sitting on the edge of the boat with Thomas and the cooky. Was that when he first had ensnared her with his siren voice? Had rescuing him been inevitable, as Aunt Maeve thought?

She shook off the idea. Although not rescuing him had never been an option, she hadn't been compelled to do so. She had chosen to save him.

And she would make the same choice again.

He gave her a small grin, and her cheeks warmed as she turned away. After a few more slices of toast, Elsbeth shooed Arick away from the stove, and she and the young lad who helped her took the final servings out to the dining room.

Arick carried two plates of food to the table and helped her drag her chair back over so they could eat. He set a notebook down beside him, and eating with one hand, he drew sketches with the other.

After managing to stab a piece of bright yellow egg and make it to her mouth without it falling off, she leaned over to see what he was drawing. A cloud? No, a storm. With extra lines coming from it. She wasn't sure what those were for.

But his next drawing she recognized immediately as the merfolk in the cavern. And his next was merfolk under the sea. Finally, he drew arrows connecting each of these in different directions. And in the middle of it all, he put a squiggle and a dot. With toast crumbs sticking to her chin, she reached over and tapped the squiggle, giving him a curious look.

He laughed. "Yes, a *question*." He gave her the same quizzical look in return.

Oh. The symbol represented asking something. She tried out the human word, her mouth struggling with the shape.

Arick repeated it and helped her until she got it right, never once laughing at her failures. Then they turned back to the drawings. She still didn't know what the lines around the storms meant, but she had an inkling of what the arrows were for.

"Question?" she said, tracing the arrows with her finger.

"Ahh," Arick said, leaning back. He pursed his mouth. "One, two, three." He held up fingers as he counted, then he tapped on the page. "One, merfolk mad. Two, storms. Three, merfolk captured." He used his hands and facial expressions to convey his meaning.

She frowned at him. That's not what happened at all.

"Orrrrr," he said, interpreting her frown. "Storms, one. Merfolk mad, two. Merfolk captured, three."

She shook her head at him and reached for his drawing, fork still in her hand. A piece of egg fell off and landed on one of the free merfolk, looking like Rona's golden hair. "One, merfolk captured. Two, storms. Three, merfolk..." She paused, unable to find the word she needed.

"The merfolk are making the storms," he said, signing at the same time so she understood him.

She glared, not wanting to agree. But... A tide pool of dread swirled in her stomach, and she pushed her plate of food away. She didn't want to think about what she had seen.

She was certain about one thing though.

"Merfolk captured," she said firmly, jabbing her finger at the image on the map.

"You think the merfolk were captured first," Arick said, then signed. "That...that would change everything."

She met his eyes, nodding slowly. Her hand lifted, her fist nodding forward once, twice. Yes.

"If we free them..." he started, his hands forming the words clumsily.

"The storms stop," she finished for him.

A RICK WRIGGLED ON THE hard wooden bench. As his uncle had said, he was permitted to join the council any time he wished, but the unwelcoming atmosphere was one of the many reasons he had refrained from doing so in the past.

But as Thomas shuffled to the center of the horse-shoe-shaped seating, Arick directed all his attention to his cousin.

"Your Majesty, ladies and gentlemen of the council, esteemed guests, thank you for allowing me to speak before you today. I bring to you a matter of national security."

As practiced, Thomas paused here, and the council dutifully filled the space with gasps and demands of explanation. Arick gave Thomas an encouraging nod. Ailsa had written out the speech for her brother, and it had been her idea to start with that captivating declaration. It had worked exactly as she had predicted.

Thomas cleared his throat and began talking again as the hubbub died down. "Beneath this very castle, there are imprisoned members of a foreign and sovereign nation."

"Eh?" interrupted Lord Murray. "What foreign nation?"

"Pishposh, the lower dungeons are flooded," Lady Quigley scoffed.

Thomas ignored the questions, focusing on the paper in his hand. "By holding these persons captive without cause, we are placing our own nation of Toravik at risk of attack."

"That's quite enough fearmongering for today, Your Highness," MacIsaac said, rising to his feet.

Arick glared at him, though he was surprised it had taken the councilman that long to protest. Maybe he had only just realized what Thomas was referring to. The king caught Arick's eye, and he was pleased to note the twinkle in the older man's face. They had spoken to Thomas's father prior to this; he had been the one to point out that the entire council had a right to know about the merfolk, but as he had already agreed to the secrecy, he couldn't be the one to reveal it.

"These people have not committed any crimes against us." Thomas raised his voice to be heard over the growing rumblings.

"This is why I petition the council here today to release the merfolk imprisoned in our dungeons and let them return to the sea!"

Silence followed the declaration as the two groups sought how to respond. Those who had been aware of the merfolk's presence were the first to recover, protesting loudly.

Donald Beattie, a confederate of MacIsaac's whom Arick loathed, thumped his fist. "How dare you accuse your betters of such duplicity?"

"Merfolk? There's no such thing as merfolk." The strident tones of Lady Quigley cut across the bickering.

Arick stood up at last, lending his strength to Thomas. "Lady Quigley, I understand your incredulity at this revelation, but if I might just point out that not all of your fellow councilmembers are as surprised as you."

She looked at him shrewdly. "What are you implying?"

He motioned to some of the more guilty expressions that surrounded him. "Would you not say that Lord MacIsaac is one of your more skeptical peers?" When she murmured her agreement, he continued. "Yet he is not scoffing at the prince's imaginings. Nay, he is protesting the sharing of what some may consider sensitive information."

She regarded her fellow council members. "You're right. What do you suppose that signifies?"

Arick hid his grin. Ailsa had promised that Lady Quigley could always be counted on to oppose MacIsaac. "That His

Highness is correct, and there are merfolk held prisoner in the lower dungeons."

"Who granted you the right to speak?" Murray demanded.

"The tradition of allowing all invited guests to hold space," Lady Quigley retorted.

"They'll let just anyone have a say in how this country runs now," Murray muttered.

"Yes, which is good for you; otherwise you would be silenced as well," Lord Jarvis pointed out dryly.

Murray sunk down in his seat, continuing to mutter into his handkerchief, but it didn't stop the continued arguing.

"You must release them, Da!" Thomas shouted, his impassioned plea heard by all.

Arick winced. Ailsa had repeatedly cautioned them not to address the king casually, but the noise and pressure were overwhelming for even him.

"You will address the king as such!" reprimanded Murray.

"This is why he is unfit to rule!" Another voice carried over the cacophony.

Arick risked a glance at Thomas's face, noting the younger man's clenched jaw, red cheeks, and trembling lip. Tears pooled in his eyes, but he refused to let them fall. Arick gave the slightest shake of his head and tilted his own chin higher. Thomas swallowed hard and copied his pose.

"Your Majesty." Arick let his sailor training flow through his voice, the words booming around the enclosed space. The noise dimmed, and he pressed on. "Sire, what the prince has proposed is for the benefit of our nation, our city."

Arguments rose again, but the king held up a hand, and for once the council obeyed, allowing Arick to continue. "If — *if* — the storms are caused by the merfolk in retaliation to the others being held captive, would it not stand to reason that letting them go would cause the storms to cease?"

MacIsaac stood, smoothing his sleeve. "Your Majesty, we all know dear little Prince Thomas and do enjoy seeing him partake in these council meetings. But, Your Majesty, matters of national security are hardly a discussion for the entire council, and a true prince would have known that."

Silence rippled through the chambers, and red filled Arick's vision for a half second. How *dare* he?

The king caught Arick's eye and nodded toward the door right before giving the order to dismiss the council. Arick hurried to follow Thomas before anyone else could crowd him. The younger man turned, tripping over his feet in his haste. Arick gripped Thomas's arm firmly and propelled him from the council chambers. He wouldn't let the prince's blurry vision cause him to stumble in front of these bigots. How could they still be so blind after twenty years of watching Thomas be the kindest, wisest, most caring person to ever walk the halls of the castle?

"Lord Arick," MacIsaac called.

Arick nudged Thomas around the corner and turned to face the small man, using his bulk to block the hall. He shouldn't have worried. MacIsaac didn't even notice Thomas's escape. "Where's that young woman of yours? Left her to fend for herself at the pier again?"

Arick narrowed his eyes. "You seem awfully concerned about her. Do you know where she came from?"

"Of course not. You're the one who brought a woman of unknown character into the castle, exposing the princess to who knows what."

Arick recoiled. Did MacIsaac intend to insult everyone around him all in one day?

"You leave my sister out of this!"

Unbeknownst to Arick, Thomas had returned. His cousin trembled, his hands balled into fists as he glared at MacIsaac. Tears once again filled his eyes, though he held them at bay. "You...you are not a nice man," Thomas managed to bite out.

MacIsaac looked affronted. "My role is to protect the crown, in whatever form that may take." He shot Arick a gloating look. "Even if that is from those brought in to tarnish it."

Thomas sputtered, and even Arick didn't know how to respond.

"MacIsaac, your role is to represent the people before the crown, not to make my son cry," the king's voice rumbled over them. Thomas gulped loudly and fled down the other hall. Arick stared at his uncle, at a loss for what to do. As the king draped his mighty arm over the narrow shoulders of the councilman, Arick understood he was free to go, and swiftly made his exit.

But his stomach churned. Nothing had been resolved, and even more problems were raising their scaly heads.

CHAPTER FIFTEEN

T HAT NIGHT, SORCHA TRAILED her hand in the cool water. The sea was impossibly calm, the waves whispering against the little boat as the stars reflected in the midnight waters. It was strange to be on the sea but not in it. She was used to seeing the water from below, or from just above the surface, her head peeking up from the depths. But now, she sat floating on it, with Arick looking at her like she was the moon.

Her throat caught, and heat rushed to her face. She had done nothing to deserve such a look, but oh, how her heart sang to see it. She gave him a tremulous smile, wishing not for the first time that she could understand him.

But no — she could understand him. She understood more than she wanted. Because that look offered something she could never have.

Tonight, they would free the imprisoned merfolk.

And at dawn, she would turn to sea-foam.

That was supposing her aunt's tales were true, of course. Maeve had said there was a way to break the bond, but it was an impossible task. Arick was kind, and being around humans wasn't as awful as she had expected, but from all she had seen, a human wasn't likely to sacrifice themselves for a mer.

Arick stowed his oars and shifted forward on his bench. She leaned toward him, even though she knew she shouldn't let her heart grow closer.

"Sorcha," he said, his voice low and husky in the night air. She couldn't resist its allure.

Taking her hand in his, he started to say something, then stopped. He looked around in frustration, unsure of himself. His calloused thumb drew swirls over her palm.

When he turned back, she gave a soft gasp. The surety of purpose in his gaze stole her breath, and she couldn't move as his hand slipped along her jaw and drew her closer.

His breath whispered against her cheek, sending thrills through her. "Sorcha," he said again, but her mouth refused to shape his name in return. Every part of her longed to close the distance between them, but she couldn't move lest she break the spell that ensnared them. Her lips fell open as she whispered his name.

He leaned closer, and every piece of her thrilled like the bioluminescents that lit up the ocean floor.

The boat rocked as it bumped against something, sending them apart. Sorcha grasped the edge of her narrow seat to keep from falling over. Her heart thundered in her chest as she panted.

"What are you doing here?" A snarky voice demanded.

With Arick's hand steadying her arm, she looked over the side of the boat to see Rona, her arms crossed as she bobbed with the waves. She smiled at her sister, pleased for the chance to speak to a family member again.

"Why are you in a boat?" Rona asked, not waiting for Sorcha to respond.

Sorcha glanced at Arick, grateful the darkness hid the blush that stained her skin. "I was looking for Ciara," she confessed.

"She's not here." Rona fiddled with her bracer, the yellow stone shining eerily in the moonlight. "She's been as absent as you of late."

"What do you mean?"

"Why do you care? Trying to get your human to trap her too?"

"What? Arick didn't trap me." She stole a look at him, only to be met with his frown. He might not understand their speech, but Rona's belligerence was hard to miss.

Rona snorted. "Then why haven't you come back? You're trapped."

"I rescued him!"

"Because you were under his spell. All humans are the same, Sorcha." She scoffed. "You were always such a naive little guppy."

"What are you doing here, then?" Sorcha retorted.

"Looking out for you," Rona said. "And it's a good thing I was here." She glanced at Arick with a knowing look. "You know what kissing him will do, don't you?"

"I wasn't —" Sorcha stopped, her ears on fire.

"You were. But don't be so stupid again — kissing a human will ensure you never return to the sea."

"How do you know that?"

"I just do. So watch yourself, little guppy." Rona smirked again, and pushed off against the boat as she flipped beneath the waves.

Arick grabbed the oars to steady the rocking. Sorcha watched him, but the moment of anticipation between them was lost. Was Rona right that kissing a human would mean...?

No. Rona was mistaken. But...why would her sister lie? And why did her heart leap at the thought of remaining with Arick?

She couldn't unravel the questions, so she sat back, watching the moon reflect on the still water as Arick rowed them toward the shore. With every stroke, his shirt stretched over his muscular shoulders. She knew from experience how strong he was physically.

His actions tonight spoke to his moral strength as well. How many people would act against their own to free prisoners? Especially ones of a different species?

And he'd been quick to grasp the unique problem of the voices — without her, the merfolk would be terrified of hearing him speak and wouldn't follow him. Indeed, without being able to understand him, they wouldn't know it was safe to follow him.

Yes, he was willing to help her people. But he wouldn't be willing to sacrifice himself like Aunt Maeve described. Maybe Rona was right. Kissing him wouldn't solve her problems.

Oh, but she wished for such a chance again.

A kiss wouldn't stop her from turning to sea-foam. But maybe, just maybe, she wouldn't be alone when she did so.

A RICK ROWED THE LITTLE boat toward the shore, weaving around the rocks that had ripped apart the lifeboat he'd seen on his first night back in Iskarraig. How things had changed since that night.

The bow scraped against the rocky coast, and he sprang out to haul the boat farther out of the waves. His boots splashed in the shallow water, but the shore was deserted. When the hull was secured above the waterline, he offered his hand to Sorcha to help her out. She stepped over the side with grace. Even though he knew her feet still hurt inexplicably when she walked, she hid it well.

But her ability to hide her feelings had him wondering what she was thinking now. He curled his fingers around hers, not letting go of her hand even though she was now safely on land. Had he been too forward trying to kiss her? She had seemed willing until the other mermaid had interrupted.

He glanced down at her, his eyes drawn to her lips. What would it be like to kiss her? Now that he'd come so close once, he couldn't stop wondering.

Time had gotten away from them, though, and they had to hurry if they wanted to hide away from the guards. The boat would stay there until later, and he was gambling on no one caring that it was there. If the rest of their plan went well, they'd need it.

The guard at the cliff door gave him a knowing smirk as he let them pass. Arick resisted the urge to set the record straight. If the guards started questioning his reasons for being on that stretch of shore at night, it would ruin everything.

Besides, the guard was only partly wrong. He had been enjoying being alone with Sorcha. Something about her belonged on the water. Even though she'd said little, she'd come to life out there, shining as if reflecting the starlit sea.

He understood why. The sea was freeing, uplifting; it embraced one's soul even as it challenged one to survive. It was unpredictable and wild, yet home lay upon the waves.

His hand tightened around hers. When the coronation was over and he returned to his training, would she come with him? Would she join him in sailing across the world? Or would she want to stay here, near her family? The idea did funny things to his insides, a reminder of the pain that nestled there any time they were apart.

Wherever they went, they would have to go together. He found he didn't mind the idea — but would she?

He opened the heavy door to the stairs and let her start the climb ahead of him. The first time they'd ascended these stairs together had been a struggle, and now he knew that it truly had been her first time ever trying steps. She'd come so far in only a couple of weeks. He laughed at himself. How could he not have known she was a mermaid from the start? The way she couldn't walk, her lack of clothing, how she tried to swim away...

At the top, he checked that the long hall was empty and guided her out onto the terrace. The wind that had caressed them on the boat was stronger here, carrying a hint of the glaciers from the Maighdeann Sea. Sorcha shivered, and he wrapped his arm around her to share his warmth. He watched for any sign of her limping, ready to pick her up should she be in pain.

If he were honest, he wouldn't mind the excuse to hold her in his arms once more.

She stumbled, and as he moved to support her, he stepped on the uneven stones. After ensuring she was steady on her feet, he knelt down to inspect the floor of the open terrace.

Although worn from centuries of use, the stones all around were as locked together as the day they had been laid. Except for right here.

Across the width of the terrace, the stones had shifted, one side lifting slightly above the height of the other.

"The storms," he breathed, running his hand over the ridge.

"Storms?" Sorcha asked with a frown.

"They've damaged..." he paused, and shifted back so she could see his hands in the moonlight as he did his best to sign the words as he spoke. "The storms damaged the castle wall, moved the rocks perhaps. We'll have to be careful."

He got to his feet and offered his arm to her again. When she tucked her hand in his elbow, they continued along the terrace to the open level below the lighthouse.

They would wait here until it was time to head below and free the merfolk.

They leaned against the balustrade and watched the distant waves. Arick thought of asking her about life under the ocean, but he didn't want to disrupt the peaceful moment with his halting use of speech and sign. She shivered again, and he drew her closer, using his body to shield her from the wind. She fit perfectly against him, her head the exact height for him to rest his chin on. Her red curls tickled his cheek, and he couldn't resist nuzzling his nose into her hair. She stiffened, and he waited for her to pull away.

When she didn't, he relaxed his arms, just enjoying holding her against him. Everything in him told him to ask her what she wanted, but he didn't know how to make her understand.

Instead, he would show her how he felt, and she could choose.

Stay or go.

Him or her family.

A life on the ocean or one below.

It would be her choice.

The note from Elsbeth's book taunted him, but he refused to believe it.

If the curse be not broke by the rising of the next moon at her height, then the mer shall return to the sea as foam.

No. That wouldn't happen. Besides, the moon wasn't yet full, was it?

The thud of the door leading onto the terrace broke through his thoughts. Quiet footsteps hurried toward them until Ailsa stepped onto the mosaic floor. Sorcha pulled away, and he didn't resist, crossing to speak to Ailsa. He had been expecting the other sibling.

She gave him a knowing look. "Sorry to interrupt, cousin."

"Nothing to interrupt," he said, not quite meeting her eyes. "What's wrong? Where's Thomas?"

"Thomas is trying to convince Father to release the merfolk."

Arick sighed. "We tried that. The council threw us out."

"I know. But he read about someone in the Edeland court holding the floor and talking for hours and hours just to prove a point, so he's doing that. If nothing more, it's a distraction, so none of the council will be down in the dungeons."

"It's night; no one should be down there anyway." Although he wouldn't put it past MacIsaac to be lurking around when he shouldn't be.

"I know, but he's trying to help." Her words carried a note of pride for her older brother.

"Who is going to get the guard to move, then?"

"I'll do it."

"Are you sure?" Arick had a hard time remembering Ailsa wasn't a small child anymore. She was still small and delicate, but she was determined and resourceful.

"Unless we want to wait until tomorrow, there's no one else." She looked at him with a hint of challenge in the tilt of her chin.

He glanced at the moon, knowing he was running out of time. "No, it has to be tonight."

"Then I'll go. I'll claim I was curious about them and hurt my ankle or something. Watch for my signal. I'll toss my handkerchief out the lowest window."

"We'll follow shortly and hide in the tower, so we'll be close if you need us."

She laid her hand on his arm. "Take care, Arick. I know you care about her, but if she's truly mer, do you know what that means?"

"Do you?"

"No. And that's what worries me."

"I'll be fine. Go, before it gets any later."

CHAPTER SIXTEEN

AILSA'S ARRIVAL SENT A subtle ripple through the
night. Sorcha stepped away from Arick, holding back
her sigh.

As anxious as she was for the evening's activities to start,
it had been nice hiding away and pretending for a few moments. Pretending that being wrapped in Arick's arms was
something she could have.

Shreds of clouds drifted past the moon, casting the terrace
into shadow. Sorcha used the cover of darkness to wipe the
moisture from her eyes. She stole a glance at Arick. He was
far enough away that her chest should have been tight, but
she could breathe without resistance.

Was the bond lessening? Was it done forcing them to be
close to each other?

But the magic didn't cause her yearning to be near him, the thrill that went through her when he said her name, nor the tingling that filled her when their hands brushed.

No, that was something wholly different.

For the first time, she let herself imagine what it would be like to stay on land — with him. To not return to Muiren would be difficult; she would miss her family, certainly. But if she were with him, would it be so bad? And maybe...maybe he would want her to stay too? Earlier, it had seemed like he wanted to tell her something, before Rona interrupted. Her face flushed at the memory, and she pushed the thought away lest he sense the way her heart was beating.

Folding her arms, she leaned against the wide rail, seeking peace from the white-capped waves below. Home had always been deep beneath the surface, and she had never thought of the wonders that lay beyond its borders. She thought of Ciara and her curiosity and desire to explore every part of the world. Is that where Ciara had gone? To find out more about the humans?

A pale head bobbed among the waves as Rona continued to search for Ciara, but there was no sign of the older sister's black hair and purple fin. Should Sorcha go talk to Rona again? Mention the chance that Ciara was on land?

No. Rona would not countenance that. And there hadn't been any storms the past few nights for Ciara to rescue a human.

Rona moved closer to shore, navigating the piles of square rocks. The moon reappeared from behind the clouds, revealing a man crouched on the rocks, inching closer to Rona. Sorcha leaned forward, ready to shout a warning to her sister, when Rona turned toward him. They spoke for a moment, Rona's arms moving in a way that Sorcha recognized as her sister's frustration. Rona turned in a huff, her hair flipping behind her, and vanished beneath the waves. The man crawled backward until he was away from the tumultuous sea and paused, glancing all around him. He looked up, startling when he saw Sorcha watching him.

There was something strange about him. Sorcha turned to call Arick to ask what he thought.

His name died on her lips as she watched Princess Ailsa grasp Arick's sleeve and lean forward to speak into his ear.

In an instant, Sorcha knew that staying on land would be the worst thing imaginable. There was no way he could love her after learning what she was. To be cursed to be near him, all the while watching him love someone else — whether that were Ailsa or a different woman, it would be a pain far greater than the shards of glass that stabbed her soles with every step or the ache that threatened to crush her heart when they were apart.

No, it would be an agony that would tear at her very soul.

Arick deserved better than her. Sorcha turned away before her traitorous heart could convince her otherwise.

The wind picked up, buffeting her in its familiar embrace, and she missed the sounds of footsteps until they were nearly upon her. She turned, unable to deny the spark of joy at seeing Arick alone.

But he didn't reach for her, stopping a few paces away to sign in the pale light of the moon. "Thomas isn't coming. He's staying to convince the king again. Ailsa will distract the guard. We should go."

His lean hands shaped the words, more confident now that he'd started practicing again. And his strange language no longer sounded so odd to her ears.

But she couldn't stay. Not when he'd fall in love with a human girl someday. No. Tonight would be her last. She'd return to the sea one way or another.

She took his offered arm, thrilling in the strength of his corded muscles one last time as they stepped into the darkness that led beneath the lighthouse to the dungeons. Down, down they went as the sea roared against the rocks and the clouds obscured the moonlight.

They paused on the stairs by one of the slit windows that overlooked the rocks. The wind, even stronger now, drove the rain inside. Arick leaned one shoulder against the edge, his head getting wet as he watched below. He still clung to her hand, his thumb tracing circles on her skin in a way that sent shivers up her arm.

They waited only a few minutes before Ailsa's handkerchief appeared at the embrasure below them. The scrap of white was immediately caught by the wind and carried away into the night. The first flash of lightning filled the stairwell as they hurried down the last few turns to the bottom.

A heaviness filled her as they neared the door to the flooded cavern. The guard was gone for now, but it wasn't the risk of being caught that made her footsteps slow. It was the dread that filled the cavern, fueled by the desperation of the prisoners who had struggled in vain for months to escape.

A haunting melody greeted them as Arick pressed open the door, a tune of longing and despair. Tears pricked her eyes as she recognized the dirge, sung only when one of the mer were sent on the current out to sea, never to return.

She rushed forward to the edge of the lagoon, desperate to know for whom they sang. Had they taken too long to rescue them? "Who? Please, who is...?"

She couldn't form the words, and they didn't give her a chance to either. Upon seeing her and Arick, the merfolk broke off singing, raising their voices in cacophony instead.

"No! It's me," she shouted above them. "I'm one of you!"

At last, two mer near her recognized she was speaking their language and signaled for the others to quiet down.

"Who are you? Why are you here?" One of the younger merfolk, his hair floating around him like seaweed, narrowed his eyes at her.

"I'm a mermaid. I..." She didn't know how to explain. "That doesn't matter. We're here to help you."

"He's a human," one of the older mer spat, his voice tight with distrust. Others drew closer, eyes narrowing as they gathered around where Sorcha and Arick stood, fins stirring the water.

"Yes, but he won't speak. He's the only one who can open the gate."

They all glared at him, not sure about trusting a human.

"I promise. He won't hurt you." She turned to Arick, and he nodded before heading to the tunnel.

"That's all well and good, but how are we going to get out of here?"

"The tunnels are flooded, thanks to the full moon tide." A few of them grumbled, but she ignored them. "You just need to climb out of the lagoon and make it through the gate." She pointed to where Arick fought with a heavy iron gate that barred the entrance to the tunnel. It had stood open when she had been here the first time, and she hadn't noticed it as she fled. Thomas had warned them of it and told Arick where the key was kept.

"It's too far," a mer — she recognized her as a Harvester, one of the mers responsible for gathering food beyond the grotto — protested.

"Come on, Sìne," a Watcher challenged. "Surely you can make it that far."

"I can — but Rian can't."

"We'll all help each other," Sorcha declared. "And once you're back in the ocean, Maeve can heal you."

"Can't you heal us now?" the Watcher demanded.

She shook her head. "I can't sing properly out of the water. But you must hurry."

A clanging came from the gate. Arick waved, a rock in his hand, showing the gate stood open. She gave him a relieved smile.

"Quickly! Help each other." The Watcher took charge, and soon mer were hauling themselves out of the lagoon and pulling themselves across the rocky ground to the flooded tunnel.

Sorcha turned her focus to the Harvester. "Who needs extra help?"

"Rian, but there are three who are chained up." She hesitated. "I don't know if Ewan will make it."

"Ewan?" Her stomach twisted at his name. She raked her eyes across the dark water until a gleam of white at the edge of the lagoon caught her gaze. A sob rose in her throat, and she clapped a hand over her mouth to stop it.

The pale, sickly mer was so changed she hadn't recognized him. Once again chained so far out of the water that he couldn't submerge, her sister's fiancé lay gasping for air against the slimy rocks.

"Arick!" She turned to him with a cry. He looked up immediately. She held up three fingers, then grasped each of her wrists in turn. He nodded and hurried over to the workspace where the humans had set up.

"Can you get Rian to safety?" she asked Sìne, the Harvester.

The mermaid hesitated, her gaze suspicious as she watched Arick. "I can."

"Ciara is my sister," Sorcha told her. "I will do everything I can to get Ewan back to her."

"Sorcha? They said you'd died in the storm."

A shiver rippled through her. Had her family given up on her?

"Surprise?" She didn't know what else to say. Had her family so easily discarded her? Or was the lie about her spread to protect the merfolk? "We mustn't waste any more time. You need to get going."

Sìne looked among the waiting mer, then grasped the arm of an older merman who bobbed near the edge, pulling him to where Sorcha waited.

"Go on, dear," he said. "I don't mind waiting."

"No need to wait." Sorcha forced cheer into her voice. She understood why Sìne was concerned. She wished Arick were here to carry him, but the sailor was busy unchaining the first of the mer on the other side of the lagoon. With a deep breath, she leaned down. "Come on, it's not far."

With some effort, the two mer were out of the water. Sìne joined the squirming line headed for the gate. Sorcha lifted the merman under his arms and dragged him as best she could. "I'm sorry, sir. This is the only way."

He grunted, doing his best to help.

The rocks were slick from the water the mer left behind, and she was just far enough from Arick that the magic made taking a deep breath difficult. Daggers pierced her feet with every step, but she didn't let on. It was nothing compared to being imprisoned here.

Over the splashing and calls from the mer as they made their way through the gate, the lilting dirge rose again, taken up by those already in the tunnel. She shuddered. Why would they choose that song to sing on their way to freedom?

Her feet slipped on the rocks, and she fell against the tunnel entrance.

"I can manage from here," the older man said. "Thank you."

With a few quick wriggles, he joined Sìne in the flooded tunnel. Sorcha sagged against the square stones while more mer made their way past her.

One voice continued to ring out over the others, the deep tones echoing through the tunnel, from someone she was sure hadn't been with the others in the pool. Her grip tightened on the stones as she recognized the voice.

"Father," she whispered in horror.

H ER GASP WAS NOTHING more than a whisper, but it snapped Arick's attention from across the cavern. Sorcha leaned against the iron gate, her skin paler than usual, her pink lips falling open as she clutched her chest.

A final twist of the key, and the last manacle opened, allowing the merman to slide into the water. Arick was moving before the splash hit the rocks he'd been perched on. He crossed the space separating them, checking for the tightness around his own chest. But it never came. Whatever the cause of her reaction, it wasn't the magical bond.

A song with the power and mystery of the sea echoed from the tunnel.

"What is it?" He signed with one hand as he clasped Sorcha's elbow.

"Father." The word was an explanation, a wish, and a cry all in one. Arick barely noticed that the word was so similar to his own language. He would have understood even if it was vastly different. The ache of family carried through.

"The singing?"

She nodded, tears obscuring her sapphire eyes.

Arick motioned for Sorcha to stay with the merfolk as he drew his sword and moved toward the voice. He wasn't fully sure why he had chosen to wear it tonight; hurting his uncle's guards wasn't something he wanted to do, nor did he wish to threaten the merfolk. But sometimes a pointy object was the best way to get the message across. And he admitted to appreciating the confidence the familiar grip gave him as he held it in his hand.

He kept his footsteps light as he neared the entrance to the second cave. The booming of the sea outside the cave kept time with his thundering heart. He sloshed across the flooded tunnel, staying clear of the escaping merfolk. Many had taken up the song, but one voice continued louder than the others.

The echoes in the cave bent around him, carrying the weight of a thousand years of torment. The voice cracked slightly at its

highest pitch, as though it were not only singing but fighting —
fighting against something unseen, something suffocating.

Arick repressed a shudder as he pressed against the square
rocks. Light spilled from the inner cave, an eerie blue-green
glow. Steadying his breath, he rounded the corner.

In the center of the cave, his fin submerged in what was barely
a puddle, the largest merman Arick had ever seen lay chained.
His broad chest rose and fell with each breath. The weathered
face, framed with long gray hair, was lined with agony, yet he
sang with all his might.

Two guards lay slumped against the far wall. They seemed
unharmed, albeit being asleep on duty meant something was
wrong. In the corner lay the odd little man, even more
mouse-like in sleep with his knees tucked up to his chest.

A wave of drowsiness washed over Arick, and his jaw
stretched with a yawn.

Magic.

He sheathed his sword and covered his ears. He hurried forward, pulling the manacle keys from his pocket as he struggled
to keep at least one ear covered. The merman's eyes flashed open
as Arick reached for the lock. Glaring, the merman sang even
louder. Arick swayed as his eyes grew heavy.

No. He mustn't sleep...

"Sorcha!" he shouted.

Whether he were calling her for help or trying to tell the
merman he knew her, he wasn't sure. He just knew he had to
say something.

The mer stopped his song, eying Arick in surprise. Another yawn split his jaw as he repeated her name. He forced his sluggish arms to lift the key and unlock the manacle holding one of the mer's wrists to the wall.

He let his eyes drift closed as the mer's hand fell.

Then fingers were wrapping around his throat. His feet scrambled for purchase on the damp floor as he fought against the iron grip.

"Father, no!"

Never had her musical voice brought such relief. The merman released Arick, and Arick fell to his knees, gasping for breath.

He expected her to run to her father, but her cool hand pressed against his cheek as her voice lifted in a question. He met her gaze, his smile a reflex to assuage the worry on her face, reflected in the flickering of the torch she held in her other hand.

"I'm fine," he reassured her, keeping his voice low. The drowsiness fell away as he pushed himself upright. She stepped back from him, and her touch left a quiet burn in its wake.

Sorcha limped to her father's side while Arick circled to unlock the other manacle. With her here, he did not expect a reprise of the attack.

The merman sagged back against the floor as his second arm was released, his face even more haggard than before.

Sorcha broke off speaking to him to sign to Arick. "My father" — she paused to spell out his name — "Alasdair. He's unwell. We must get him to the water."

He nodded, taking a deep breath. The merman was as broad of shoulder as Arick himself, with a tail several feet longer. Arick knelt beside him and helped him into a sitting position. He then turned his back and drew the mer's arms over his shoulders. With Sorcha helping him balance, he pushed to his feet. Arick took a staggering step toward the opening of the cave. The flooded tunnel wasn't far, but if he fell now, he wouldn't have the strength to lift himself and Alasdair. The mer's long indigo tail dragged across the rough floor, but he made no complaints. Behind them, Sorcha began to sing, her song full of life and hope, so different from the lament the others had been singing. Arick pressed on, his muscles not aching as much and the lingering fire in his throat fading. He risked glancing over his shoulder at her. Was she...*healing* him?

She gave him a quirk of a smile in reply, pausing to lean her hand against the cave wall. "I'm okay," she signed in reply to his look of worry. "Breathing is different."

He nodded and continued on. If she was lending him her strength in any form, he wanted to complete his task quickly to not draw on her too long.

He reached the edge of the flooded tunnel and knelt carefully. Lowering his burden into the water, he and Sorcha helped the older mer fully submerge. He saw the moment when oxygen once again filled Alasdair's lungs, the grayness leaving him and his movement becoming stronger.

"He is well," Sorcha signed after a brief exchange with her father. Arick's shoulders sagged in relief, but he'd already known from the smile that lit her face.

A rumble of thunder drew his attention to the opening of the tunnel, where several mer were milling around. They hurried forward, Sorcha calling out.

He spotted the problem before she could relay their answers.

The tide was receding, and with the storm rising, the water wasn't high enough for them to swim out. He saw no sign of the three he had unchained, and his suspicions were confirmed when the other merfolk pushed an elderly merman ahead. They were ensuring the ill and weak ones were rescued first.

He stepped down into the creek, the water immediately sloshing into his boots. Arick grabbed the older mer and pulled him along. His feet stumbled on the rocks, but he kept going, until the water reached his waist and the merman twisted free. The mer caught his eye and clasped his fist over his heart, then he was gone beneath the waves.

Arick hurried back over the rocks as quickly as he could, stopping to lift a younger mermaid over the shallowest part. She stared at him in fear the whole time, then slithered away as quickly as she could once he released her.

The final three mer were arguing, but there wasn't time. He looked to Sorcha, who pointed to the woman. Arick caught her eye before lifting her under her shoulders, doing his best to keep as much of her in the water as he could. The other merman followed, propelling himself by his arms. Once past the rise,

Arick set the woman down, then hurried back to get Sorcha's father.

She was singing again, her voice wrapping around him, and he wondered again about the truth that humans had the voices that enchanted merfolk. When she sang, every part of him longed to draw near to her.

She sat at the edge of the tunnel, her feet in the water. Her father held her hand, and the look of longing on her face made Arick pause.

As much as he yearned for her to stay with him, she deserved to go home. To be with her people.

Chapter Seventeen

T HE WIND SOUGHT HER out before Sorcha stepped from the shelter of the cave, snatching her song away even as the words left her mouth. The rough rocks of the shore bit through her boots, and the hem of her skirt was soaked from the flooded tunnel. The Watcher and Sìne slithered down the beach to the ocean, their whoops of freedom mingling with the thunder and pounding waves. Sorcha pushed her dripping hair out of her face and laughed with them. *They'd done it!*

After all the heartache of knowing her people had been held captive, hope shone through. The storms didn't matter. Her curse didn't matter. She had spent her last night doing something worthwhile.

Arick was helping her father, and then the last of the mer would be free.

The storms could stop.

Her people would be safe.

"What is going on here?"

Sorcha turned to see her aunt bobbing at the edge of the large rocks.

"We've freed the mer from the humans!" Sorcha cried triumphantly.

"Everyone?" Maeve asked, her voice strange.

"Yes, even Ewan," Sorcha said excitedly. She couldn't help the joy and pride that seeped into her voice. "We rescued them all. It's over."

But Maeve didn't smile. Her expression shifted, something unreadable flickering behind her eyes. Not guilt. Not relief.

Something like...worry.

A whirlpool churned in Sorcha's gut, and something clicked in her mind. All the times her aunt had been on the surface during storms. Her constant warnings about humans. Her understanding of human magic.

Fury filled Sorcha. How dare Maeve protest them freeing the merfolk?

Her heart broke a little bit. She hadn't wanted to believe it was her aunt. Maeve, who had spent her life protecting and helping others. Who had taught Sorcha how to be a Healer and use her magic for good. Who had been the first to find her on the beach, broken and human.

But it explained so much. "Why?" she cried. "Why would you do this?"

Maeve's eyes widened. "Sorcha, I..."

"No!" She couldn't bear to listen to excuses. "They're all free now. You can stop the storms."

Maeve's mouth opened as if to speak, but before she could answer, lightning ripped apart the sky, and a cry rang out behind them.

"Sorcha!" Arick's voice, hoarse with panic.

She spun.

Arick stood just outside the tunnel entrance, her father slung over his shoulders like before. She leapt toward them, feet sliding on the wet rocks, pain shooting through her soles.

The ground trembled beneath her feet. A crack sounded like the splitting of the sky.

Boulders tumbled down from the cliffs above, crashing into the beach in a cascade of stone.

Sorcha's knees hit the ground, salt and rainwater blinding her. Her back and shoulders were pelted with stones. She rolled into the tunnel opening as more rocks fell amid the cries of human and merfolk alike.

The rumbling ceased, and for a moment, even the storm stilled. Dust choked the air. The crash of waves felt distant now, muffled by stone. Her ears rang with silence. She tried to move — but the tunnel pressed close, narrow and dark.

A shriek pierced the stillness — one not of fear but of anguish.

A RICK HELD TIGHT TO the powerful arms wrapped around his neck. Sorcha's father was much larger than the other mer he had helped, and the few minutes submerged in the water had helped restore his strength. But the retreating waves meant he still needed Arick's help to get past the rocks.

Arick stepped from one rock to the next, ensuring his footing was sound before continuing. Rain poured all around him, pooling on every surface until he no longer knew whether he was walking in freshwater or salt. He shook the water from his eyes, glimpsing Sorcha speaking to a mermaid he didn't recognize from the cavern. As soon as he knew her father was safe in the sea, he would encourage Sorcha to retreat to the tunnel. They could speak to the merfolk in the morning, when the storm had passed.

Lightning cracked overhead, shooting through the lighthouse and sending shards of light in all directions.

And Arick became aware of three things all at once.

Firstly, the cliff face above him was collapsing.

Secondly, he was about to lose his footing on the rocks.

Thirdly, he loved Sorcha with his whole being and would do anything for her.

And that truth hit him harder than the rocks cascading around him did.

The next moment, he was in the water. His hand slipped from Sorcha's father, and his feet scrambled for purchase on the slick creekbed.

He grabbed for anything he could hold onto, his fingers scraping against stone. But the waves kept crashing over his head, making it impossible for him to break free. With his lungs screaming for air, he let go.

The undertow jerked him below the surf. His shoulder slammed against a rock, then he was twisted around and flung farther from shore. He stole a breath in the instant between waves. The sea was as angry as it had been on the night of Thomas's birthday party.

Furious. Unrelenting. Vengeful.

And Arick was in its thrall.

He knew better than to fight against the current, but the darkness made it impossible to know which way was up, where he was being taken. He could only hope it wasn't out to sea. A face appeared, a flicker of a magenta fin. Both were gone before he could follow.

His chest ached, and his stomach roiled from the spinning. Was this his end? Had he been saved by one mermaid just so he could die rescuing her friends?

No.

He had to get back to Sorcha. He wouldn't leave her to turn to sea-foam without him.

He kicked as hard as he could at right angles to the pull of the water. After several agonizing moments, the water loosened its hold on him, and he broke the surface.

Blessed air filled his lungs, even as rain did its best to fill the space. A wave washed over him, and he was carried along before managing to surface again. This time, he was able to see the lighthouse.

He had been pushed away from the shore, but instead of being carried out to the Maighdeann Sea, he was nearing the harbor entrance.

The storm wasn't finished with him yet, and the next wave pushed him back under. A mer appeared out of the blackness — a face Arick recognized from the cavern.

He swam toward Arick, who reached out a desperate hand. The mer froze, unsure. His mouth parted as if to speak, then he clamped his hands over his ears and twisted away into the depths.

Another wave slammed into him, flipping him sideways and plunging him back into darkness. His ribs cracked against a submerged stone. His vision swam.

He couldn't breathe. Couldn't see. Couldn't think.

His legs kicked weakly, but the current spun him in circles, dragging him deeper with every heartbeat.

A mer with black hair and dark tail swam alongside him for several heartbeats, her expression undecided. Blackness edged his vision as he fought to reach the surface. His sluggish fingers shaped the words "Help me," but it was too late. She was gone.

Bubbles burst from his mouth, and he clamped his lips shut again. Another swirling wave tossed him to the side, and he slammed into an unforgiving wall. He was pinned, water pouring past him, driving him against the stone.

Something shifted against his ribs, a shape firm and slick. He twisted, disoriented. And the creature nudged him again. A sleek gray body, longer than his.

The dolphin nudged him around the side of the pillar of rock, enabling him to kick free of the current. His shoulder throbbed, his limbs screamed, but he rose toward the surface.

Air met him like a blow. He sucked it in between coughs, blinking against the stinging rain.

Then he saw it.

The rowboat.

It floated just beyond the harbor's mouth, bobbing in the swell.

The dolphin held it steady, its powerful body pressed against the hull.

And floating just beyond it was the mermaid with the purple fin and black hair.

Chapter Eighteen

W ITH BLOODIED HANDS, SORCHA shoved at the rubble
blocking the tunnel. The passageway echoed with the
howl of wind behind her and the gurgling rush of water at
her feet. Every crash of thunder shook the stone around her,
vibrating through her bones like a warning. Rain drove in sideways through the narrow opening, and the frequent flashes of
lightning lit the passageway in jagged bursts. Her hand slipped
on a stubborn rock, wrenching her finger as she pawed faster at
the barrier. She had to get out.

Had to get to Aunt Maeve.

To Arick.

To Father.

Despite her continued calls, she hadn't heard anyone since
Aunt Maeve's anguished cry. Was she okay? Was everyone else?

More debris tumbled from the pile, bouncing off her legs and feet, adding to the shards that pierced her every time she adjusted her position. She shouted again, no longer knowing whether she was calling for Arick in his tongue or for help from the merfolk in hers.

The tightness in her chest caught her off-guard amid the other aches that consumed her body. "Arick!" she cried again, his name cut off when she couldn't get her breath to finish it.

Where was he? Why would he have left?

Her fingers bled as she clawed at the rocks holding her prisoner. Dust from crushed stone clung to her tongue, gritty and sour. The wet grit bit into her palms, grinding into torn skin with each frantic shove. The bond had been lessening. He must have gone farther than the boat if it hurt this much. And it was getting worse.

At last the hole was large enough for her to scramble through. Her dress snagged, the skirt ripping, but she barely noticed as she struggled to her feet.

The shore was empty.

No merfolk bobbing in the turbulent waters. No Arick standing tall and strong against the wind. Only the rhythmic boom of waves and the moaning wind threading through the broken rocks.

She stumbled toward the water, following the pull in her heart that always pointed to him.

Lightning cut across the sky, blinding her.

But not before she saw what lay at the edge of the rocks, framed by the crashing waves.

Scrambling, slipping, crawling, Sorcha found herself beside him. At every step, the wind sought to shove her over, and the hungry hands of the waves clawed at her ankles.

He lay so still. Arm reaching for the open sea. Face turned to the water.

A dark streak leaching away from his head and onto the rocks.

He looked more like a statue than a man. Rain slid down his skin in rivulets, pooling in the hollow of his throat. His eyes didn't flutter. His chest didn't rise.

"Father!" The word was a sob.

She collapsed over him, her tears mingling with the driving rain.

What had she done?

She sought for a song, anything to heal him, but her sobs stole what breath she had left.

Where was Aunt Maeve? Even though she knew there was no saving her father now, Sorcha cried out for her aunt.

But her aunt was gone, and so was Arick.

The invisible bands around Sorcha's heart pulled tighter with every breath. He was getting farther away, but where? And why?

She clung to her father's hand, limp and heavy.

Alone. Abandoned. Strangled by the bond.

Sorcha bowed her head as her tears spilled, letting her sorrow mingle with the rain that washed over her.

The air around her charged, waiting for lightning that never came.

A faint glow pierced the edges of her vision, and beneath the thunder came another sound.

A voice.

Low and rhythmic. Chanting.

Not her aunt. Not Arick.

Sorcha lifted her head, blinking through rain and tears.

A yellow light pulsed in the storm, growing brighter with each word. The waves surged higher. The wind sang a broken harmony.

She turned, holding her arm up to shield from the bright yellow light in her sister's hand as the mermaid rode high in the waves.

"Rona? What are you doing?"

Rona ignored her, continuing to repeat the rising litany of words, until the light narrowed its glow into a beam that pinned the lighthouse in its path. The wind keened in answer, almost harmonizing. The hair on her arms lifted.

"Rona!" Sorcha called again, forcing the words past her aching lungs. What was this?

"This is beyond you, little sister," Rona said, voice sharp with contempt. "Stay in your tide pool, where it's safe."

Sorcha climbed closer so she wouldn't have to shout over the storm. "We freed everyone. The storms can stop."

"Oh, you innocent little guppy. This was never just about them being captured. The humans need to pay." Rona raised her hand, and the yellow light pulsed as though trying to escape.

"You have to stop this. Fath—" She choked. "Father's been killed. The storm... More people are going to be hurt."

Rona sent her a hard look. "The humans killed Father when they took him. Just let me finish this, and I promise they'll get what they deserve."

Sorcha flinched like she'd been slapped. "No," she breathed. "You can't."

Arick. He was still out there — *one of them*, in her sister's eyes.

Lightning sparked overhead, spearing toward the lighthouse. Thunder cracked. The cliff groaned. Glass exploded as the beam of hope snapped out.

Sorcha staggered, her foot slipping on the slick rocks.

The ground vanished beneath her.

She hit something hard as the world tilted around her and breath jolted from her lungs.

A wall of water crashed down, swallowing her whole.

She clamped her mouth shut, seeking the oxygen from the water as she always had done.

But she had no gills now.

The swells spun her around, pulling her from shore. Her skirts, so warm and fitting as a human, entangled her legs so she couldn't kick. Up. Where was up? The sea pressed from every side, turning the world inside out.

Her chest burned. She thrashed in the darkness that should have felt like home, but the sea treated her like an outsider. Unable to breathe, unable to swim, she flailed, sinking deeper to where the storm didn't reach.

Every sound was muffled, warped. The roar of the waves became a low, pulsing thrum in her ears. Her hair tangled in her face. Her skirts twisted tighter. Salt stung her eyes.

Then a pale shape appeared out of the gloom. She blinked, unsure whether she should trust whatever it was. Struggling to stay upright, she waited as the shape became a mer. The Watcher she had rescued swam near, holding out a bundle of algae. She took the rubbery bladderwrack, pressing the bulbous end to her mouth and sucking the precious air.

Using his hands, he framed the question: "Human or mer?"

"Mer. But human bound," she signed back.

He nodded slowly, then reached for the end of the strands of algae. She held on tightly as he swam toward the surface. Even though she couldn't kick, she moved her hips just like she had as a mer and helped propel herself.

The Watcher stayed close until she pulled herself up onto the pillars of stone, gasping. Her limbs trembled as she rolled free of the water.

Then he crossed his fist over his heart, nodded once, and slipped back into the dark.

She pushed herself up on one elbow to scan the vacant shore. Rona had vanished, and her father lay still on the rocks above the lapping waves. Sorcha collapsed to the ground, barely noting that the moon once more lit the shore.

And Arick was still beyond the magic's reach.

A RICK HAULED HIMSELF INTO the rowboat as the mermaid held it steady. There was something familiar about her, though he knew they had never met. A fire in her eyes reminded him of Sorcha. She gave him a slight nod, then sank beneath the surf.

The oars were still stowed in the hull, and he lifted them into the oarlocks. His muscles ached as he rowed; he struggled for breath with every stroke.

But the pain drove him onward. He wasn't a fool. As much as she tried to hide it, any time he and Sorcha were separated and the pain arrived, it was much worse for her than him.

The sea fought him for every boat length. His arms shook with every pull, yet the ache in his chest drove him back to Sorcha. Magic or love — he needed to be with her.

Although the distance wasn't far, the tide and wind were against him. Waves washed over him, soaking him again and again. He shivered uncontrollably.

The lightning fizzled out first, leaving the sea in darkness. The beacon atop the tower was out, the cupola a broken silhouette against the brightening sky. Thunder faded over the distant hills, and he breathed in relief. Being on open water in a storm was a frightening proposition. The rain stopped, and the wind stopped pushing him toward the open harbor, but the stillness was unsettling.

He dug deep, and after a few minutes of hard rowing, the bottom of the boat scraped the shore. With a reluctant glance at the waves, he stepped out. The water sloshed over the top of his boots, adding to the damp already there. Glancing around, he took stock of where he was, surprised to see the shapes of the town looming nearby. He could fight his way across the rocks back to Sorcha, but cutting through the castle would be faster.

He staggered toward the cliff door, hand digging into his chest as if he could rip out the bands trapped there.

The entry was unguarded, but his pounding was quickly answered by the guard sheltering inside.

"Apologies, sir. I should have stayed out there."

"No, you were right to seek shelter," Arick reassured him, already moving past.

"Yes, sir. I'll go back out now that it's calmed down."

Arick hurried through the castle halls, leaving a trail of wet footprints in his wake. The pain accompanied him, and it gave him an odd comfort. Surely if Sorcha were dead, the magic wouldn't be drawing them back together. He slipped past the guardroom where several of the king's men were gathered around the roaring fire, speaking in low voices and casting frequent glances at the narrow window.

He reached the tower and pulled open the door and stopped.

MacIsaac stood there, just as surprised as Arick, until a sneer took over his face. "You fool," MacIsaac hissed. "You've doomed us all." An odd sound, almost like a giggle, came from the tower below.

"What are you talking about?" Arick didn't want to deal with the dour man. He wanted to get back to the shore to find Sorcha.

"The storms will only get worse, thanks to you."

"Much worse!" came an odd echo.

Arick pulled himself upright. "Freeing them was the right thing to do."

"Maybe for you and that soft-headed little prince, as neither of you can see what isn't right in front of your eyes. But I was protecting this city."

"How was starting a war with mer — who have magic — protecting anyone?"

"Because while we had prisoners under the tower, they tempered their attacks." His words were punctuated by a shriek of wind through the narrow embrasures.

Arick struggled to concentrate on MacIsaac's words around the aching pull. "Why? What does the tower have to do with it?" A deep creak echoed through the spiral stairwell, as if the tower knew they were speaking of it.

"The mirror holds the key!" The voice was high and eager, coming from the shadows behind MacIsaac. A stooped figure shuffled into the light — the odd little man from the caverns, all twitchy fingers and darting eyes. He had recovered, then, from the sleep spell Sorcha's father had placed upon him.

Arick hesitated, his brow furrowing. "The mirror that's part of the beacon? How is that a key?" He had so many questions, but none of them were bringing him back to Sorcha.

MacIsaac glared at the mouse-like man before addressing Arick once more. "*That* is none of your conc—"

"Magic in the mosaic!" He giggled again, rubbing his hands over his face as though smoothing whiskers.

"The mosaic..." So not the lighthouse. But what did the oddly shaped piece of glass in the middle of the terrace floor have to do with the storms? "Why not just give it to the mer if they want it so desperately?"

"Fool. It's held in by magic. And only magic can remove it."

"The storms are caused by magic," Arick said slowly, the truth settling like cold iron in his chest.

"Yes," MacIsaac said grimly. "And now that they don't have to protect their own..."

He stepped aside, nodding toward the window. "They'll destroy the tower to take it."

CHAPTER NINETEEN

THE SUN'S EARLY RAYS did little to disperse the fog that clung to the harbor. Gray light stole across the water, turning dark shadows to hazy shapes. The harbor rocks loomed out of the mist like grave markers. The air was thick with the damp scent of seaweed and salt. In the distance, circling gulls called to each other.

Sorcha paid little mind to the arrival of the day. Her red-rimmed eyes remained fixed on the damp rocks where her father had lain, her throat raw.

The Watchers had taken his body back to Muirin along with the freed merfolk. The king would be given the traditional parting ceremony, and she wouldn't be there for it. She wouldn't get to say goodbye to her father, nor apologize to her mother for not being able to save him.

"What day is it?" she asked suddenly, lifting her head from her folded arms.

Arick started a reply, but he hadn't understood her. He'd appeared beside her sometime in the last hours, silently offering her support.

"The moon. Was it full last night?" This time, she signed as she spoke.

"No, tonight." His hands bore the marks of the night, covered in scrapes and bruises.

She'd been wrong. Last night hadn't been her last. The moon's betrayal stung like saltwater in an open wound. She should have been sea-foam by now — washed away by the waves as the sun kissed the shore.

Now she had to live one more day. A day full of pain knowing her father was gone. A day knowing Arick would never be able to break the curse.

Because it was unbreakable.

She'd held out hope. As much as she'd tried not to, her traitorous heart had refused not to wish it were possible.

But he had risked himself for her. Had helped her at every turn. Had nearly died helping her.

And he'd come back to her.

Yet she was still here. On land, with two feet and no tail.

She stood, unsteady as always, as the shards of glass pierced her feet. Arick joined her, dusting the dirt from his trousers.

If she only had one day left to live, she would spend it finding a way to stop Rona. Whatever she was trying to accomplish wouldn't save the merfolk. It would only hurt the humans.

And the humans would continue to blame the mer. They'd start a war the mer could not hope to win.

And the rest of her family would die.

Rona's power came from that strange bracer she wore. But Sorcha couldn't hope to get it from her — she couldn't go in the water, and Rona would never come close enough to land to let her take it. Her best option would be to get help. But with Ewan and the other prisoners back in the grotto, Ciara and Maeve would be too busy to come to the surface.

They wouldn't anyway. Not with Father's funeral to prepare for. She shivered, the sea's soft mourning echoing in each retreating wave.

A warm arm wrapped around her, and she sank against Arick's chest. His heart beat a steady rhythm, and she clung to him lest he vanish like everything else in her life.

"My sister, Rona, is responsible for everything," she finally confessed. She signed the words with one hand, the other buried in Arick's shirt, stiff with the dried saltwater. Her eyes burned, her tears locked away.

"I know." He turned them toward the cliff door, away from the tunnel.

Rona, not Maeve. She couldn't help but feel a wave of relief that her aunt wasn't the one trying to kill the humans Sorcha had grown to care for. But her stomach churned. She should have known it was Rona, with the way she despised humans and called them weak. Where had that hatred come from? The mer generally had no ill will toward the land-dwellers and preferred to keep their presence a secret. And until a few months ago, Rona had been no different.

Something had changed. Where had Rona gotten the bracer? Contained magic like that was a human creation. Had she found it on the seafloor the same way Sorcha had found many of her own treasures? Or in one of the shipwrecks? But none of her curios had ever held hidden magic.

"I'm worried she's not going to stop," she signed, her footsteps slowing. "I think she wants something."

Arick nodded, his arm firm around her. She waited for him to elaborate, the deep lines between his brows indicating he was thinking of something, but he stayed silent.

Sorcha buried her head against him once more. She needed to stop Rona from starting a war with the humans. But she didn't know how. She wasn't a Watcher or trained in any sort of battle magic. She was only a Healer.

A poor excuse for a Healer at that. She couldn't even heal herself from this curse.

And it had led to her father's death.

A RICK WANTED NOTHING MORE than to scoop Sorcha into his arms and carry her over the rocks, to protect her from pain, to shield her from all he could. But though she leaned into him, frail and trembling, he sensed a deep brittleness in her. One wrong word, one wrong move, and she'd shatter like glass.

And so he supported her quietly, swallowing the words he longed to shout from the foremast. Telling her how much he loved her would have to wait. First, he would have to face the fallout from releasing the merfolk. And tonight was Thomas's coronation ball. He would be there for his cousin.

And after the ball, before the moon set, he would bring Sorcha back to the water and hold her until the tide took her from his arms.

He hadn't found a way to break her curse. The knowledge of his failure was a knife through his heart. He couldn't lose her. He'd already lost Daniel, and this would be so much worse.

Tucking her closer under his arm, he lifted her other hand with his free one, clinging to whatever part of her he could. She glanced up at him, her sapphire-blue eyes wide and shimmering in the early summer sun. How had she claimed his heart so completely in only a few short weeks?

No, he corrected himself. His heart had been hers from the moment she'd first looked at him and trusted him.

They drew near the castle entrance, and he took a steadying breath. As much as he wanted to, they couldn't hide on the shore all day. Time to face up to what he had done.

The guard nodded to them as she let them pass, and they were immediately enveloped in the bustle of the castle. Despite the early hour, the staff were alight with the preparations for the evening's festivities. They dodged past a pair of servants juggling a ladder and several table-lengths of fabric, maids scrubbing the floors, and a harried footman struggling to balance a tray of goblets. The sharp scent of vinegar warred with the delicious aromas wafting from the kitchens.

They found no sign of Thomas or his father in the small sitting room nor in the family's dining room, so they continued toward the bedchambers. Sorcha leaned more heavily on him as they went, and if it weren't for his own exhaustion, he would have carried her up the steps, but he feared dropping her. The stairs led to a quieter hall, with only a few maids slipping in and out of the guest rooms. A door creaked open behind them, and Arick barely had time to turn before Ailsa descended upon them.

"There you are!" She squeezed Arick before turning to Sorcha, her hands flying as she spoke. "I was so worried about you both! After I convinced the guard to leave his post, he was so concerned about me, he followed me all the way back here, but Mother was waiting and I couldn't get back." She swatted Arick's arm. "Where were you? I expected you to send word hours ago!"

She paused long enough to take in their appearance, her eyes narrowing as she noted their torn and filthy clothing, the dried blood on Arick's hand, the weariness etched on them both. "What happened? Were you harmed?"

Arick shook his head, his tongue heavy as he sought how to tell her. "We weren't anticipating the storm to be as bad as it was. Sorcha's...one of the merfolk was killed."

Ailsa froze, her hands stilling for once. "Oh." Her hands moved first, a fist circling tightly against her chest. "I'm so sorry."

She took a deep breath, meeting Arick's gaze once more.

"You must both be exhausted. Arick, your room by Thomas's is still free, and Sorcha can come with me. I'll order a bath, and you can rest." With that, she whisked Sorcha back through the door whence she had appeared, supporting the red-haired woman despite being several inches shorter.

They were gone before he could say anything, and his side was suddenly cold where Sorcha had stood for so long. Funny how perfectly she fit against him.

A yawn cracked Arick's jaw as he contemplated Ailsa's offer. A bath and a nap would both be sorely welcome, but he ought to first find the king and speak to him. He swayed, undecided, as another door opened, and a noble he recognized from the Edelish court passed by, wrinkling his nose. Although such an expression wasn't uncommon for the Edelish, Arick surmised his own appearance had much to do with the current derision.

Perhaps today was not the day to look like he'd been pulled out of the sea in a fisher's net.

He hurried down the hall, passing his room long enough to rap an almost-forgotten rhythm on Thomas's door, before returning to the bedchamber Ailsa had said was free. If Thomas were there, he'd come.

Arick stumbled through the door and collapsed in a chair, where he forced his boots off. The scent of the sea mingled with his own sweat.

Yes. A bath, then he would tackle the consequences of doing what was right.

SORCHA SAT ON A low stool while Ailsa flitted about the room, gathering items. Servants hurried in and out, lugging buckets of steaming water behind a screen. Sorcha watched it all through a fog, barely responding as Ailsa and a maid with a pleasantly lined face helped Sorcha out of her damp clothing, peeling off her boots and soggy stockings to reveal her pale toes, the skin wrinkly and sore. They gave her privacy to remove her underclothes and climb into the little pool. She sank into the steaming water, which wrapped around her like a hug. The chill clung to her until the heat sank into her bones.

The woman approached and, with gentle hands, massaged flakes into her hair that turned into a sea-foam, fragrant with the scent of the heather-strewn moors. Sorcha rubbed the bubbles between her fingers, wondering distantly if she would vanish as easily as this foam did.

Would Arick try to hold on to her the way she held the foam in her palm? Or would he walk away, leaving her to disappear on the waves with the rising of the sun?

She pressed a hand to her sternum, where the ache so often marked their separation. No, she knew better. He would wait. His own kindness wouldn't let him walk away. But even more so...the magic had been trying to tell her something for a while, and though she wasn't sure he even knew, she was sure of it — he cared for her as much as she cared for him.

Strange how comforting that was — to know that she mattered to someone. That someone would miss her. Not just as an extra Healer or as an annoying little sister wanting to tag along, but as her.

Yet...there was no point. In less than a day, she'd be gone. Washed away as though she'd never existed.

Her mind refused to go near that thought. Ailsa and the woman spoke around her, sometimes asking questions, their voices drifting in and out like the waves on the sandy shore. She lifted her arms when prompted, though the movement didn't feel like hers. The woman scrubbed her skin, but the pressure barely registered. She rose when beckoned to do so, and they wrapped her in a robe as soft as the cooky's fur, then they tucked her into the bed, where she lay in silence, eyes dry and burning.

She avoided thoughts of Arick, as though they were guarded by a ring of electric eels, poised to sting her if she drifted too close. Instead, she thought of her father. Of her mother and sisters. Of Rona. Of anyone other than Arick.

And then she couldn't stop thinking of him. The memories came unbidden, precious and sharp. She gathered them jealously, pouring over each one like a pearl.

The stranger who had pulled her from the water and immediately found something for her to cover herself with. Who had carried her despite his own exhaustion. Who had offered her a safe place to stay.

The man who had introduced her to his friends, never minding that she could barely walk and spoke not a word of his language.

The friend who had made her part of his world. Who had laughed with her after being soaked in the rain. Who had risked everything to help her family.

Who had fought his way back to her, even injured and in pain.

A sob escaped as she pictured the way his hazel eyes crinkled when he laughed. The sun shining on his curly hair. His quiet strength, which he offered her when she needed it. His lean, strong hands that he'd used to find a way to speak with her. The way his face lit up when he noticed her enter a room.

The way he had wanted to kiss her.

The tears came at last, hot and drowning. She rolled onto her side, burying her face in the pillow. Sobs wracked her until she couldn't breathe. And the familiar ache tightened ever so slightly around her heart, reminding her she wasn't alone.

A RICK CLOSED THE HEAVY door on the flurry of preparations and schooled his features to hide his own swirling
thoughts.

The central hall held the usual mix of nobles and visiting
dignitaries. Guests were already starting to arrive for the ball
in a few hours, and servants passed around trays of light re-
freshments, a teaser of what would come later during the formal
supper. Banners in the kingdom's blue, green, and gold tartan
hung from the balcony railings, and garlands of ivy and summer
blooms wrapped the columns in cheerful defiance of the storms
that had plagued the coastal city.

Arick kept his head down as he crossed the hall. A bath and
a few hours of rest had soothed the worst of his exhaustion but
not his thoughts. After a brief conversation with Thomas, he
had set out to find the king. Thomas had wanted to join him,
but his steward had insisted the prince needed longer to prepare
for the ball, seeing as it was in his honor.

The king hadn't been in his private chambers, so Arick
sought him in the more public offices. But to get there, he had
to pass through the central hall. Exhaustion still tugged at him,
but he needed to talk to his uncle as soon as possible. He passed
a guard, refusing to make eye contact lest the man shout for his
arrest. What would his punishment be for freeing the merfolk?

MacIsaac and his cronies had made their stance clear, but King Craig had been tight-lipped on the topic.

Either way, Arick was prepared to face the consequences. He'd gone against the council, so there was every chance they would imprison him for it. He only hoped his uncle would take pity on him and allow him one last night with Sorcha before locking him away. One last chance to break her curse.

Tightness wrapped around Arick's chest, but he no longer resented it. It was a welcome reminder that Sorcha was nearby. He adjusted his path so as not to cause her extra discomfort and turned down the corridor to the council chambers, the bustle of the hall fading behind him. A servant with an empty tray was just leaving the receiving room beside the main chambers, so Arick quickened his steps to catch the door before it swung shut. Upon seeing the occupant of the room, he sought to slip out again without being noticed, but it was too late.

"Arick! Come here, lad," the rotund Lord Beattie called out to him, scone crumbs flying as he beckoned with a hand full of his snack.

Groaning inwardly, Arick stepped back into the room, schooling his face to not betray his eagerness to leave. "Lord Beattie, how are you today?"

"Good, I'm good," he said, pausing briefly to stuff the scone into his mouth as more crumbs dusted the front of his well-adorned jacket. "You're just the man I wanted to see."

Arick folded his hands behind his back and adopted the relaxed but attentive stance he'd learned in the navy. But inside, his thoughts churned. This was wasting time when he had so little of it left with Sorcha. "Why is that, sir?"

"Well, I was hoping you'd have an answer for us today. We haven't got much time left, you know."

Arick took a deep breath to control his impatience. He didn't have time to rehash this argument. "I believe I made my answer perfectly clear already. I will not commit treason by taking my cousin's throne."

"I can understand where you're coming from. You love the boy. And MacIsaac — well, I can't blame you for getting a stick up your spine around him. The man does the same to me by times. But you have to look at the facts. Thomas's recent attempt at convincing the council that merfolk exist is a clear indication that he's not ready to be king."

Arick opened his mouth to protest, but Beattie waved him off. "Let me finish my points before you argue." He helped himself to another scone, smearing liberal amounts of clotted cream and jam on it before taking a massive bite. A glob of jam stuck to his beard. "Where was I? Oh yes. Young Thomas. You were there. Even with your help, he could barely finish his speech, and, well...the council ripped him to shreds, didn't it? Is that what you want for him for the rest of his life? Wouldn't it be kinder if you stepped in? Saved him from all that?"

Arick shifted his feet. Seeing Thomas humiliated like that had been hard to watch. He'd give a lot to ensure that never happened again.

"Ah, I can see it on your face. You know I'm right. You can do some real good. The people respect you. And without the stress of the crown, Thomas may even thrive. Spend more time with his animals. He's a good lad; I'm not denying it. But he's not ready to be king."

Arick dragged a hand over his face. He'd tried so hard to help Sorcha. They'd stopped the storms, yet she was still a human, still in pain. If he couldn't save the woman he loved, maybe he could help his cousin instead. Maybe doing something would ease the helplessness clawing at his chest.

He shifted his weight, rolling the idea around in his mind. Could he do more good if he took on the role of crown prince? More than as an advisor? More than Thomas could?

Beattie slurped the last of his tea. "Look, I won't push you to give me an answer right now. But you need to decide. The coronation is tomorrow. The king will need to know before then."

He lumbered out of the room, humming to himself, and shut the door behind him.

Leaving Arick alone.

With his thoughts.

And that was the worst possible thing he could have done.

CHAPTER TWENTY

WHEN SORCHA AWOKE, THE room was dimly lit with soft sunlight. Heavy pink curtains were pulled across the windows, giving the cream walls a rose hue. Gentle strains of music filled the room, and Sorcha turned to see Ailsa in the corner, a tall wooden instrument cradled against her. Her fingers flew up and down the strings, plucking and strumming. The princess smiled and nodded at her, finishing the song before setting the instrument upright and bouncing from her chair.

"I'm so glad you're awake! I'll have a late lunch sent up right away, as I'm sure you're starving, then we've got plenty of time to prepare for the ball."

She signed as she spoke, her hands shaping the words almost faster than Sorcha could keep up. Still, she couldn't help but smile at the younger woman's exuberance. Thankfully, she was growing more accustomed to the humans' language and could understand many of the words — namely "lunch," which made her stomach growl in response.

"Yes...food, please," she said, forming the words with care.

Ailsa's eyes lit with wonder, and she clapped her hands. "Oh, I'm so glad you're learning!" She crossed to the fireplace and pulled a heavy gold cord. In the distance, three gongs chimed. "I love having someone to sign with, but learning more will make things so much easier for you. And I can teach you a few words and phrases you may need this evening."

Sorcha gave a small smile. There wasn't much point in learning more. Not if she was going to turn to sea-foam before the next dawn. She sat up, pushing the blankets away.

Ailsa swept open the curtains, flooding the room with the afternoon sun. She gestured to a basin and pitcher on a carved white stand. "You can freshen up there, then I'll show you some dresses while we wait for lunch to arrive."

Sorcha stepped carefully across the soft carpet, inlaid with dainty pink and purple flowers on delicate green vines. The soles of her feet still hurt, but the cushioning of the carpet relieved some of it. She took her time splashing cool water on her face and scrubbing away the dried tears. Thoughts of the ball swirled in her head. She missed the freedom of dancing underwater, but it wouldn't be the same on land, where gravity pulled at every step. And there would be so many more humans there to laugh at her if she got things wrong. But Arick would be there, and dancing would mean his arms wrapped around her... She bit her lip to hide the smile that threatened. Ailsa hummed as she moved between her wardrobe and the bed, carrying four different white linen dresses.

"I've got two for you and two for me. We can decide together which ones we love best!" Ailsa clasped her hands together and spun in a circle.

Sorcha cocked her head, frowning at the identical shapeless dresses. Did they even have sleeves? The only difference she could see was that two were much longer than the others. Judging by the length, the longer pair must be for her, as Ailsa was nearly a head shorter. After regarding them a moment longer, she turned to Ailsa, who was dragging two chairs closer to a small table.

"They're...same?" she asked, unsure if she had the right words.

Ailsa looked up. "What? Oh! They're covered — see?" She lifted the bottom of the white skirt to reveal a glimpse of a rich material the color of heather in bloom.

A knock on the door gave Sorcha a moment to hide her embarrassment over not realizing the white linens were just covers. The gentle maid from before entered when Ailsa opened the door, a covered tray balanced in her hands. She set it down on the little table and lifted the cloche.

Sorcha drifted toward the chairs, drawn by the warm, savory scent of stew that curled through the air like an invitation.

"I asked Cook to send something hearty," Ailsa said as they dug in. "I never get much chance to eat at these parties, so I like to have a good meal beforehand so I don't get faint."

Sorcha didn't care the reason — she hadn't eaten since the day before, and the warmth of the stew removed the last of the chill that had lingered. The soft rolls were dripping with melted butter, and the cold milk soothed her parched throat.

The maid moved silently around the room as they ate, and when their bowls were empty, she lifted two of the dresses from the bed to show them. She had removed the coverings, and the long skirts draped across the floor.

One was the heather Ailsa had shown her before, the bodice woven with a subtle tartan of violet, gray, and green. The other gown echoed its shape, but in shades of sea-glass blue and kelp green. A row of pleats ran down one side of the skirt, sweeping back to reveal a contrasting underskirt. White lace trimmed the bodice and the cuffs of the bell-shaped sleeves.

"They're beautiful," Sorcha signed. She loved that the styles matched, so she knew she wouldn't stand out. The dress would allow her to blend in with the other ladies. And the colors of the one meant for her reminded her of home.

"Oh, I'm so glad you like them! But don't decide yet! I want you to see this next one first!"

"You had two dresses made for me? How?"

"Of course I did — I knew Arick would invite you to the ball, and I wanted to be sure you had something appropriate to wear. Elsbeth helped me with the measurements."

Sorcha swallowed back tears. These two women she barely knew had accepted her and treated her with such kindness. She tucked her head to wipe her eyes.

Warm arms wrapped around her. "You're one of us now."

Sorcha returned the hug. "Thank you," she whispered around the lump in her throat.

Ailsa returned to her seat and nodded to the maid, who lifted the other two dresses. One was a delight of pink and gold, but the second had Sorcha gasping, tears springing to her eyes.

The rich sapphire silk spilled to the floor in gentle waves, a myriad of tiny iridescent gems twinkling in the sun. The bodice draped off the shoulders, right where her scales had started, crisscrossed with threads in varying shades of blue. Two swathes of sheer, shimmering fabric cascaded from the sides, fanning out like the sea curling at her feet. It was a dress for a mermaid, an exact match of her scales and fin, and it made her heart break from longing for what she had lost.

"That one," she whispered in her own language. "I want to wear that one."

Lord Beattie's words hung heavily over Arick, clinging to him like damp wool as he made his way back to the central hall. The piercing call of bagpipes drifted in from the courtyard, a lively tune at odds with the churning in his mind.

Inside, the noise had doubled since he'd passed through earlier. The hall now brimmed with velvet and brocade, polished boots and practiced laughter. Guests lined up for admittance to the ballroom, their voices rising with the clatter of heels and the rustle of silk.

Arick accepted a goblet of cordial from a passing server out of habit, but the scent turned his stomach.

He was expected to smile. To dance. To make conversation.

But all he wanted was to find Sorcha.

And still Beattie's words echoed: *Wouldn't it be kinder if you stepped in?*

He straightened his shoulders and wove through the crowd, trying not to look like a man with a decision weighing down every step.

"That's a long face to be wearin' at a party, lad."

The familiar voice cut through the din like a warm fire on a stormy night. Arick turned, his lips tugging into a smile. "Elsbeth! You're here."

"Of course I'm here," she said, wrapping him in a hug that smelled of tea and cinnamon. "I might only be an innkeeper, but I still remember Craig in his nappies long before he became king." She drew back, peering up at him. "But tell me what's bothering you. Is it Sorcha?"

"No, no. She's well. There was...a lot. But she's with Ailsa now, getting ready together." Now was not the time to explain all that had happened the previous night.

She waited for him to continue, and he took a deep breath, wondering how much to tell her. But Elsbeth had been the grandmother he'd never had, being far more approachable than his own socialite mother. As a child, he'd never been able to keep anything from her. And now, with everything weighing on him, he found himself wanting her counsel more than ever. He drew her to the side and into a concealed alcove, where they wouldn't be overheard. "It's Thomas...well, not him exactly. But the council." He rubbed his neck, unsure how to say it aloud. "They want Thomas to abdicate his position as heir to me."

Her brows rose, then drew together as her tone turned probing. "And you're considering this?"

"No! I mean, yes. Maybe?" He dragged a hand through his hair. "I don't know what to do."

"You'd best explain yourself, then." Her voice held a hint of censure, softened by concern. "You know how much he looks up to you, but he's also a good prince."

Arick winced. "I know. The speech the other night was a disaster. Thomas did a decent job, all things considered, but the council ripped him to shreds. Then MacIsaac and his lot laughed the whole thing out of consideration." He looked away, jaw tightening. "You should have seen Thomas."

Elsbeth's tone gentled. "And you think taking his place will protect him from all this?"

Why did Beattie's argument feel like logic but Elsbeth's make it sound like betrayal? The conflict churned in his gut. Arick groaned, scrubbing a hand over his face, caught between guilt and duty.

"If you do take this role, how will you feel in two years? Five? Ten?" Elsbeth's voice was gentle, but her gaze didn't waver. "Will you be satisfied staying in one place? Holding meetings? Playing politics?"

Arick shifted, the question twisting in his chest. "I...I don't know." He rubbed his thumb along the edge of his sleeve. "Daniel would have been perfect for this. He always knew what was expected of him." The words caught unexpectedly in his throat.

Elsbeth's eyes softened. "Aye, Daniel was a fine lad. But he was a homebody, through and through. He liked routine. Found comfort in predictability. You" — she poked him lightly in the chest — "you were never made for that. From the moment you could walk, you were trying to climb the stables or sneak off to the docks."

Arick huffed a short laugh, but it held no real humor. He sipped the cordial, his throat dry.

She stepped back to look him over. "You're not like your brother, lad. And that's no failing. Your heart doesn't belong to stone walls and council seats. You're made for adventure. For wildness. Which is exactly what someone in love with a mermaid ought to be."

He choked on his drink. "How...how did you know?"

Elsbeth gave him a sly look. "Besides the fact you left the book open on my table?"

He paused his attempts to clean his sleeve to give her a chagrined look. "I should have cleaned up. I'm sorry."

She waved his apology aside. "I already knew."

"But how?" He hadn't figured it out on his own.

Elsbeth's smile tugged at one corner of her mouth. "She speaks the Old Tongue. And she watches you like you hung the stars."

"I knew you understood her!" His heart did a funny little jig at Elsbeth's words. Did Sorcha love him in return?

She shook her head. "No, but it's not the first time I've heard it spoken."

The skirl of bagpipes echoed through the hall, quieting the hum of conversation. Arick and Elsbeth turned as the herald stepped forward to announce the opening of the ball. Thomas stood beside the king, with Cookie leaning against his knee. The guest of honor was resplendent in his formal attire, which matched the blue and green tartan that adorned the hall, but his hair already showed signs of him being unable to keep from mussing it up.

There he was. The prince Beattie wanted to replace. The cousin Arick had loved his whole life.

He exhaled slowly. Elsbeth's words wrapped around his heart, tugging him to something more. To the life he'd always longed for: adventure on the open seas.

But a glimpse of Beattie speaking to Lord Murray tore at him. Could he leave Thomas to their machinations?

He didn't know. But for now, he wanted nothing more than to find Sorcha.

S ORCHA STARED AT HER reflection in wonder. The maid, who had finally shared that her name was Joanna, had managed to tame Sorcha's curls into a design that lifted her hair onto her head in twists, with only a few choice curls falling around her face.

"Thank you," she said in the human language, drawing her hand from her chin outward at the same time.

Joanna smiled and adjusted one last curl before stepping back to allow Sorcha to admire her reflection in the full-length mirror a moment more.

The gown shimmered with every breath she took, its deep-sapphire silk catching the sunlight and scattering it across the room in tiny stars. The sheer side panels fluttered when she moved, like waves lapping against the shore. She looked like herself — and yet not. Human and mer, all at once.

"Almost perfect," Ailsa said, a hint of mischief in her voice.

Sorcha shot her a questioning look and the princess stepped forward, holding out something that sparkled in the last of the afternoon sun.

"I found your necklace. I meant to give it back sooner, but it took me a while to find the right ribbon for it." As always, one of her hands shaped the words as she spoke.

Sorcha gasped and took the pendant gently, clutching it to her heart. Even though the trinket was human-made, it reminded her of home. The silver cage gleamed softly, the sapphire within catching the light.

And the ribbon...

She pointed to the blue and green tartan that formed the crest Ailsa had pinned to her chest. "Same?" she asked softly.

"Same," Ailsa said, smiling. "Now you carry a piece of both worlds."

Sorcha nodded, blinking hard. She fastened the necklace around her throat, the cool metal settling like a steady heartbeat. Something whole again. Something hers.

Something that was both human and mer.

Joanna helped them both into dainty slippers that matched their dresses. Sorcha winced as she stepped. Unlike the boots, the flimsy footwear did little to stop the stabbing pain that shot through her feet with every step. But the tight pull in her chest that had lingered the whole afternoon was growing more insistent, so she refused to delay any longer.

The women hurried out of the room and down the carpeted halls.

The corridors were empty.

"We're not late," the princess reassured her with a grin. "Everyone else is expected to arrive before us, while we're to make an entrance within the ballroom proper."

None of which made sense to Sorcha, but she followed her friend's lead anyway.

The tightness in her chest eased, alerting her that Arick was near. But the closer they got, the more her hands grew damp and her stomach fluttered.

This was her last night on land and her first human ball.

What if she made a fool of herself?

She nearly stopped to laugh at herself. So what if she made a fool of herself? She'd never see any of these people again.

The thought steadied her. Lightened her steps.

Head held a little higher, she quickened her pace, suddenly eager — eager to see Arick, to feel his arms around her one last time, and to learn what dancing on two legs was really like.

The women paused outside a set of double doors at the prompting of the herald stationed there. As they waited to be announced, Sorcha took in her surroundings with wide eyes — the muted strains of music drifting through the polished wood, the delicate scent of fresh blooms woven into the garlands, the flicker of golden light on polished stone.

Below, in the central hall, a few guests still mingled — and among them stood a tall, broad-shouldered sailor, whose gaze found hers like a beacon.

Arick looked up and froze.

His jaw slackened as his eyes swept over her. She raised a hand in a small wave, beckoning him up, but he didn't move.

Didn't even blink.

A smile tugged at the corner of her lips. At last, he seemed to shake himself free of whatever spell he'd fallen under and took the stairs two at a time until he stood, breathless, at her side.

"You look like a mermaid," he murmured, unable to take his eyes from her. He shifted to face her more fully, then signed a single word. "Beautiful."

Heat bloomed in her cheeks, and suddenly she wasn't sure of anything. What was she even doing there?

But then he offered his arm, and she slid her hand into the crook of his elbow, letting him steady her.

Together, they stepped forward, and the herald's voice rang out above the music as their names were announced to the assembled guests.

Heads turned, curious eyes following their descent down the shallow steps to the ballroom floor. But Arick didn't falter. His hand stayed firmly on hers, anchoring her as the polished floor opened before them.

"Dance with me?" he asked, his voice low.

She hesitated.

"Your feet hurt, don't they?" he asked gently.

She nodded, wishing it weren't true.

"Come on, then. I have an idea."

He led her to the dance floor, drawing her close. With a grin, he tucked her feet atop his boots, his arms holding her tight.

They moved with the music, a gentle sway that soon had them gliding across the ballroom floor. She tucked her head against his shoulder, the world slipping away.

It wasn't the same as dancing under the sea. But it was close. If only she could stay in his arms forever.

One song melted into the next, and then another, the music wrapping around them like waves. Arick whispered something now and then, making her laugh softly as they danced, her heart full that she could understand him. The ache in her feet faded beneath the glow of being seen, cherished, held. The music shifted, a brighter rhythm taking hold. Arick's arms loosened as he began to guide her toward the edge of the floor.

"May I have this dance?" a voice cut through her dreamy haze, sharp and unwelcome. Arick's sudden stiffness warned her before she noticed who it was.

MacIsaac stood there, his hand outstretched, his face bearing a practiced smile. She glanced at Arick, unsure. But Ailsa had warned her about such occurrences and that it would be considered an offense to refuse. Arick's jaw was tight, but he gave her hand a gentle squeeze before releasing it.

Sorcha nodded and placed her fingers lightly in MacIsaac's hand, following him toward the forming lines of dancers. Her limp worsened with every step, but she did her best to hide it.

The music picked up, lively and structured, allowing more space between them. MacIsaac guided her into the steps with stiff precision, his palm heavy at her back.

He spoke as they danced, long droning phrases she couldn't follow. Then he turned her, brought her back to face him, and said in slow, clipped tones, "You don't belong here."

Sorcha blinked, trying to follow the rest, but his voice dropped, and the music swelled around them. She caught *Ailsa...Arick...*and something that sounded like *proper match*.

His condescending gaze told her enough.

She tried to step away, but his hand tightened on her waist — not enough to draw notice, but enough to warn her.

"You're not a noblewoman. You're not even a lady."

Sorcha stared at him, and to her own surprise, laughter bubbled in her chest. No, she wasn't a noblewoman.

She was the daughter of the queen of the ocean. That made her more than his equal. A princess.

Tossing her head back, she let go of his hand and stepped away.

Before she could find the right words in his language to tell him exactly what she thought of him, the ballroom doors burst open.

CHAPTER TWENTY-ONE

A RICK HAD LONGED ALL day to be near Sorcha — and now, with her finally by his side, he hated that etiquette compelled him to let her dance with another. From outside the tall windows, twilight crept in, swallowing the edges of the sea in shadow. It was a reminder of how little time she had left.

He drummed his fingers against his leg, fighting the urge to walk over and cut in. The sharp tinkle of glass made him turn. A young servant girl was crouched near the wall, gathering shards from a shattered goblet.

Before Arick could move to help, Thomas was already there, kneeling beside her. The prince offered a few quiet words as he helped collect the fragments, and the girl smiled as she carried the pieces away.

Thomas looked around for Cookie, spotting the little dog making friends with the young son of the ambassador from Fenmere. Thomas joined the party, and soon their indifferent expressions vanished as everyone lit up around the prince.

Arick shook his head. People *loved* Thomas. He carried an infectious joy that drew others to him. But was that enough to stop the naysayers?

"He's going to be a great king someday," a soft voice at his elbow said.

Arick glanced down at Ailsa, a delight in a pink shimmering dress similar to Sorcha's but with skirts twice as wide. The determination in her eyes belied the frothy confection of her gown. He nodded.

"Yes. He will."

And he meant it.

"Father's about to make the speech. Unless there's a reason he shouldn't?" The words were a challenge.

Arick looked chagrined. "You know."

"Of course I know," she scoffed. "It's my castle. I live here."

He laughed. Of course she knew. And of course she believed in her brother. Just like he had — before everything had gotten so complicated. With Ailsa on his side, Thomas could hardly fail. "Excuse me," he said with a slight bow. "I need to speak with the next king of Toravik."

With one eye following a head of red curls above a shimmering blue dress among the dancers, Arick threaded his way through the crowd toward Thomas.

"...dog in the ballroom," the Edelish representative muttered, just loud enough to draw attention.

Arick's fist clenched as he spun around, intent on cutting off the man before Thomas heard.

But the prince was already smiling up at the gaunt, angular man towering over him. "Cookie isn't just my pet," he explained. "He's trained to help me if I have trouble with my breathing or other difficulties."

His lips curled in mockery. "A prince who needs a lapdog to steady him? Charming."

Arick stepped up beside his cousin. "Support isn't weakness. Even you serve your king in your own way."

"Are you comparing me to a dog?"

"If I am, then I'm comparing myself as well. I am here to support and advise Thomas in any way he sees fit."

The man looked between the cousins, then moved off with a sniff.

Thomas turned to him, hope flickering behind the uncertainty. "Do you mean that?"

"I do," Arick assured him. "You are the true prince. And I will stand by you — as an advisor, on your council, whatever you need. This kingdom wasn't built by bending to pressure, and we're not going to start now."

Thomas's whole face lit up, and for a moment Arick thought he might throw his arms around him on the spot.

But before either could say another word, the ballroom doors slammed open.

A guard stumbled in, breathless, his uniform dripping. He halted at the top of the stairs, panting.

"The city is flooding!"

The guard's shout rang across the ballroom. A shriek from the violins cut through the swell of startled chatter.

Arick and Thomas surged forward, slipping through the edge of the startled crowd. Across the room, the king was already moving, his expression grim. Several men joined them around the dripping guard, and the king took charge of questioning them.

"Start the music again," King Craig barked over the rising murmurs, after a brief moment of discussion. "We won't let a little water ruin the night." The herald took over the forced cheerfulness of the king and shepherded the partygoers back to the dance floor.

Once the crowd turned back to the dancing, the king moved swiftly. Pages were dispatched with messages. Guards were ordered to the port to secure the ships, others to assess the castle's defenses, and still more to begin flood barricades.

Thomas turned to his father. "What about the people in the city?"

"Not now, lad." The king waved him off, focused on ensuring the needed infrastructure was in place to protect the city.

Rebuffed, Thomas hurried out of the ballroom, a stubborn tilt to his jaw. Arick followed on his heels.

"We have to help them," Thomas said, worry creasing his young face. "The nobles are safe in the castle, but the others have nowhere to go."

Arick nodded, his heart filled with pride. "We will help. Whatever it takes."

WITH THE BALLROOM DOORS thrown wide, the storm was no longer a distant threat. Thunder cracked overhead, shaking the castle to its foundations. Lightning flickered in the tall windows, illuminating startled faces. Tables rattled, and a tower of sugared pears crashed to the floor.

Many of the guests continued to dance, but an undercurrent of fear grew, as did the lightning outside.

Rona.

She was back.

With no merfolk in the castle, there was nothing to stop her sister from destroying it. She didn't care about the humans.

Or me.

Sorcha shoved the thought aside and followed the tug in her chest that led to Arick. Gathering her skirts, she hurried up the stairs past the king holding a murmured council.

"Sorcha!"

She turned, breath catching in relief. Arick and Thomas stood in the hall, both wide-eyed but resolute. The cooky stood beside them, his ears perked and tail aloft.

Servants rushed to secure doors that banged open on the wind. Rain streaked the flagstones, puddling in the corners of the hall. Somewhere far above, the groan of shifting stone set the chandelier swaying.

"It's Rona," she told them, her hands forming the letters of her sister's name. She hated how it still felt like a betrayal. "I have to stop her. She's going to destroy everything — this castle, the city, everyone in it. But I don't know why."

Arick looked shocked, then determined. "She's trying to take down the tower to get the mirror from the mosaic."

"The mirror in the floor?" Thomas asked.

A memory of white-hot magic flashed through her. "It holds powerful magic. I touched it once, and it..." She struggled for the right word. "...bit me."

"It bit you?"

"Yes...like fire." She pointed to the flickering torch on the wall to emphasize her point.

"Oh. Burned!" Thomas said, showing her the sign at the same time.

"If it has magic like that, we can't let her get it," Arick agreed. "MacIsaac said it was held in by magic, hence the storms."

"The townspeople could be hurt. There's so many houses close to the water," Thomas interrupted. "I have to help them get to safety."

"Go," Arick urged him. They gripped arms, then Thomas raced toward the courtyard, the cooky at his heels.

Then he turned back to Sorcha, entirely focusing on her.

The storm pressed against the stone walls beyond, thunder muttering at a distance, but in this narrow corridor, the world held still. The echoes of running feet faded. Candles flickered, but the light between them stayed steady.

Her breath hitched.

"I need to find Rona," she signed, torn.

"You don't have to do this alone," he replied, his voice quieter, rough. "It's not your fault."

"But what if I can stop her and I don't? Then it is my fault." She looked at him, this man who had accepted her into his life and carved a place in her heart. Tonight was supposed to be spent in his arms. But she couldn't be selfish, no matter how her heart ached for her to give in.

"Sorcha?" His steady hand on her arm belied the uncertainty in his voice. But when she looked in his eyes, she saw her own desire reflected there.

He leaned down, his thumb on her chin. She tilted her head up, delicious shivers running up her arm. His lips claimed her own before she could think, then all thought was gone in the wonder of his kiss. Warmth spread from his fingertips as they grazed her jawline, sending sparks all through her.

She clung to him, her fingers curling into his jacket. If only this moment could last.

But the storm shook the walls again, and a painting crashed to the floor. She broke off with a gasp. "I have to go."

CHAPTER TWENTY-TWO

A RICK GRIPPED SORCHA'S HAND as they raced down the corridor, his sword bouncing against his leg. As soon as he turned the handle, the terrace doors slammed open, and a wall of rain drove them back.

"We should take the long way," he shouted over the howling wind, pointing back along the corridor.

She shook her head. "Faster!"

She was right. He took a deep breath, tightened his grip on her hand, and together they plunged into the storm.

They fought their way onto the open terrace, rain slashing sideways like knives. The covered walkway offered little shelter — just enough to funnel the wind into a howling tunnel that screamed in their ears. Water sheeted from the roof above and poured down in torrents between the stone pillars, turning the flagstones into a slick, treacherous path.

Arick squinted against the downpour, blinking rapidly to keep his eyes clear. Each breath felt like trying to swallow the storm, the air thick with water and the taste of salt and lightning. Sorcha stumbled beside him, her skirts whipping around her legs like angry seaweed. He tightened his grip on her hand and hauled her closer, his other hand skimming the stone railing to keep them both from being tossed into the void below.

She shouldn't have to face this. The thought stabbed through him as another gust nearly knocked them off their feet. This wasn't bravery — it was desperation wrapped in love and fury. But when he looked down at her, at the fierce resolve in her eyes, he knew he could no more talk her out of it than he could stop the sea itself.

A flash of lightning split the sky overhead, so bright it burned his vision white for a heartbeat. Thunder cracked immediately after, shaking the walkway beneath their feet. Ahead, the terrace shimmered in the rain, barely visible through the curtain of water.

They pressed on, leaning into the wind.

His feet slipping on the smoother tiles told him they'd reached the mosaic. He forced his eyes open again.

"Still there!" Sorcha pointed to the center of the swirled tile pattern.

The piece of broken mirror lay embedded in the center, its surface dull and pitted, reflecting the storm in fractured shadows. Time had stripped it of its shine, but not its purpose. Arick sighed in relief to see it still in its place. He touched it, but it felt like any other part of the mosaic. Wet. Cold. Empty.

Sorcha dropped to her knees beside the mirror while Arick staggered to the railing. He peered into the dark as he clung to a pillar slick with rain. The sea below was a churning blur, barely visible through the sheets of water. Only the brief flare of lightning revealed the jagged whitecaps far beneath.

Where was Rona?

There was no sign of anyone on the water. No glow of magic, no hint of movement. And even if Rona was singing, he'd never hear it over the constant thunder. He turned back to Sorcha.

A bolt of blinding white exploded overhead, so bright it seared through his eyes. The tower groaned. Stones rained from above as the lighthouse began to collapse in on itself.

"Arick!"

Sorcha's scream cut through the chaos. He lunged toward the sound, still half-blind, just as the pillar he'd been leaning on splintered and toppled over the edge.

He found her by instinct more than sight, his vision still smeared with afterlight and rain.

"The stairs!" he shouted, gathering her against him. Her fingers grasped his sleeve with reassuring firmness.

The narrow stairwell was a risk, but it was closer than the open terrace, and offered at least some protection from the falling stone and driving rain.

Chunks of debris bounced off his shoulders as they barreled down the narrow, spiraling stairwell. The walls trembled with each distant rumble of thunder, but after several turns, the shaking eased, and they slowed their pace, breath catching in ragged gasps.

Sorcha leaned out of one of the embrasures. "Rona...under," she said in his language, her hands sketching the movement.

Arick winced. "Won't she crush herself if it collapses?" he asked.

Sorcha let out a short, breathless laugh and switched back to her own tongue, her hands translating for him. "She always could wriggle her way out of trouble. Even as a guppy."

"Then we need to get there first," Arick said grimly.

They pressed on, feet pounding against stone as thunder and waves hammered the cliff just beyond the walls. Arick halted when his boot splashed into the cold water pooling on the steps. The last few were already submerged.

"The cavern's flooded." The words stuck in his throat, dread curling in his gut. How powerful was this storm, to send water this far through the tunnels?

They waded through the rising water and splashed across the submerged landing to the door at the bottom. It stood unguarded. Had the king pulled the guards away once the prisoners were gone? No, this was still a vital access point. They wouldn't have left it unprotected.

He reached for the handle and shoved. The door didn't budge. He tried again, harder. The heavy wood flexed, then bounced back.

"It's blocked somehow," he told Sorcha, breathing heavily.

"Open it!" she cried, pointing to the yellow glow seeping through the cracks.

He braced his shoulder and drove into the door with all his weight. Sorcha joined him, both of them pushing against the barricade. His boots skidded on the slick stone, and he nearly went down into the rising water.

Arick motioned her to stand aside. He drew in a deep breath, his heart pounding. Then he planted his hands and shoved. Muscles straining, jaw clenched, he pushed with everything he had. The door edged open, groaning against whatever blocked it. With another heave, he heard something crash behind it. A final shove, and the door gave way, swinging wide enough for them to squeeze through. Water surged around his knees as they slipped inside. A searing yellow glow filled the cavern, and a haunting song rippled off the walls. A low groan pulled his gaze to the left.

A guard lay slumped against a pile of rubble, his arm twisted at an unnatural angle. Sorcha was already beside him, tearing one of the sheer mantles from her gown. She met Arick's eyes briefly, then helped him secure the man's arm against his chest.

"I'll get him out of danger. Wait for me."

She nodded, but uncertainty flickered across her face. He hesitated. Had she truly understood?

But he couldn't delay. He hefted the man over his shoulder, muscles protesting as he waded through the flooded passage. Every step was a battle. Lightning split the sky outside, and the stone trembled beneath his boots.

He couldn't take the man all the way to the top. He turned at the landing to the barracks and lowered him carefully, ensuring his chest still rose with breath. Then he cupped his hands and shouted down the corridor.

"Coo-ee!"

His call echoed, hollow and unanswered. No time. He couldn't leave Sorcha alone.

With a final glance at the wounded guard, Arick turned and plunged back down the stairs, each step heavier than the last, fear clawing deeper into his chest with every heartbeat.

What would he find when he reached her?

WITH ARICK GONE, SORCHA hesitated, the cavern's yellow light flickering across the rising water. She wanted to follow him. To wait. But there wasn't time.

Every note of Rona's song fed the storm. Magic flared from the bracer's core, the yellow gemstone casting its beam upward, summoning the storm to strike the cliff above.

Sorcha picked her way around the fallen stones, drawn by the sound and the glow.

But when she reached the open cavern, Rona wasn't alone.

It was Ewan holding the bracer aloft.

Sorcha's breath caught. The bracer's beam shone from his hand, steady and deliberate, the yellow light painting cracks in the cavern ceiling.

The hard, bitter line of his jaw was almost unrecognizable.

What was Ciara's fiancé doing back in the place where he'd been imprisoned? And worse — why was he floating in the flooded cave beside the wrong sister?

Did Ciara know he was here? Did she know what he was becoming?

Sorcha's gasp drew their attention. Rona turned first, and the cruel triumph on her face sent a ripple of dread through Sorcha.

What was her sister planning? Did she even understand where this would lead?

"Come to join us, sister?" Rona's voice dripped with mockery. Beside her, Ewan picked up the eerie chant, feeding the gem in the bracer with each syllable.

"Never! You're going to get people killed." She forged her way closer, but they were in the center of the deepest part of the pool, where she couldn't go.

"Humans, maybe," Rona said with a shrug.

"Humans are people too!"

Rona scoffed. "What would you know? You're just a little Healer. A poor one at that."

More rock tumbled from the ceiling. The beam from the bracer grew brighter.

"Attacking the tower is only going to bring it down on our heads!"

"In case you haven't noticed," Rona drawled, "I can't exactly walk up there to get what I need." Her eyes gleamed. "Unless, of course, you're volunteering?"

"Over my dead body."

"That," Rona murmured, "can be arranged."

She resumed the chant, her voice joining Ewan's. The glow pulsed brighter, sharper. Water surged in response, slapping against Sorcha's legs.

She shivered, her ballroom gown soaked and clinging, the cold floodwaters tugging at her like ghostly hands.

"Why do you even want it?" Sorcha asked, her voice rising above the chaos. If she could make them talk, it might break the rhythm of the chant and disrupt the spell's power.

"It's magic," Rona said with a scoff, as if that should be enough. Her tone was flippant, dismissive — because of course Sorcha couldn't possibly understand.

But she'd felt the magic in the mirror. She knew what it was.

"Now," Rona added with a sneer, "run along to your little corner and heal someone, why don't you?"

Heal. She wasn't a strong fighter. She couldn't command storms or break stone. But her magic still mattered. Maybe, just maybe, she could heal the damage the bracer was doing. If she couldn't stop them outright, maybe she could slow them. Hold the spell at bay. Just long enough.

Sorcha lifted her chin and began to sing. She shaped the magic into every note, letting it rise from her chest with steady resolve. Rona shot her a glare, but Sorcha didn't stop. She'd learned how to breathe like a human, learned how to stretch each phrase between ragged inhales. It wasn't as easy as singing with gills, but she could do it.

She focused on the stone above, seeking the deep cracks, the fractures weakening the cliff. If she could calm them, seal even one...

Nothing resonated.

Maybe she needed to touch it? But it was too high. Too far.

She shifted her attention to the floodwaters around her feet. Sang to them gently, coaxing, reminding them of their home, the ocean, not this shattered cavern.

Still nothing.

Her song faltered for a breath. Why wasn't it working?

"Can't heal? Or won't?" Rona mocked.

The familiar flush of shame flowed over her. Rona had always pushed her to heal in ways she couldn't.

Or could she?

She'd been trained to mend wounds of flesh and bone. But how many times had Rona tried to get her to soothe a frightened mer's panic, to calm the aching hearts of those who felt forgotten? Back then, Sorcha had thought it beyond her skill.

But maybe...maybe this was her moment to try.

She shifted her song.

Not to the stones. Not to the sea.

To Rona.

She reached with her magic, not toward the storm but toward the storm's maker. She poured her power into a new melody, one that carried not resistance but hope. A lullaby, soft and gentle, spun from childhood memories: the hush of the grotto, coral-light flickering on the walls. The sound of laughter echoing through sea tunnels. Her sisters spinning in circles, hair streaming like kelp in the currents. Lessons by their mother's fin, her voice a steady anchor in the shifting tides.

She offered all of it in her song. Peace, safety, love.

Would Rona listen?

Her sister's melody twisted, sharp and jagged, clashing against Sorcha's like a coral reef battering a tide.

Sorcha flinched at the resistance. She recognized it — the way a Watcher's body fought healing when the pain ran too deep. But she didn't let go. She pushed more of herself into the song, drawing from the aching core of her magic, from every tender note of peace she could conjure.

Rona's voice rose higher, harsher. Her tune turned discordant, weaponized.

A rushing filled the cavern.

A wave shot toward her down the tunnel like a living beast. Sorcha barely had time to suck in a breath before it crashed over her, slamming her to the stones. She tumbled backward in a surge of freezing current, limbs flailing, dress dragging like seaweed around her legs.

Gasping, sputtering, she clung to a rock, the chill biting through to her bones.

As the waters receded, a flash of movement by the door danced in her periphery.

Her head snapped up. Through the mist and crashing spray, a familiar figure slipped into the cavern, keeping low. Water swirled around his boots.

Arick.

Hope flared in her chest, sharp and sudden.

He was here. He'd come back.

Maybe now they could stop them.

Or maybe they'd only buy the world one more breath before it shattered.

ARICK LOCKED EYES WITH Sorcha, relief and fear crashing together in his chest. She wasn't injured. That was all that mattered — for now.

He pressed a finger to his lips and shifted sideways, boots sloshing quietly through the ankle-deep water. The rumble of thunder and the low hum of magic masked the noise, but every splash still made him flinch. He kept low, eyes fixed on the two figures floating at the center of the large pool.

His pulse raced as he took them in. He'd known magic existed — couldn't deny it with the presence of merfolk and the bond tethering him to Sorcha — but seeing it before him now made it irrefutable. Magic may have vanished for a hundred years, but there was no question now. It had returned.

Sorcha stepped forward, rising from the flood with water trailing from her ruined dress. But instead of confronting Rona, she turned toward the other mer.

And that's when Arick saw him clearly.

The one who'd been chained up during each of Arick's visits to the prison cavern.

He barely recognized him. Gone was the drawn, silent captive. The mer before them now radiated purpose and cold fury. Yellow light flared from the bracer wrapped around his hand, its glow painting long shadows across his face and casting cracks into the cavern ceiling above.

Scars ringed his wrists, dark and raw, proof of what he'd endured — but they didn't explain why he stood at Rona's side. And Sorcha's voice, sharp with disbelief and something like heartbreak, told Arick she didn't understand it either.

He kept one eye on her as he went, for even drenched and shivering, her dress in tatters, Sorcha was the most beautiful creature he'd ever seen. But then he noticed her hands. They moved with purpose, fingers forming shapes against the yellow glow. The merman was too distracted to notice.

She was signing for him.

"Why would you do this, Ewan?"

Her hands moved deliberately as she asked the question, even as her voice carried it into the cavern.

The merfolk's chant broke off. Ewan's expression twisted with something darker than anger — resentment. Regret. Rage.

Arick couldn't understand his bitter words, but Sorcha's signs filled in the gaps, his own limited knowledge helping him bridge the rest.

"Why? Ha. At first, it was just a job. Get the mirror, get paid. A lot of gold, too. Enough for Ciara and I to disappear. To start over. Somewhere far from duty and rules and all the people and their expectations."

His voice scraped like broken coral.

Arick slipped another step closer, water swirling around his boots as he drew his sword from its sheath.

"But you disappeared months ago," Sorcha said.

"And if I'd succeeded then, none of this would have happened." Ewan's voice dripped with bitterness. "Merfolk wouldn't have been captured, and the humans wouldn't have found out about us. But some fool human was where he didn't belong."

Arick's grip tightened on the hilt.

Ewan sneered. "There was a shipwreck. I got trapped inside. The humans found me before the Watchers even knew I was missing."

A laugh, low and cold. "How...unfortunate the human died. Couldn't tell anyone what I was doing. So the mosaic stayed unguarded. And no one saw the next storms coming."

Arick froze, his mind cycling through the words Sorcha had signed.

Shipwreck. Human. Killed.

Months ago.

Only one human had died in that storm.

Daniel.

Arick's breath caught, the world narrowing to a single, awful truth.

Ewan was talking about Daniel.

His brother.

The perfect son. The heir. The man everyone expected Arick to become.

The one who should've been here tonight.

Not lost to the sea. Not an accident.

Murdered. By the traitor floating smug in the water.

Something inside Arick cracked.

A surge of grief, love, and pressure came to the surface. Rage and hurt blinded him.

He roared, lunging forward, water crashing around his legs as he plowed toward the pool, sword raised.

"Arick!" Sorcha's cry pierced the chaos, startled and afraid.

Rona's song shifted.

The cavern trembled.

A rumble shook the walls, and a shower of stones fell from the ceiling. Arick halted just short of the pool, sword poised, when a great crack of stone drew his eyes upward.

A slab of stone the size of a man hung suspended.

Right above Sorcha.

No.

He spun, driving himself back through the rising water. It dragged at him like hands trying to hold him back. He pushed harder.

She didn't see it.

She was still looking at him.

He reached her just as the stone broke free.

He hurled himself forward, catching her around the waist.

"Down!" he shouted, and flung her clear with every last ounce of strength.

The boulder struck.

The force of the impact lifted him off his feet.

Stone and water exploded around him.

He slammed into the far wall with a sickening crack and crumpled to the ground as blackness swallowed him.

"ARICK!"

Her scream tore from her throat as the rocks slammed him across the cavern.

His body hit the wall, then he slumped to the ground, motionless.

Sorcha staggered forward, but agony ripped through her legs.

She screamed, crumpling as fire shot up through her bones. Something in her chest snapped.

Her vision swam. Her breath caught.

And then...

The pain vanished.

She lay panting on the cold stone, chest heaving.

Why couldn't she breathe?

Something wasn't right.

Her dress clung strangely to her skin. Her limbs felt wrong. Heavy.

A hand grabbed her leg and jerked her into the deeper water of the pool.

No. Not her leg.

She gasped, flailing — then froze.

In the dim light, her sapphire scales shimmered beneath the ragged hem of her gown. Her fin gleamed, long and strong, slicing the water with every panicked kick.

She stared at her fin — her real fin — and couldn't process what it meant.

She was free. The curse was broken. She was a mermaid again.

But at what cost?

"Huh. Guess he was capable of it after all," Rona said coolly. "Too bad for him."

Sorcha's breath hitched.

"He...he broke my curse."

The words caught, fractured by sobs she couldn't hold back.

Arick's act of selflessness — throwing himself between her and the falling stone — had shattered her curse.

And shattered everything else with it.

She turned toward him.

He didn't move.

His chest was still. Blood streaked the stones, seeping into the rising water in dark tendrils.

The band around her heart clamped tighter, not loosening with the broken curse but locking into place forever.

He was gone.

Because of her.

No.

Her gaze snapped to Rona.

Because of *her*.

"Why are you doing this?" Sorcha demanded, fighting to keep herself afloat. Her skirts kept dragging her down, and she suspected Rona was doing something to add to that.

"I told you. We need that piece of glass."

"Find another way! If you kill the humans, they're going to start a war against the mer. How are our people going to protect themselves against the weapons humans have?"

Rona smirked. "Once we have the mirror, then we won't need to fear the land-dwellers any longer."

She looked around, desperate for some way to stop them. Maybe, if she could disrupt the magic, even for a moment, the storm would weaken.

Sorcha set her jaw and dove beneath the water. She shot toward Ewan, hoping to disrupt his focus — anything to stop the bracer's magic.

But Rona was ready.

A sudden current slammed into Sorcha's side, hurling her into the stone wall. Pain burst through her ribs, and the impact left her reeling. She twisted back into the flow, but the water fought her at every turn. Rona's magic surged through it, turning the cavern into a trap she couldn't escape.

Again and again, she tried — racing forward, singing, clawing for anything that might give her the edge.

But she couldn't reach them.

Not on her own.

Another boulder crashed down into the cavern pool, sending a wave surging over her. The thunder outside was now loud enough to be heard, and the ceiling groaned, cracks spidering out from the bracer's beam. The cavern couldn't take much more.

Sorcha surfaced, gasping, the water stinging her eyes, her limbs trembling from cold and exhaustion. Her gills flared, desperate for breath.

A sob cracked in her throat.

Nothing I do is enough.

She'd tried to heal, to reason, to fight. But she couldn't win. Not like this. Not without Arick's help.

And Rona was going to destroy everything.

How could one little Healer fight against such hatred?

CHAPTER TWENTY-THREE

H ER LIMBS TREMBLING, SORCHA clung to a rock at the edge of the pool. There was no way to stop both Ewan and Rona. Too late, she realized the only weapon that could have worked was Arick's voice — the human voice that could have lured them out of the water, silencing their song.

But he was gone.

No one else knew they were down here.

No help was coming.

"Stay where you are while I finish this," Rona mocked. "Be good, and I might let you live."

Arick's sword lay caught among the rocks, just out of reach.

Arick, who had cared for her since they'd first met. Who had never known her as anything but herself. Who had given his life to save hers.

Who had loved her.

"At least you're back to being a mer," Rona said with a curl of her lip. "No more of those disgusting human legs."

Her voice turned sharper. "Humans are weak. Selfish. Now shut up and let us finish."

Sorcha shook her head slowly.

She had always thought she had to choose. That she had to belong to one world or the other. But she didn't. Her heart had space for both.

Her fingers brushed the sapphire necklace Ailsa had repaired for her. "No, they aren't," she said slowly. "Before, I wanted only to be a mermaid. Then I came to love being a human. But the truth is — I'm both."

Closing her eyes, she wrapped her hand fully around the pendant, clinging to the words Ailsa had told her. *"Now you carry a piece of both worlds."*

She didn't just carry a piece of both worlds. She was part of them.

She concentrated on everything it meant to be human. Every new thing, every heartbeat, every step she had learned to take. Bracing for the pain, she clenched her jaw.

It came. Sharp, but not unbearable. Not like before.

Her legs reformed beneath her, unsteady and smooth. As soon as her feet touched stone, she pushed herself out of the pool, staggering past Rona's reach.

Arick's sword glinted amid the rubble. She lunged for it, fingers wrapping around the hilt. It was heavy, but she had never been weak physically.

Ewan's and Rona's voices twisted together, the cadence of the chant changing as the gem glowed brighter. Whatever was going to happen when they finished would surely bring the tower and the cliff down on top of them.

It was now or never.

Sorcha raised the sword overhead and hurled it with all her strength.

The blade spun through the air, end over end, aimed straight for the bracer.

A crack of sound split the cavern, sharper than lightning.

Water exploded upward in a furious wave.

The stone beneath her feet shook.

Light consumed everything.

Sorcha collapsed to the ground as the blast swallowed her whole.

THE VOICE OF AN angel pulled Arick from the dark.

"Hush, little mermaid, close your eyes," sang the voice, each word brushing against him like a wave.

The melody wrapped around him, familiar and haunting, threading through the cracks of pain like a balm. He floated in it, adrift in sound, until something warm and alive tugged him back toward himself.

The scent of salt and rain lingered in the air, cut through with a faint metallic tang. A chill clung to the damp stone beneath his back, and water lapped softly at his boots.

The burning pain in his side ebbed, replaced by a deep tingling that spread through his chest and limbs. Breathing no longer felt like being stabbed. He drew a slow, shaky breath and let it settle.

"Rest in the embrace of the starlit sea," the song continued, each note more powerful than the last.

The words had healed him once before, when he was half dead beneath the ocean's surface. He'd thought it a dream. A final mercy. But now it wove through the air again, real and raw and impossibly gentle.

He forced his eyes open.

Shadows danced across the stone from a flickering brazier somewhere nearby. The distant roar of the storm was gone, replaced by gentle lapping as the floodwaters receded.

And kneeling beside him, haloed by curling red hair and firelight, was Sorcha.

Not an angel. A mermaid.

Her lips moved with the lullaby, her voice trembling slightly but sure in its melody. Her soaked dress clung to her frame, the fabric torn yet glittering still.

She looked like the sea come to life. Fierce. Fragile. Unbreakable.

He lifted a hand, brushing a damp curl from her cheek. The strands slipped through his fingers like silk, and he smiled faintly. Too bad more of it hadn't fallen loose from the intricate updo she wore.

"You save me," he whispered, voice rough with wonder.

She paused mid-note and met his eyes, her own brimming with unshed tears. She smiled, that beautiful shy lilt to her lips that made him want to kiss her.

"You saved me first," she countered.

He gave a lopsided grin. "Well, I was trying to be a brave protector. Pretty sure I just ended up as ballast."

She laughed softly, smoothing his hair back from his forehead.

"How did you heal me?" he asked after a moment.

She shrugged, a touch of weariness behind it. "You weren't truly dead. I can heal wounds but not bring someone back." He could hear the ache in her voice, knew how she had longed to save her father. Her hand found his again, squeezing gently. "But you weren't gone."

He tightened his fingers around hers. "I couldn't leave you alone." He shifted slightly, glancing past her. "What happened?"

"I threw your sword at Ewan."

He blinked. "You didn't."

"I did," she said, a hint of pride in her voice. She handed him Rona's bracer, the metal twisted and the gemstone cracked and dull. "I hit the bracer. The light exploded."

He laughed, the sound echoing around the cavern. "Remind me not to hand you sharp objects when you're mad."

She smiled, but the light in her eyes dimmed as he asked, "Where are Ewan and Rona now?"

"I don't know. They were gone when I woke. And I was more worried about you."

He brushed a stray hair from her cheek. "I'm here," he promised her.

She gave a watery smile as she nodded.

"The bond is broken now, isn't it?" he asked softly.

"You broke it," she said, "when you sacrificed yourself for me."

"I'd do it again in an instant." His thumb brushed across her knuckles. "But how do we know it won't come back?"

"We can ask Aunt Maeve," she said. "I suspect she knows a lot more about the bonds than she's let on."

"Later," he said, his voice rough with something deeper. He wasn't ready for more answers. Not yet.

"What?" She looked at him, confused by the shift in his tone.

"Kiss me," he said, breathless. His heart pounded as he waited for her to decide. Their last kiss had been amid chaos and fear. Would she want to again?

She chose him.

She leaned down slowly, the soft red halo of her curls framing her face. Her eyes never left his. He reached up and cupped the side of her neck, drawing her closer, her hair brushing his hand.

Her lips met his, and everything else fell away.

Warmth bloomed through him, brighter and fiercer than the bracer's light. The cold, the ache, the fear that she might vanish all melted away. There was only her, only this. Her kiss tasted of the sea, of hope and healing and home.

CHAPTER TWENTY-FOUR

T HE BEACH WAS NEARLY deserted, save for a few gulls
wheeling above the foam-streaked shore. In the distance,
the broken lighthouse pierced the frothy clouds that dotted the
bright-blue sky. Waves lapped against the rocks with a steady
rhythm, and the scent of salt and sun-warmed stone hung in the
air.

Sorcha stepped behind the rocks, her bare feet splashing
through the cool shallows. She untied her outer dress and
draped it carefully over one of the guarding stones to keep it dry,
her hand lingering on the tartan waist.

She sat on a low rock where the tide crept in, waves lapping
over her calves. Clutching the sapphire pendant at her throat,
she pictured her underwater home — the coral grotto lit with
filtered light, her sisters' songs weaving through the currents,

chasing Ciara past blooming anemones as their fins flashed like sunlight.

The ripple of transformation came, a twist of pain that she braced for. This time, it didn't overwhelm her. A gasp of breath, a flinch, then it was gone.

Her legs had fused once more into a shimmering sapphire tail, bright and strong beneath the sun-dappled waves.

For a moment, she simply floated, letting the saltwater cradle her. Her tail flicked gently, adjusting to the shift, her gills fluttering open as the sea welcomed her.

She unbuttoned the shirt and tossed it over the rock with the dress. It felt strange to be without clothes again, but she wasn't cold. Her scales shimmered in the sun, cloaking her in more than enough modesty.

"Are you decent?" called the voice that she loved most.

Slipping fully into the water, she pushed out until she could float freely, her fin stirring the surf. "I am," she called back.

Arick stepped from rock to rock until he was level with her, balanced with the quiet confidence she adored.

"You're not sea-foam." His smile twinkled, relief clear in every line of his face.

"I'm not. You're stuck with me on land."

He looked out to the open harbor, the calm waves belying the civilization that lay beneath. "Just for the day, right?"

She smiled at his anxiousness. "I'll be back by sundown," she reassured him.

"I'll be waiting," he promised in return.

She gazed up at him, memorizing the curve of his smile, the way the sun gilded his ruddy curls, the hazel eyes that always made her feel seen.

She drifted back into deeper water, resisting the tug to swim closer. To kiss him. To stay.

But first, she needed to go home.

He stood tall on the uneven stones, legs braced wide for balance, watching her with a look that warmed her even through the chill of the tide.

She struck out for the open harbor, her body remembering the rhythm of the sea, the effortless grace of swimming with the current. Each movement came naturally, as if she'd never left.

She turned for one last glimpse of Arick. He stood on the rocks, still watching. She lifted a hand in farewell. He waved back.

Then she dove beneath the surface.

The cliff by the castle would have been a shorter route to the grotto, but she couldn't bear to return there, not after all that had happened. Besides, the king's guards were crawling over the wreckage, investigating the events of the night and inspecting the foundation for cracks.

Instead, she'd chosen the beach where her legs had first taken shape, where her life had first split in two.

Where Arick had found her.

Her journey this time was far different than the one she'd made that stormy night. The sea was calm, the sky above bright with morning. No shipwreck, no howling winds, no people in the water.

She slowed as she neared the grotto entrance. She'd left in anger, tired of chasing expectations she could never meet.

Rescuing Arick had more than proven that she was capable of so much more. And though she regretted the anger, she couldn't imagine what would have happened to Arick had she not been on the surface in that storm, if Thomas and the cooky hadn't pointed her to him.

With a deep breath, she crossed one arm over her chest and nodded to the Watcher at the gate. Strands of black seaweed hung from his spear in solemn respect for her father, the fallen leader of the Watchers.

The grotto was hushed, the usual choral of voices subdued. Merfolk went about their business, their movements restrained.

Then came a cry of welcome, and Sorcha was swept into Ciara's embrace. "You came back!"

"Just for a visit," Sorcha said, the hug grounding her more than she expected. "I have a message for Mother from the human king."

Ciara pulled back, blinking at her. "But you're a mer again."

Sorcha straightened the tartan ribbon around her neck. "Somehow, I'm able to change." She paused, giving her sister a deep look. "How are you? Tell me everything that's happened."

Ciara hesitated, glancing around at the other merfolk weaving through the grotto. "Let's swim a little. It's quieter near the kelp beds."

Sorcha nodded, and the two of them slipped through the water together, gliding past coral shelves and waving kelp.

Only when the sounds of the main grotto faded did Ciara speak again, her voice low and tight with emotion.

"I don't even know where to begin," Ciara said softly. "A number of us were on the surface last night as the storm started, ensuring there were no humans or other dangers. As it worsened, we were ordered to fall back. But that's when..."

She paused, her voice catching. Her gaze found Sorcha's, pleading for confirmation. "It was them, wasn't it?"

Sorcha nodded, unable to voice the truth any more than Ciara could.

"I saw Rona and Ewan," Ciara whispered. "They entered the cave beneath the castle. They had...magic. Human magic." Her eyes fell to Sorcha's pendant.

"And after?" Sorcha prompted gently.

Ciara drew a steadying breath. "After a flash of yellow light brighter than the sun, the storm just...stopped." She blinked, remembering. "We swam for the surface, all of us. But it was already over. Ewan found me. He tried to convince me to leave with him. He said we could start over, somewhere no one knew us."

Her voice faltered.

"I couldn't," she finished quietly.

Sorcha touched her arm. "And Rona?"

Ciara shook her head. "No one's seen her since the storm ended."

A hush fell between them, heavy with all they hadn't said. Together, the sisters turned toward the cavern where their mother reposed, the water cool and hushed as they glided side by side. Ahead, Maeve and a few others waited quietly at the queen's side.

True smiles broke over the faces of the mermaids as they spotted Sorcha, and she found herself passed around until each had hugged her. Aunt Maeve squeezed her tightly, a knowing glint in her eye. "I knew he would do it," she whispered.

Her mother held her the longest. "My dear girl," she murmured. "You've returned to us."

Sorcha pulled back, her fingers clutching her mother's hands. "I can't stay, Mother. But I needed to come home. To see you. To...say goodbye." Her voice trembled on the final word. She hadn't been able to say goodbye to her father, but here, in the quiet of the sea, she felt him near. Her mother gave her an understanding look, and they all settled down for a time of sharing their stories. Sorcha settled into her usual spot in the sand by Ciara as Queen Cliodna returned to her seaweed-draped divan.

After a pause, Sorcha drew a deep breath. "I also bring a message from the king of Toravik."

Her mother tilted her head, one elegant brow rising in amusement. "Do you, now?"

"He hopes to speak with you. Perhaps to renew the pact that once existed between our peoples."

"A curious thought. Tell him I will meet him near the shore three days hence." She paused. "I'm assuming you can get a message to him in return?"

Sorcha nodded slowly. "Yes. I'm going back, Mother."

"But we need you here!" cried one of her younger cousins, who had until now only stared at Sorcha in silent awe. "You're our Healer."

Sorcha gave a soft smile. "And you'll still have one. Maeve is here, and you're about to start your own training, aren't you?"

"You know you are valued here, Sorcha," Mother said.

She shook her head. "I know you love me; all of you do. But here, my worth has always been tied to what I can do. I want to be somewhere I'm not measured by what I can do but where I'm wanted simply for who I am."

"What will you do up there?" Aunt Maeve asked.

"I'm going to school. I want to learn, to explore. To see the world beyond the sea. And to find out who I am in it."

"And the sailor?" her mother asked.

Sorcha couldn't stop the warmth that rose across her cheeks.

"Ah. I understand how it is." She gave her daughter a benevolent smile. "You will always have a place among your people, Sorcha. But your home must be where your heart lies."

Sorcha left them then, circling the grotto one final time in quiet farewell. She passed the coral palace, pausing at her hidden nook to retrieve her old jar of trinkets. Each piece was a memory, a thread of the life she was leaving behind.

Ciara joined her as she swam through the gates. "I had to stay, you know," she offered. "For Mother. I couldn't leave her. Not now."

Sorcha squeezed her sister's arm. "Thank you. The Watchers will have the perfect leader when you're ready."

"You'll visit?"

"Often," Sorcha promised.

They said one last goodbye, then Sorcha headed for the surface, and for the sailor who waited for her there.

A RICK WATCHED THE SHIMMER of iridescent scales vanish beneath the water until he could no longer pretend he still saw them.

Sorcha was on her way to visit her family. And though every part of him protested watching her disappear into the sea, he knew she would be safe.

He let out a long breath and turned away from the surf. The wind carried the tang of brine and seaweed, mingled now with something warmer — sunlight on drying sand, and the hush of waves no longer whipped by storm.

He crossed the sand and unhitched the horse from the buggy. It would be faster to ride than to take the buggy, as they'd had to take the long way to avoid the streets still choked with storm debris and shattered crates. He shortened the reins and swung up without a saddle. The horse stamped once, then settled. They set out down the road at a comfortable trot, the horse easily able to navigate around the deeper puddles as the sun dried out the mud. The breeze tugged at his collar, but it carried the promise of summer, not the threat of storms.

A flurry of people bustled about the Coorie Inn as he drew near. The scent of smoke and salt lingered in the air, mingling with the sharper tang of fresh-cut wood and damp stone. He reined in the horse and swung down, pausing just long enough to find Elsbeth.

Like he and Sorcha, she had spent the night at the castle. But she'd already left by the time he awoke. Now, she stood by the kitchen door, directing a pair of sailors as they arranged a table against the wall. Her sleeves were rolled, and her hair was tied up with more practicality than style.

She spotted him and offered a smile, though her eyes immediately swept him head to toe.

"Alright, lad?"

"Aye," he said. "Sorcha's off to visit her family." He let the words carry more weight than they seemed to on the surface.

Her eyes widened with quiet understanding. The corners of her mouth lifted knowingly. "We were right then. She'll be back?"

"Yes, this evening." He took in the movement around them. "The inn was undamaged?"

"A bit of water on the floors," she said, waving it off. "Nothing a mop and a bucket couldn't handle. But others weren't so lucky. And the clean-up crews need to eat."

His grin widened. "So you're feeding the whole harbor?"

"Not alone," she said briskly. "Others are pitching in."

"I'm heading to the castle now. I'll let the steward know you could use more supplies."

She reached into a basket on the table and handed him a tidy stack of shortbread, still warm. "Then take these for the road. Can't have you facing royalty on an empty stomach."

He gave her a grateful smile. "You're a treasure, Elsbeth."

She shooed him off with a wave.

Navigating the cluttered streets was slow going, with debris piled high and fabric banners still clinging to broken windows and railings. The air smelled of rotting seaweed, but the breeze from the hills brought with it the wild moors. His horse skittered sideways every time a scrap of cloth flapped in the breeze, ears twitching.

At the castle, Arick returned the borrowed gelding to the stables, offering a few quiet words to the stable hand before making his way to the king's large office beside the council chambers.

Inside, the atmosphere was tense but orderly. Thomas, King Craig, Queen Freya, and Ailsa were seated around the long polished table, joined by Lady Quigley, Lord Beattie, and two other council members Arick didn't immediately recognize.

"Ah, Arick," King Craig said, gesturing for him to join them. "We've just been discussing MacIsaac and his future serving this country."

Arick slipped into the seat beside Thomas, giving the prince a nod. He leaned forward, resting his forearms on the table. "Sir," he began, but faltered as Lady Quigley leveled a look of smug satisfaction at him across the table. "I'm anxious to hear all that's happening," he said instead, steadying his voice.

"Yes," the king said dryly, casting a glance around the table. "As I was saying, MacIsaac has been stripped of his position on the council and encouraged to retire to his estate in the northern hills."

Beside Arick, Thomas gave a barely contained wriggle of delight.

Arick flicked a glance toward Lord Beattie, noting how the man's mouth tightened. Beattie's gaze dropped to the table, avoiding Arick's entirely.

Across from them, Ailsa signed "wait," her expression calm but firm. Arick settled back in his seat. Now was not the moment to challenge a second councilman.

"Given MacIsaac's continued efforts to sow discord among this council," King Craig continued, "his reckless provocation toward the merfolk, and worst of all, his attempt to manipulate succession by undermining the rightful crown prince, I exercised royal prerogative and bypassed a full council vote."

A sharp intake of breath from Beattie drew all eyes to him.

"Well," the man began, his voice brittle, "with so many — ah — complaints stacked against him, I suppose it was inevitable."

The king leveled a steely look in his direction. "It was necessary."

Silence stretched.

Arick let out a slow breath, a quiet satisfaction rising in his chest. No more would MacIsaac be lurking in the shadows, twisting words and bullying Thomas.

"Now to our next order of business," King Craig moved on. "A number of prisoners were released from the dungeons without authorization."

Arick's stomach churned. He had known doing so could lead to trouble. If there were consequences, he would face them. He squared his shoulders, waiting for his chance to speak.

"Prisoners, Father?" Ailsa interjected smoothly, her tone crisp and composed. Despite her petite frame, she radiated command. "The merfolk were being held in the lower levels — a section the steward's report previously deemed unfit for long-term confinement. So it's possible whoever released them was merely rescuing them from unsafe conditions." She paused, flipping through a few neatly stacked papers. "Either that, or we may need to investigate why the crown was holding prisoners in such inhumane conditions."

The king blinked.

Then he barked a laugh, loud and genuine. "Very well, then. Does anyone wish to challenge the princess's interpretation?"

Silence.

"Good." He dipped his quill and made a note on the parchment before him.

Arick let out a slow breath. Across the table, Ailsa remained composed, but a tiny triumphant smile curved the corners of her mouth.

He shook his head in quiet admiration.

"Now, if that is all, I believe we're all eager to return to the business of cleaning up after the storm," King Craig said, his gaze sweeping the table.

Queen Freya slid a parchment toward him.

"Ah, yes," he said, peering at it. "How forgetful of me. The official presentation of the next crown prince of Toravik will be moved back a few days to allow for storm recovery. However, now seems as good a time as any to confirm one small detail." His voice sharpened. "The identity of the person who will be presented."

He looked around the room, gaze lingering on each face. Lord Beattie shifted uncomfortably, refusing to meet anyone's eye. Arick met the king's stare evenly. He'd already told Thomas his answer and had nothing left to apologize for.

Thomas rose to his feet. His fists were clenched at his sides, and his ears flushed red, but his voice rang clear.

"It's me. I am the crown prince. It's my birthright, and I will work hard to prove myself worthy of it."

Arick nodded at him in pride. Thomas had never been a coward, but now he was ready to take charge.

The king turned back to the table. "Any objections?" His tone dared anyone to speak.

Beattie twitched as if tempted, but the silence that followed was heavy with warning. No one else moved.

"Excellent. No changes to that, then." King Craig signed the parchment with a flourish and passed it back to Queen Freya.

"Well," he said, standing. "Meeting adjourned. Let's get back to work. If necessary, we'll convene again to address the flooding and what our people need most."

Arick stood, ready to join Thomas on an inspection of the damaged tower, when the king's voice stopped him. "Arick, a quick word before you go."

He stepped aside as the other council members filtered out. The queen and his cousins remained, lingering nearby.

King Craig moved to the window, hands clasped behind his back, staring out over the city and the harbor stretching beyond.

"Thomas knows this, but I think it's worth stating plainly," the king began. "My son will always have my support should he choose to be king."

He paused, then turned to face Arick, his gaze steady.

"But I'm not blind to his difficulties. Or to the fact that there will always be men like Beattie and MacIsaac, waiting to exploit any weakness." He stepped forward. "So I ask you plainly: Will you support him? Will you take your brother's place on the council?"

Arick drew in a sharp breath. He'd already offered Thomas his loyalty, but this — this was a formal promise. A lifelong one.

"It doesn't have to be now," Queen Freya added gently. "By the Creator's grace, Craig and I intend to be around a good while longer. But it would ease our hearts to know Thomas has trusted voices at his side."

Arick smiled and squared his shoulders. "It would be my honor." He hesitated. "But..."

"Out with it, lad," the king said, though his tone was kind.

"I want to finish my training. I want the chance to earn my own command. To captain a ship." A flicker of something filled his mind: sapphire scales, red hair, and a smile that lit the morning brighter than the sun. "To show Sorcha the world."

Before he could say another word, Thomas pulled him into a tight hug, knocking the air from his lungs.

Arick froze — then wrapped his arms around his cousin, holding on just as tightly.

He couldn't help but remember that first night back in Iskarraig, standing together on the open terrace as the storm raged around them. Thomas had looked so young then, weighed down by expectations and fear.

Now, he stood tall. Surrounded by family.

By love.

"You're going to be the best king," Arick whispered, voice thick with emotion. "And I'll be there — whenever you need me."

The storm had passed. And for the first time, Arick believed what came next might actually be peace.

CHAPTER TWENTY-FIVE

A RICK PACED THE DAMP sand, its grains slipping beneath his boots as the waves whispered against the shore. The sun was still two handbreadths above the horizon, casting gold rays across the water, but he was anxious for Sorcha to return.

Deep down, he questioned whether she would. But she had promised. And if she chose to stay with her family, well...he'd find a way to be with her anyway.

He rubbed his chest. The ache of separation no longer tore at him, but he didn't need a magical tether to tell him how much he adored being by her side.

Not quite a month had passed since he had woken up on that beach after the storm that had nearly killed him and Thomas. And he'd found her there — lost, alone, and unclothed.

He hadn't understood it then, but something had compelled him to bring her with him. And he knew without a doubt that it was more than just magic that kept drawing him back to her.

The soft strains of her lullaby floated across the waves. He turned, and a smile meant for her alone curved his lips.

She was back.

The setting sun reflected off her shimmering scales as her powerful fin sent droplets flying, scattering rainbows through the air. She swam close to shore, until the rocks kept her from coming closer. Once again, he splashed out into the shallows to lift her from the sea's embrace. She fit perfectly against him, her arms sliding around his neck as if they'd always belonged there.

"You came back," he whispered, his forehead pressed to hers.

"I said I would," she teased, her voice as soft as his.

The sunset painted the horizon in hues of gold and rose, streaking the water with molten light. The broken silhouette of the castle stood sentinel in the distance, a reminder of all they had survived.

Sorcha turned her face up toward him, her sapphire eyes wide. "I'm choosing the human world, but do I really belong here?" she whispered, her voice trembling ever so slightly. "I've never really fit in anywhere."

His thumb drew circles on her back where scales turned to skin. "You fit with me."

She drew a shaky breath. "But I want to explore...do things...see the world. I don't want to hold you back — I don't want to force you to follow me."

"You wouldn't be." His grip tightened just a little. "I'd follow you wherever you wish to go or wait for you to come back, if that's what you need. Because I want you to be yourself, whatever that looks like."

Her lashes glimmered with unshed tears. "And if I get lost? Unsure of my purpose...unsure of who I really am... What then?"

He drew her close. "Then I will be there. I'll be your siren amid the storms. I'll call you back to me, no matter how far you roam. I'll be your safe harbor, your ship upon the waves."

He tightened his embrace, feeling the softness of her damp curls against his cheek as she turned up her face to him, smiling with pure, vulnerable love. His pulse thundered in his veins as he paused just a breath away, letting their noses brush in a fleeting caress. When she leaned in, he captured her lips with his own, gentle at first, then deepening, until there was no space left between them, only warmth, connection, and the promises that anchored their hearts. Her hand slid along his jaw, burying in his hair, drawing him even closer. And in that kiss was their vow — that no matter how far they strayed, they would always find their way back to each other.

**The waves may have calmed...
but the story isn't quite over.**

Join my newsletter for an exclusive bonus epilogue — set sail
one last time for an underwater wedding and a shipboard cele-
bration that brings Sorcha and Arick's journey full circle.

https://RobynSarty.com/WhispersBonus

W HEN I FIRST IMAGINED this world, it was sparked by a series of what-ifs:

What if the little mermaid didn't rescue the prince?

What if she didn't want to be where the people are?

What if it was the humans who had siren voices?

This story grew from those questions — into a tale of sacrifice, storm-bound destinies, and a love that must prove itself through selfless action.

But a story like that needed the perfect setting.

In 2019, I had the privilege of visiting the land of my heritage — Scotland. As I explored its rugged landscapes, lost myself in the mists, and wandered through ancient castles, the magic of the land beckoned me to write stories that captured the myth and lore that linger in the hills and ruins.

Setting *Whispers of the Starlit Sea* in Scotland just made sense. The wild beauty and whispered myths of Scotland became the heartbeat of this story.

But no story finds its voice alone. It's shaped by whispers and sparks gifted by many — moments of encouragement, words of wisdom, quiet gestures of belief. To those who stood with me, lent their talents, and shared in the magic, this book owes its heart.

To Sìne Màiri MacDougall, Angela Nurse, and Jackie Kirkham, thank you for sharing your Gaelic help and Scottish knowledge with such generosity. You gave this story roots it would never have found on its own.

To Liz and Nic, thank you for listening to a year and a half of rambling (and ranting), for reading chapter after chapter, and for asking the hard questions that pushed this book to be its very best.

To Matthew Schroeder and his family, for helping make Thomas feel like a real person, for sharing insights, laughing at ideas, and for naming Cookie.

To Alora, Amanda, Ashley, Dana, Elaine, and Scarlett, for beta-reading and offering feedback that strengthened this story and encouraged me when I felt lost. You guys did more than help the story; you lifted me up when I needed it the most, encouraging me when I was sure I couldn't figure it all out.

To my Ream supporters, especially Linda Jackson, DaLeena Taylor, and Terry Juell French, thank you for quietly cheering me on every step of the way, reminding me that every chapter was worth finishing.

To every one of my amazing, incredible, and wonderful Kickstarter backers — the special editions would never have come to life without you. You brought joy, hope, and belief to this book just by being here. And I am so deeply grateful for each of you.

To Nicole Schroeder, for once again being the world's greatest editor as well as the best accountability partner, who encourages me at every turn. Thank you for making this story brighter, for patiently listening to countless hours of rambling, and for knowing how to make words truly sing. And for putting up with editing the nice things I say about you every time!

To my husband, my Captain and my anchor, who supports every wild dream I have — even when he doesn't quite understand it — and still shows up every morning with fancy coffee and a quiet, steadfast love that keeps me going.

And, above all, to my Heavenly Father, who gave me the gift of storytelling and placed this book upon my heart. To Him be the glory.

Robyn

June 2025

Robyn Sarty is an avid fan of all things Disney, and she loves stories with happy endings, where good triumphs over evil. She tries to incorporate these elements into all of her writing, stories that feature women who refuse to back down from a challenge. She lives in rural Nova Scotia with her very own Prince Charming, where she is easily distracted by sparkly things and glitter. When she's not reading or writing, she can be found baking cakes, rearranging her library, or playing with her Bernese Mountain Dogs, Toblerone and Otto.

Sign up for a free short story, updates, and exclusive content here:

https://robynsarty.com/ebook-giveaway/

www.robynsarty.com

https://www.facebook.com/RobynSartyAuthor

https://www.instagram.com/robynsarty/

*M*ACISAAC OPENED THE HANDKERCHIEF *and let the first rays of dawn glimmer across its surface. If anyone saw him, they'd think he was inspecting a pocket watch, not the stolen artifact that glowed faintly within.*

The shard of mirror was so much more than that.

He'd pried it from the mosaic without anyone noticing, the storm's chaos dislodging its magic just enough for him to extract it.

It called to him — a faint, almost unheard song.

He tightened his grip. Her warnings still rang in his mind.

He was not a fool.

He would not let temptation dictate his fate.

He turned toward the water's edge.

A ripple passed across its surface, a fleeting shadow gliding just beneath as his counterpart appeared.

He reluctantly held out the handkerchief. "You'll get it to her immediately?"

The nod was accompanied by a confident grin. "My absence won't be noted. In fact, it would be welcomed."

He turned away from the shore, reluctantly. All his careful plans rested upon this moment.

He hated allying with a mer, yet there had been no way around it.

At least he would be well rewarded when she had the mirror safely back in her possession.

Then, and only then, would the real games begin.